STRANGERS IN THE VILLA

ALSO BY ROBYN HARDING

The Haters

The Drowning Woman

The Perfect Family

The Swap

The Arrangement

Her Pretty Face

The Party

STRANGERS IN THE VILLA

A Novel

ROBYN HARDING

GRAND CENTRAL

New York Boston

This book is a work of fiction. Names, characters, places, and incidents are the product of the author's imagination or are used fictitiously. Any resemblance to actual events, locales, or persons, living or dead, is coincidental.

Copyright © 2026 by Robyn Harding

Cover design by Olga Grlic. Cover images by Getty Images and Shutterstock. Cover copyright © 2026 by Hachette Book Group, Inc.

Hachette Book Group supports the right to free expression and the value of copyright. The purpose of copyright is to encourage writers and artists to produce the creative works that enrich our culture.

The scanning, uploading, and distribution of this book without permission is a theft of the author's intellectual property. If you would like permission to use material from the book (other than for review purposes), please contact permissions@hbgusa.com. Thank you for your support of the author's rights.

Grand Central Publishing
Hachette Book Group
1290 Avenue of the Americas, New York, NY 10104
grandcentralpublishing.com
@grandcentralpub

First Edition: March 2026

Grand Central Publishing is a division of Hachette Book Group, Inc. The Grand Central Publishing name and logo is a registered trademark of Hachette Book Group, Inc.

The publisher is not responsible for websites (or their content) that are not owned by the publisher.

The Hachette Speakers Bureau provides a wide range of authors for speaking events. To find out more, go to hachettespeakersbureau.com or email HachetteSpeakers@hbgusa.com.

Grand Central Publishing books may be purchased in bulk for business, educational, or promotional use. For information, please contact your local bookseller or the Hachette Book Group Special Markets Department at special.markets@hbgusa.com.

Library of Congress Cataloging-in-Publication Data

Names: Harding, Robyn author
Title: Strangers in the villa / Robyn Harding.
Description: First edition. | New York : Grand Central Publishing, 2026.
Identifiers: LCCN 2025043795 | ISBN 9781538774007 hardcover | ISBN 9781538774021 ebook
Subjects: LCGFT: Thrillers (Fiction) | Novels
Classification: LCC PR9199.4.H366 S77 2026 | DDC 813/.6—dc23/eng/20251121
LC record available at https://lccn.loc.gov/2025043795

ISBNs: 978-1-5387-7400-7 (hardcover), 978-1-5387-8054-1 (Canadian trade pbk.), 978-1-5387-7402-1 (ebook)

Printed in the United States of America

LSC-C

Printing 1, 2025

For the TWs:
Jo, Chris, Dirk, Mike, and John
Thanks for an inspirational trip to Spain.

STRANGERS IN THE VILLA

COSTA BRAVA HOUSE FOR SALE
Catalonia, Spain

    This jewel of tranquility is located on Mount Peni high above the picturesque town of Cadaqués. The property offers stunning views of the town, the sparkling Mediterranean, and the pretty boats floating in the harbor. Though it is less than a three-hour drive to Barcelona, you will feel you live in a private oasis. Surrounded by trees, you will wake each day to the sounds of birds singing and leaves rustling in the gentle breeze. Each day will begin full of joy!

    Built in 1963 in traditional Spanish style, this home has original Spanish tiles and wooden ceiling beams. Natural light floods into the spacious living-dining room through a bank of arched windows. French doors open up to the sunny pool and terrace, perfect for relaxing and sunbathing. Two bedrooms are on the main floor with one bathroom. The house is perfect for a couple, but the downstairs has three more rooms with the potential to be turned into space for a family.

    Does this house need some TLC? Yes, of course. But it is a large plot of land and one of only a handful of properties on the hillside. It offers the utmost privacy and serenity, with a security system for peace of mind. With the right attention and devotion, this could be a truly magical villa. A perfect home to fill with love and happy memories!

SYDNEY AND CURTIS

1

It was a remarkably romantic description for a house, especially when one considered the author was a chain-smoking Realtor with a pot belly and an unconvincing dye job. But this is Spain, where the people are passionate and poetic... even the real estate agents, apparently. José Sainz could not have known he was crafting the perfect blurb to entice an American couple to leave their jobs, give up their apartment, and start over in this secluded hillside locale. He couldn't have known he'd sell this house to a couple desperate to save their marriage.

Sydney Cleary takes a drag on her cigarette and exhales the smoke into the sluggish morning air. She's sitting out back next to the kidney-shaped pool, facing away from the house and its lauded arched windows. Her eyes drift over the distant, whitewashed buildings of Cadaqués (pronounced Ca-da-kes, not Ca-dacks, as she and Curtis had called it when they first visited). The Mediterranean sparkles beyond it, small boats bobbing lazily in the bay. The view is stunning, just as José's ad promised, but it's wasted on her. The chirping birds and beautiful vistas were supposed to have her waking each day "full of joy." But as she sits here in her bikini and cover-up, sunlight filtering through paintbrush clouds, Sydney just feels numb.

"You've been through an extremely painful experience," the couples' therapist had told her. "It's not unusual to suffer symptoms of PTSD... Anxiety. Depression. Insomnia." Sydney had felt so weak, so pathetic. She hadn't been attacked or raped or bombed out of her house in a war. That was *real* trauma. But according to the sleek and stylish Dr. Ellen Dwyer, what Curtis had done to Syd had destroyed her sense of safety. Her sense of self. She didn't know who she was anymore, who *they* were together. Her entire world had been knocked off its axis. It was going to take a while to get over it.

The timing of her husband's betrayal had compounded the pain, amplified it to eleven. Syd's mom had just passed, and the loss had knocked Syd out of her orbit. Never had she felt so singularly and spectacularly alone, a tiny planet adrift in a vast universe of nothingness. She'd consoled herself that she had a meaningful job, many friends, and her brother, Reid. Most importantly, she had Curtis.

They'd been together fifteen years, married for twelve. They'd tied the knot when Syd was a baby lawyer, when Curtis's business was just getting off the ground. They both wanted kids but agreed they would wait until they were more established in their careers, until they'd done some traveling, until they had a bigger apartment... Suddenly, Syd was forty and the window was closing. They tried naturally for a while with no luck, and then they explored their options. The physical, financial, and emotional tolls of pursuing parenthood had felt overwhelming.

"I'll go along with whatever you decide," Curtis said. "But we don't need kids to complete us, Syd. You and me together... We're still a family." His words had warmed her, made her realize that a strong, happy marriage to her best friend was enough for her.

Unfortunately, it hadn't been enough for Curtis.

When it all fell apart, Syd's family doctor (Ellen was a doctor of psychology, prohibited from prescribing medication in New York) had prescribed a low-dose antidepressant. Ativan, to be taken at night, as needed, helps her sleep. The drugs have taken the edge off the darkness, muted her anger, but Syd wakes late each morning feeling groggy and fuzzy. That's why she's out here in her bathing suit at 9:45 a.m. A bracing swim shakes out the cobwebs and makes her feel almost normal.

Taking a last pull on the cigarette, she stubs it out on the flagstone and drops the butt into the empty jam jar she keeps tucked under her lawn chair. One cigarette a day, that's all she allows herself. Syd had smoked her way through college and then law school but had given it up after she got married. When her mom died, the cravings returned, but she held strong. Then Curtis ripped her heart out and she caved, smoking over a pack a day. It had been a mindless salve, a habitual crutch. She knows it's deadly. When they moved to Spain she vowed to quit. Reducing to one a day is a start.

As Syd stands and stretches, there's a crash in the kitchen—a dropped pot or a metal lid. Curtis is making an elaborate breakfast. He does this now, juicing oranges, cutting up fruit, making French toast from thick crusty bread he buys at the bakery in town. He's always made sure she ate in the morning. Back home, that meant handing her a bagel sandwich as she hurried off to work. But in Spain, he's upped his game. Part of her appreciates it. Another part of her wants to throw his fancy breakfast across the room and scream: *You think café con leche and some fucking eggs will compensate for blowing up my life?* But her anger, while understandable, is not productive. She doesn't need a therapist to tell her that she's chosen to stay and salvage this marriage. She can't keep punishing him.

In these quiet, reflective moments, Sydney wonders why she accepted the arduous task of forgiveness. Does remaining in her marriage mean she's weak? Or does it mean she's strong? Everyone back home had an opinion. Staying meant she was a doormat; leaving was giving up on a lifelong commitment after one mistake. She'd blocked them all out and made her own decision. But did she stay because she truly loves her husband? Because she knows their relationship is worth this monumental effort? Or is she simply afraid of being alone so soon after losing her only parent? The reasons don't matter now. She's here.

Moving to the pool, Syd wades into the cool water. It needs to be skimmed—bugs and leaves litter the surface—but the temperature is brisk. The pool is unheated, and given their elevation, it's still too cold for Curtis until the afternoon. But Syd's grandparents had a cottage in Ontario. She's used to swimming in chilly lakes, frolicking in frigid streams. She knows the adrenaline rush of a cold plunge, the improved clarity and mood. She takes a deep breath, is about to go under, when she feels something swish against her legs.

She startles, splashing at the surface in a panic, legs churning fruitlessly to move her toward the edge. There are venomous snakes in Spain, and she'd been warned to be vigilant. She should have checked the pool for vipers looking for a place to escape the impending heat. But when she looks down, she realizes she's still wearing her cover-up, the light fabric swirling around her body like seaweed.

Without removing it, she dives under and swims to the end of the pool.

2

Curtis glances out the window to see his wife swimming lengths in her nightgown. This would have been alarming before everything happened—Sydney was a buttoned-up attorney, so capable and put together—but now she's cloudy and distracted. Some of it's the medication she takes, some of it's the depression, and some, according to their couples' therapist, is her body's response to the emotional pain Curtis inflicted on her. Sydney's gone numb to protect herself from future suffering. If she feels nothing at all, she can't be hurt again.

Guilt squeezes his heart as he watches his wife climb out of the pool. She's still so elegant, a cool patrician beauty, but now she looks fragile, brittle, a husk of the vibrant woman she used to be. He did this to her, and he hates himself for it. But she's given him another chance, and he's going to fix everything. As Syd reaches for a towel, he realizes she's wearing not her nightgown but the white gauzy shirt she wears over her bathing suit. Still, he wonders why she didn't take it off. He knows enough not to comment.

The toast pops, and he hurries to butter it while it's still warm. They're having scrambled eggs today, with blistered tomatoes and fresh-squeezed orange juice. The eggs are fresh, the bread made at a quaint little bakery. He wonders if Sydney tastes the quality like he does, or if his thoughtfully prepared meals are sawdust in her mouth. Some days, she's fine and everything feels almost normal. Other days, she's sad, or sullen, or outright angry. But she's here. And he's going to make her love him again.

He hurries outside, where Sydney is wringing out her cover-up, a towel wrapped around her torso. "Brunch is served, m'lady. Do you want to eat inside or outside?"

"Doesn't matter."

"Come in. You'll get a chill out here."

While Syd changes, Curtis sets the table. The dining room is his favorite space, maybe because it needed the least amount of work. Morning sun slips in through the sheer white curtains, warming the terra-cotta tiles. The massive farmhouse table, left here because it's practically immovable, is a soft timber, etched with the memories of family meals. He sets down cloth place mats, forks, knives, and the pitcher of freshly squeezed orange juice. The scene is idyllic... with only the faintest thrum of discontent under the facade.

Moving to Spain had been Curtis's idea. Even with couples' therapy, Syd was struggling to heal in New York. There were too many reminders, they were too close to the scene of the crime, and Sydney had told too many people what Curtis had done. He knew some of Syd's friends thought she should leave him. Her brother, Reid, did. Reid had told Sydney to get her own place or move in with him and his husband upstate. Reid was protective, Curtis got that, but he couldn't force his sister to abandon her marriage.

Ellen, the therapist, with her blunt bob and fashionable outfits, had insisted they ignore the advice of outsiders, not let shame or judgment drive them apart. Sydney had struggled to shut out the well-meaning chirping, the constant feedback loop. Syd still loved Curtis. He knew she didn't want to give up on the life they'd built together. And Curtis loved her more than ever. And so, Curtis had made the grand suggestion, an extravagant gesture to show just how committed he was to a fresh start.

"Spain?" Syd had laughed, incredulous. It had seemed so random. But they'd spent their honeymoon there twelve years ago and had fallen in love with the country.

"I found a house," he said, bringing up the listing on his phone. "It's not far from Girona, above Cadaqués. It needs some TLC, but we can afford it if we sell the apartment."

"What will we do for work? How can we just *move* there?"

"This place has some property," he said, passing Syd the phone. "We could plant some grapes. Start a little vineyard. Spain offers a golden visa if you invest in real estate or start a business. And the cost of living is way cheaper than in New York."

"I'm a lawyer," Syd countered. "A public defender. I can't just retire when I'm in my forties."

"But they work you to death at the PD's office. You're stressed and exhausted. And you've always been interested in wine. It'll take a while to get started, but this could be a new career for you." His voice had sounded almost childlike with hope. "For *us*."

Syd's brow had been furrowed with skepticism, but it softened as she scrolled through the photos, saw the potential of the place. He knew she could envision a new kind of life, just the two of them. They could rebuild their relationship in this hilltop home. Syd could see it, too.

"And I don't want you to touch your inheritance," Curtis had added. "Your mom left that money to you, and I think we can manage without it."

But they couldn't, of course. (Has a reno ever come in under budget?) It soon became clear that they'd need more funds. Curtis had wanted to do most of the renovations himself, but there were limits to his skills. They'd had to hire an electrician to upgrade the panel to support the air-conditioning, and a plumber to replace cracked underground pipes from the well to the house. They could live with the chipped countertops and dated cupboards in the kitchen, but the fridge was leaking, and the stove was a fire hazard. And Syd didn't think she could bear the Spanish heat without fixing the pool, so repairing the crack in the concrete had been a top priority. Starting over, building a new life, was expensive. But it was worth it.

Syd approaches the table then, her wet hair slicked back, her face free of makeup. Her expression is placid after her bracing swim, and she looks beautiful. Healthy. The May sunshine has kissed her cheeks, and thanks to Curtis's cooking, she's gained back some of the weight she'd lost when everything happened. She'd arrived so thin and fragile, and now she's more robust. More like the strong, self-assured woman she was.

Curtis fills two crockery plates with scrambled eggs, halved tomatoes, and thick slabs of toast. He sets one in front of his wife and another across from her.

"Thanks," she says, digging in heartily. He sits and watches her enjoyment for a second, absorbing the wonderful normalcy of it.

Scooping up a forkful of buttery eggs, he says, "I think we should start clearing out the north quadrant of the property, where the fence is coming down. It would be a good spot to plant our vines."

"Depends which grapes we want to grow," she says, biting into her toast with a crunch. "Airén vines can handle full sun and dryer soil. But if we want to grow Tempranillo, they prefer more shade."

Syd's been researching. It means she's investing in their plan. The therapist said that it could take years for Sydney to fully heal, but this move, this new venture, will expedite the process. One day in the not-so-distant future, Curtis will be able to wake up without worrying that she'll be gone. That he'll look for her by the pool, on the steep path that leads down the mountain, in the shops of Cadaqués, and discover that she's left him. That she's returned to the States. That she's given up on them.

"We should grow whatever you like to drink," he says. "There's going to be a lot of tastings in our future."

"Airén, then," she says. "I get less hungover from white." Her smile is small, even begrudging, but it bathes him in warmth, safety, and optimism. Until he hears it: a light but insistent knock at the door.

"Who's that?" Syd asks, setting down her toast.

"I don't know." They are so alone here, so isolated, which is just how they wanted it. They've made no friends, are only on wave-and-smile terms with their distant neighbors. So, who the hell is at their door? It must be a wrong turn, a lost tourist or maybe a local selling fish or jamón. It's nothing to worry about.

So why, as he scrapes his chair back across the tiles, does Curtis feel this sense of dread?

Sydney Cleary and Curtis Lowe, Couples' Counseling Session
Ellen Dwyer, Psychologist, PsyD
June 24

TRANSCRIPT 1.

Ellen:
What brings you two in today?

Sydney:
Tell her, Curtis.

Curtis:
I... was unfaithful. I love Sydney more than anything, and I made a huge mistake. The biggest mistake of my life.

Ellen:
I can hear that you're hurting. How are you doing, Sydney?

Sydney:
I'm broken. And I'm devastated.

Ellen:
That's completely understandable. Infidelity is incredibly painful and can even be traumatic... Curtis, does it feel okay to tell me how it happened?

Curtis:
Syd and I were going through a dark time. We weren't connecting. Sydney's mom had been sick for months, and she'd been caring for her. She was exhausted and overwhelmed. I wanted to be there for her, but I felt like I couldn't reach her.

Sydney:
So, it's *my* fault you had an affair? Or is it my mom's fault, for getting cancer and dying?

Ellen:
Sydney, your anger is so valid. Could you tell me more about what you're going through?

Sydney:
I'm hurt. And I'm disappointed. And I'm so fucking angry. I was grieving. My mom had just died, and he slept with one of his clients. When I was at my lowest point, when I needed him the most, he betrayed me.

Ellen:
Grief can have a huge impact on a relationship. Your emotional suffering was likely all-consuming.

Sydney:
It was. My mom and I were really close. Losing her destroyed me.

Ellen:
Curtis, did you feel shut out of Sydney's experience? Like there was no role for you in her suffering?

Curtis:
Yeah, I did. Sydney's a strong person. She didn't need or even want my comfort or support.

Sydney:
If you're going to keep blaming me for this affair, I'm going to leave.

Curtis:
I'm not blaming you. *I* did this. I know I did. I'm just trying to explain my headspace.

Sydney:
You weren't the center of my attention for once in our marriage, and you couldn't handle it.

Ellen:
There's no excuse for infidelity. But it's usually a symptom of something more going on. If we can understand it, we can make sure it never happens again.

Curtis:
It won't happen again. Ever. I hate myself for what I did to us, Syd. That's why I came clean. I couldn't live with what I'd done.

Sydney:
I knew you were hiding something. Even through my grief, I could tell.

Curtis:
The guilt was eating me up inside. It was torture. I'll never hurt you like that again, Syd. I swear on my life.

Sydney:
I want to believe you, Curtis, I do. I just don't know if I can.

3

Sydney takes in the couple standing on their doorstep: late twenties, good-looking, drenched in sweat as if they've been hiking in the late-morning heat. They appear to be tourists in their shorts and sandals, well-worn T-shirts. The woman steps forward, smiles beseechingly. She has dark-blond hair; tanned skin; an open, approachable face. There's a small jewel in her nose, a Japanese symbol tattooed on her forearm. Three gold necklaces of varying lengths adorn her throat. "*¿Habla inglés?*" she asks hopefully.

"We speak English," Curtis responds tightly. His fists are clenched in some macho display of protectiveness, and Syd can feel the tension emanating off him. Does he think this attractive pair is here to scam them? Or rob them? Or worse? Syd is surprised by the intrusion too, but she's not worried about it. Maybe she just sees the good in people. Or maybe the antidepressants are muting her fear response.

"Thank God." The young woman smiles, presses a hand to her chest. "My name's Bianca. This is my partner, Damian." She has an accent, Australian or maybe Kiwi. It suits her girl-next-door energy.

"We've had some car trouble," Damian says, his accent unmistakably Aussie. He has dark hair under a ball cap, broad shoulders, and well-developed traps. If he's here to harm them, Curtis, with his slim, urban physique, will be no match for him.

"We pulled over to take some photos," Bianca explains. "And now the van won't start."

"I'm pretty sure the fuel pump's shot," Damian says, adjusting his cap. "We've been trying to call mechanics for over an hour. None of them speak English, and our Spanish is terrible."

"We were using Google Translate, and now our phones are dead." Bianca holds up a useless device as evidence.

"So, what do you want?" Curtis asks, and Syd feels embarrassed by his hostility. Why is he being so rude? And so paranoid? She steps forward.

"Do you want to charge your phones?" Sydney offers. "Or borrow ours?"

"We hate to impose on you," Bianca says, twisting open a metal canteen. "Maybe you could charge one of our phones, and we can wait somewhere in the shade." She takes a drink of water, clearly the last in the vessel.

"Come inside," Syd offers. "We have air-conditioning." She feels Curtis's eyes on her, but she ignores him. Syd gets a good vibe off this girl. And Damian seems fine, too. Until this moment, Sydney hadn't realized how starved for company she's been. She and Curtis have been on their own for four months, "rebuilding" and "connecting" and "finding their way back to each other." It's tedious, frankly. Sydney craves outside stimulation, laughter, and interesting conversation. She's been lonely.

Bianca's pretty face lights up. "Really? You wouldn't mind?"

"We really appreciate it," Damian adds.

"Of course," Syd says brightly, looking over at Curtis. He's not comfortable with this. It's evident in the set of his jaw, the prominent vein pulsing in his temple. But he won't go against her.

"Come on in," he says tightly.

One of the benefits (or hazards) of never having visitors is a certain laxity in housekeeping. Syd's eyes rove over the jumble of blankets on the sofa, the pair of shoes abandoned in the middle of the living room, and of course their half-eaten breakfast cooling on the dining table. She hadn't noticed the layer of dust coating the TV and coffee table, the book splayed open on an ottoman. But Bianca seems immune to the mess.

"Oh my God..." she says, voice tinged with wonder. "It's so beautiful. The arched windows are incredible."

"They were a major selling feature," Sydney says, watching Curtis as he leads Damian down the hall to plug in the dead phones. The two men appear to be chatting amiably. Curtis must be warming up, dropping his guard, realizing this attractive young couple isn't here to murder them.

"I love all the built-in details." The Aussie woman pauses to admire a small curlicued nook where Sydney has placed her mother's favorite porcelain vase. The piece isn't expensive, or particularly stylish, but it is precious.

"The Spanish architecture is so charming," Sydney agrees.

"How long have you lived here?"

"Just over four months. We still have a lot of work to do."

"The place looks great." Bianca smiles at her. "You're living the dream."

A muscle twitches in Syd's jaw, but her grin stays in place. "First time in Spain?" she asks.

"First time anywhere. Australia is so bloody far away." Bianca strolls into the dining room. "I love this old table."

"It was here when we moved in," Syd replies, whisking the neglected plates to the kitchen counter. "It weighs a ton. They probably had to build the house around it."

"You've done an amazing job with the decor. It's modern without sacrificing the old-world Spanish charm."

"Thanks." Syd glances around at the pale overstuffed sofas, the low coffee table, the battered credenza that she plans to refinish. She's not sure the aesthetic is working yet, but she appreciates the compliment.

"I really admire you guys," Bianca says, taking in the postcard view from the dining room windows. "Starting a new life in a new country is such an adventure." She turns to face Syd. "Damian would never leave Australia permanently, but I would. I've got nothing there anymore."

"Oh?" Syd doesn't mean to pry, but Bianca opened the door.

"My dad's been out of the picture since I was little. And my mom died a couple of years ago. Skin cancer."

"I'm sorry," Syd says. "I recently lost my mom to cancer, too."

"It's so hard, isn't it?" Bianca's eyes are shiny. "I mean, my mom and I didn't always see eye to eye on everything, but your mom is the moon in the sky. She's like your gravitational force. And when she's gone, you just feel...adrift. Like you're not really tethered to the world anymore."

Syd's throat tightens. This stranger has articulated exactly how she's felt since her mom passed. No one in her circle has understood her, not even Reid. Her brother has always been so strong, so independent. But this young stranger gets it. Syd forces words past the lump of emotion.

"Can I make you a coffee? We can get to know each other while the phones are charging."

Bianca smiles. "I'd love that."

4

With the cell phones plugged into a power bar in the guest room, Curtis leads Damian up the hill behind the house to the north corner of the property. He knows Damian's type: an uber-masculine bro into MMA, cars, and listening to Joe Rogan while he pumps iron at the gym. Damian strikes him as a beer drinker with no palate for wine. But he'll be more interested in their plans to build a winery than in Syd's furniture choices.

Near the top of the slope, they stop. "Eventually, we'll plant vines on this hillside," Curtis says, pride in his voice. It's such a cool plan. He and Syd are creating a dream life, and he can imagine how impressive it must sound to this van-living Aussie.

"Nice," Damian says, looking over the vista. "And what a view."

"We're going to build a small winery and a tasting room. I've been working on a business plan."

Damian points to the derelict shed to their right. "You could fit a couple of steel tanks in that building over there. Depending on your scope, that could be your winery."

"Except the shed's about to fall down."

"Maybe not." Damian trudges through the tall grass toward the abandoned building, Curtis in tow. When they reach the shed, the younger man presses the outside wall, leans his shoulder against it. "The structure seems pretty sound. The roof needs new shingles, but that's no big deal." He pushes open the door, the rusty hinges creaking and catching in protest. The two men peer inside at the cobwebs, the abandoned pieces of lumber, a few dusty coffee cans full of nails and screws. "You'd just need to replace some of the rotting boards. And then you could build a nice deck out front for your tastings."

Why hadn't Curtis thought of utilizing this shed before? Now that this backpacker has pointed it out, he can visualize it. The distance from the house would allow him and Syd privacy. And the view from up here is spectacular. Even if their wine is subpar, people would come for the scenery.

"Are you an architect, Damian? Or a builder?"

"Nah. Commercial diver. But my dad was a general contractor. I worked summers and weekends on construction sites since I was fifteen. You pick up a few things."

As they stroll back toward the house, Curtis asks, "What part of Australia are you guys from?"

"Western Australia. Fremantle, near Perth."

"Never been."

"It's a bloody long way. Most isolated capital city in the world."

"I've heard it's beautiful."

"Best beaches on earth."

"Really? Better than Spain?"

"Can't complain about the Med, but WA has white sand, turquoise waters. And the beaches aren't crowded like in Europe."

"Because the sharks do a cull every now and then?" Curtis jokes.

"They mostly snack on surfers. Swimmers don't worry about them too much."

"Commercial diver sounds like a pretty dangerous job."

"It is. But it pays well. Enough for me to take Bianca away for a few months. She's been through a rough time recently."

"Sorry to hear that."

"Yeah. Her mom died a couple of years ago. Her dad buggered off when she was a baby."

"Syd's mom passed recently, too."

Damian's pace slows a little. "It's hard, isn't it? Being the support system. Dealing with their grief all the time."

The young Aussie knows how exhausting and lonely it is to be in a relationship eclipsed by constant pain. But during Bianca's suffering, had Damian ever made an enormous error in judgment? A mistake so monumental that his partner would struggle to forgive him? Probably not. Curtis had been selfish and stupid, and he'd broken Syd's heart. Now, he must make amends.

"They'd do the same for us," Curtis says, and he means it. "For better or for worse and all that."

"B. and I aren't married, but I feel the same way." Damian's smile looks slightly forced. "It's all part of the deal."

They've reached the pool now, where the women are deep in conversation over mugs of milky coffee. Damian lowers himself onto the end of the lounge chair next to his partner, drapes an arm around her shoulders. "They're going to have a great little winery here."

"So I hear," Bianca says. "I reckon it'll be a huge success."

Curtis pulls up a cheap plastic deck chair, addresses his wife. "Damian had some great ideas for that shed out back."

"Perfect." Syd seems delighted. "Coffee, Damian?"

"I'm okay." He looks to his girlfriend. "We should go. The phones are probably charged by now."

"Call from here," Sydney suggests. "It's too hot to sit in your van."

"All our stuff is in the van," Damian says. "We shouldn't leave it alone too long."

"We could push it into the driveway," Syd offers. "And then we could have an early lunch. Curtis makes a great frittata."

Irritation tenses Curtis's jaw. Without even consulting him, Sydney is inviting these interlopers for lunch and suggesting he cook. She clearly doesn't want them to leave, doesn't want to be left alone with her husband. Curtis swallows his annoyance, pushes it down. He wants to keep his wife happy. Syd and Bianca can bond over their dead mothers, and Curtis can pick Damian's brain about converting the shed.

"Stay," Curtis says. "I got some Manchego cheese at the market the other day."

Bianca and Damian exchange a look. "I *am* hungry," Bianca says.

Damian turns toward Curtis. "If you're sure it's not too much trouble."

But it's Syd who answers. "No trouble at all." It's the happiest she's sounded since before her mom passed. She jumps up. "Let's go get the van."

Sydney Cleary and Curtis Lowe, Couples' Counseling Session
Ellen Dwyer, Psychologist, PsyD
June 24

THERAPY PROGRESS NOTES—SESSION 1.

Curtis is open and vocal about his love for his wife and his desire to save the marriage. He'll need to be patient with Sydney. Before she can even try to forgive, she needs to know that Curtis understands the pain he has caused her and the damage he has done.

Curtis admitted the affair to his wife. Why? He claims he couldn't bear to lie to her, but was he fearful of getting caught? Curtis may have been trying to get ahead of it so he could control the narrative. Or was it an effort to assuage his own guilt? Curtis seems to consider his admission to be proof of his devotion to Sydney. She doesn't appear to see it that way.

5

"It's nice to have company," Syd says as the foursome trudge up the hill. "Curtis and I have been cooped up alone for months. If we don't have some outside stimulation soon, we're going to murder each other." It's a joke, but she sees Curtis smart from her words. She feels guilty for a second, and then she remembers.

"I get it," Bianca says. "Damian and I have been living in a van for nearly a month. He's had to sleep with one eye open for the past two weeks."

"Oh, I haven't been sleeping," Damian responds, and they all laugh.

The van sitting idle on the side of the road is an old Volkswagen Westfalia. Sydney is no expert on camping vehicles, but her auntie Jean had a similar van when she married her second husband, Uncle Murray. They drove all over North America in it, sleeping in the back, eating sandwiches at their little table. As a child, Sydney had thought it was romantic, bohemian. But she can't imagine living like that now.

"Let's see if it starts," Curtis says, walking up to the driver's-side door. "Maybe it was flooded."

"It wasn't flooded," Damian replies, but he gets in, turns the key. The engine sputters but refuses to catch. He climbs out again.

Curtis peers inside. "You've got a manual transmission. We could try to push start it." His tone is confident, knowledgeable, bordering on macho. Since when does Curtis know anything about cars? They had a Range Rover when they lived in New York, a luxury vehicle that they stored in an expensive garage. It was washed, buffed, and maintained for them. It's not like Curtis spent his weekends tinkering under the hood.

"That only works if the battery's flat," Damian tells him. "The engine wouldn't respond at all if it was."

"Right," Curtis says, like he knew it. He didn't.

Damian ushers Bianca into the driver's seat. "It's in neutral, babe. You steer it into the driveway. The three of us can push."

Bianca takes the wheel, and the rest of them move to the back of the vehicle. "Release the hand brake!" Damian calls to his partner.

"Done!"

"Okay, let's push." Damian gives Sydney a quick wink that makes her feel like part of the team, though they probably don't need her. Months of anxiety and depression have taken their toll on her physical self, and she's light and weak. But the three of them lean against the rear end of the vehicle, the two men grunting with the strain of getting it off the verge, back onto the asphalt. Sydney pushes with all her might. She's enjoying this. For the first time in weeks, she feels fully awake, fully present.

"There we go," Damian says as the van begins to roll. "Don't push too hard on this incline." The van moves forward, Bianca steering it back onto the road. Syd's hands are planted on the warm metal surface, her head down, eyes on the ground beneath her. It feels good to be physical. She's felt so frail and powerless. Suddenly, the vehicle evaporates under her touch. She looks up to see the van gathering speed, cruising down the hill.

"Hit the brakes, B.!" Damian calls.

"I can't reach!" the girl cries from inside the van. "The seat's too far back."

"Fuck!" Damian swears and breaks into a run. "Pull the hand brake!" he yells, sprinting after the speeding vehicle. "Pull the hand brake!"

Curtis and Syd run after them, eyes on the van careening down the hillside. Syd's stomach twists with dread. Bianca's not wearing a seat belt. If she hits a tree or a fence at this speed, she could be hurt. Badly. The van is almost at their property line now, still traveling at a dangerous pace. Suddenly, there's a screech of metal, a cloud of dust, and the back wheels of the van lock up. It skids to a stop, coming to rest at the mouth of their driveway.

Damian runs up and opens the door. Bianca climbs out, falls into his arms. He holds her, stroking her hair as she trembles in his embrace.

"Are you okay?" Syd puts a comforting hand on the girl's shoulder.

Bianca turns toward her, looking shaken but also exhilarated. "I'm fine. But I could use a bloody drink!"

With the van parked safely in their driveway, Syd digs in the fridge for a bottle of cava. "We're seriously drinking?" Curtis asks. There's a hint of judgment in his tone, like she's offering their guests a bag of cocaine.

"Bianca's been through a trauma," she says breezily, popping the cork. "And we live in Spain now. Day drinking is perfectly acceptable." She rinses the dusty flutes and pours the bubbles as Curtis puts the frittata in the oven. He hustles around the kitchen, making his excellent pan con tomate and tossing a bright, citrusy salad. If he's annoyed that Syd's invited their guests to stay, he's hiding it well. Curtis is the consummate host.

Sydney takes the flutes to the dining room, where Damian and Bianca sit side by side at the timber table. "Brilliant," Damian says as Syd sets a glass in front of him.

Bianca accepts the flute and sips the cava. "Thank you. I needed this."

Damian turns to face his girlfriend. "I thought you were going to roll away and leave me forever."

"Never." They kiss. It's so tender and intimate that Syd looks away.

Curtis enters with the frittata and a plate of crusty tomato bread. "Lunch is served."

* * *

They fill their plates, all of them famished from the day's excitement. Compliments fly around the table as they tuck into their meal, and then Bianca says, "I'm so sorry you're stuck with our broken-down hunk of junk in your driveway. I told Damian we should *rent* a vehicle, not buy one."

"It was such a good deal, though," Damian says, crunching into a piece of bread.

"Because it's a piece of crap!" Bianca cries good-naturedly.

"You're definitely having an adventure," Syd says, smiling at the younger couple. "What made you decide to come to Spain?"

Damian opens his mouth to respond, but Bianca talks over him. "My mom was obsessed with Spain—the food, the language, the people. But she never got to see it. She never had the chance to travel." The blonde takes another drink of her bubbly. "I didn't want to make the same mistake."

Syd meets her gaze, and they share a moment, an understanding. They are two motherless daughters who have been shaped by their losses.

Curtis grabs the bottle to top up Damian's flute, but there's only a dribble left. He surveys the table. "Should I open another?"

"Why not?" Sydney says. She's enjoying discussing topics besides renovations, grapevines, and their troubled relationship. A couple of glasses of cava in, she almost feels like her old self.

Bianca looks at Damian. "We need to sort out the van," she says.

Damian groans, leans back in his chair. "Yeah, we do. I should make some more calls."

Syd checks her watch. "Everyone will be having lunch now. And after that, they have siesta."

"I keep forgetting they sleep all afternoon." Bianca's face is creased with concern.

"Spend the night," Syd suggests. "Curtis can drive you to Girona tomorrow. It'll be easier to communicate with a mechanic in person."

"That's so generous," Bianca says.

Damian turns to Curtis. "Really? You wouldn't mind?"

All eyes are on Syd's husband. His expression is unreadable and she's afraid he'll say no. He'll tell Damian that they're too busy working on the property, fixing up the house, and trying to rebuild their marriage. That the two travelers should move along.

"Stay," Curtis says, and he almost sounds like he means it. "I'll take you to a garage tomorrow."

Sydney smiles at her partner, her chest warm with gratitude. "I'll grab some more bubbles."

On light feet, she moves to the kitchen.

6

The city of Girona is just over an hour's drive from the hillside house. With a population of over one hundred thousand, it has an airport, a hospital, and all the services of a midsize city. It's a picturesque town, with medieval walls, colorful buildings, and narrow winding streets. *Game of Thrones* fans flock to Girona because several scenes of the popular show were filmed there. The first time they'd visited, Curtis had marveled at the expansive stone steps of the Girona Cathedral, remembering how Jaime Lannister had ridden his horse up the Great Sept of Baelor. But Syd didn't watch the series. She wasn't into fantasy, and she'd heard the sex and violence were over the top.

"I really appreciate this," Damian says as Curtis navigates a wide roundabout. "Hopefully I can buy a new fuel pump for the van and install it this afternoon."

"You know how to replace a fuel pump?" Curtis is impressed. Growing up in the city, working in the business world, Curtis had little opportunity to develop those hands-on skills.

"I know my way around an engine," the Aussie says. "And YouTube can help me if I get stuck."

"Hopefully one of the garages has what you need."

"I hope so."

They lapse into silence then, both dwelling on the likelihood of that. At least Curtis is. What are the odds that a mechanic will have a fuel pump for a Volkswagen Westfalia from the 1980s on hand? If he doesn't, how long will a part take to arrive? What will Damian and Bianca do in the meantime? They can't sleep in Curtis and Syd's driveway for days on end. They'd spent last night there, and it had felt a little awkward.

"Stay in the spare room," Syd had offered.

"It cools off at night, so we're totally comfortable in the van," Bianca replied. She was making pasta for dinner, had insisted on cooking to make up for the intrusion. Syd had opened a bottle of wine despite complaining of a cava headache earlier.

Damian spoke up. "We don't need a bed, but I'd take a shower if it's on offer."

"Of course." Syd hurried to a linen closet for fresh towels, delighted to be playing hostess to these strangers. Curtis was okay with it—it couldn't be helped—but when the pair had gone to bed in their van, he'd slept fitfully. They'd left the front door unlocked in case their guests needed the facilities. It was perfectly safe—probably—but still Curtis felt restless.

Now, as he maneuvers his Citroën C4 onto the Girona exit, his eyes check the digital clock on the dashboard screen. It's 8:56 a.m. All the garages will be open by the time they arrive. There are several mechanics in town; surely one of them can get Damian his fuel pump in a timely manner.

The GPS directs them to the first garage, and Curtis pulls up out front. "I've got some errands to run," he says, car still idling. "Text me when you're done."

"Thanks, mate." Damian climbs out of the vehicle. "I'll get this sorted as quick as I can, and we'll get out of your hair."

"No problem," Curtis says, but the car door slams on his words. He drives off.

His first stop is the hardware store. They need more white paint, painter's tape, and new rollers for the basement walls. The main bathroom shower needs re-caulking, so he gets the supplies. While he's there, Curtis checks out lumber for fixing the old shed and turning it into their winery. He didn't have time to take measurements before this emergency trip, but he does some rough cost calculations on his phone.

Next, Curtis drives to the market to pick up milk, fruit, and a whole fish for dinner. He knows the odds that their guests will leave tonight are slim. With the groceries in a cooler bag, Curtis heads for a café. He orders a coffee and a traditional pastry with a name he can't pronounce and sits at a small table outside. The sidewalk is shaded, and he's pleasantly cool despite the morning sun promising another hot day. He sips his coffee, tears off a piece of deep-fried pastry, and observes the locals heading to work, speaking their Catalan dialect that seems to vary from town to town. And then he pulls out his burner phone.

He'd like to leave what happened in New York behind him, but it's not that simple. Things got complicated. Messy. And Sydney can never know about that. He gave her the passwords to all his devices—an effort to regain her trust—but his wife doesn't know about this phone or the secret email address he keeps. He's one hundred percent devoted to repairing his marriage, but he can't just ignore the disaster he left in his wake.

"It's me," he says, voice lowered, though the Spanish couple at the next table likely can't understand him. "Just checking in."

But the response, distant and tinny, barely registers because Curtis sees Damian's muscular form moving down the sidewalk toward him. "I'll call back," he says, abruptly hanging up. He turns off the phone and shoves it deep into his pocket. Curtis's pulse is ragged due to nearly getting caught. Damian was supposed to text when he was done with the mechanic. When Curtis checks his regular phone, he sees that he has.

Wrapped up. Going to grab a coffee. Want one?

"Hey," Damian calls as he approaches. "Not great news, I'm afraid."

"What's up?"

The Australian pulls out the wrought iron chair and sits opposite Curtis. "I checked three mechanics, and they all said they'll have to order in a fuel pump. It'll take a couple of weeks. One guy said maybe ten days, so I went with him."

"Damn."

"But don't worry," Damian says quickly. "I can have the van towed into town, and Bianca and I can get a hostel here."

Phew. "Sure, whatever. No rush."

"We won't wear out our welcome. You and your missus have done enough for us already."

"Syd's loved the company." Curtis takes the last bite of his pastry. "And me too. Did you still want to get a coffee?"

"Nah, I'm okay. I should get back and explain the situation to Bianca."

Their chairs scrape across the pavement as they stand, move down the street toward the Citroën. They've only gone a few yards when a woman's voice calls out.

"*¡Señor!*"

Curtis turns to see an attractive Spanish woman standing, waving at him. She has long hair, a bone-colored dress, impressive cleavage. She'd been seated at the table next to him, but he'd been so engrossed in his phone call that he hadn't noticed her.

"*¿Sí?*" he responds, taking a step toward her.

She says something in Spanish so rapid he doesn't understand. He looks to Damian, who shrugs, then winks. "Maybe she likes you?"

Curtis snorts, but his ego swells. He can't help it. Since Sydney learned of his affair, she's been physically repulsed by him. They've only had one intimate moment in their new home—after *a lot* of wine—but it hadn't gone to plan. The pressure of the encounter, combined with the alcohol, had inhibited Curtis's performance. Syd had pulled away from him, disappointed and hurt. He'd tried to explain, to blame the booze, but she'd gone inward. Since then, Syd hasn't shown any sexual interest in him, let alone desire. And now, this beautiful

Spanish woman is calling out to him. It's normal to be flattered by the attention.

"*Aquí. Tu bolsa,*" she says, pointing toward the table they just vacated. The cooler bag sits forgotten under it.

"Almost forgot your purse!" Damian jokes, but Curtis ignores him.

"*Gracias,*" he mumbles, hurrying back to retrieve his groceries.

7

Ellen, the therapist, had been extremely clear with Sydney: "You don't want to know the details of Curtis's liaison. That kind of information paints a mental picture that can be re-traumatizing." So, Syd had never asked about Curtis's lover's background, personality, or sexual proclivities. She didn't want to know what attracted him to Collette, the irresistible quality that had led him to sleep with a virtual stranger and risk a twelve-year marriage. That knowledge would only hurt her more. She knows this. But Sydney wouldn't be a normal human being if she didn't check out Collette on social media.

Curtis had been forthcoming with only the most superficial details. Collette Jasper was around forty, divorced, the COO of a biotech startup looking for office and lab space in any of the five boroughs. She was white, attractive, with dark hair and tawny skin. It wasn't much, but it was enough for Sydney to find her on Facebook.

Syd's still in bed, sipping the coffee Curtis made before he left for Girona, her laptop warming her legs through the sheets. Whenever Curtis leaves Sydney alone in the house, she indulges her curiosity. She knows it isn't healthy, that it may impede her healing, but she can't help herself. Setting down her mug, she types the name of her husband's mistress into the Facebook search bar.

As she waits for Collette Jasper's profile to load, Sydney wonders why she continues to visit this page. She already knows Collette's privacy settings are tight, that there's virtually no personal information available, only a handful of photographs. (Like a masochist, Syd has screenshotted them, saved them to her camera roll for accessible torture sessions.) And yet, Syd returns to the site like it's a lifeline, her only link to the woman who nearly destroyed her. It's twisted and disturbing.

Collette's profile pic is seared in Sydney's mind. It shows a sexy woman with a dark, shoulder-length blowout, dangly earrings, and a curvaceous figure. In another photo, Collette laughs while holding a whimsical cocktail: tiny umbrella, fresh fruit, curly straw. In the next, she stands in front of a tropical resort, her floral sarong matching the peach tones of the stucco building as if it were staged. Curtis's lover appears fun, light, the kind of woman who vacations on Miami Beach and orders a double piña colada. Was it Collette's vivaciousness that attracted Curtis? Or was it simply those big boobs?

As always, the mental image of her husband's mistress prompts an unpleasant comparison. In contrast to Collette, Sydney feels pale and scrawny, bland and reserved. She's lost too much weight since the infidelity. The emotional pain and the medications have made her dull and listless. Sydney used to be vibrant, sexy, and confident, didn't she? And yet Curtis still found this other woman with her sparkling smile, her curves, her bright colors, impossible to resist. Maybe Syd shouldn't have worn so many neutral pantsuits.

The page is loading slowly, the Wi-Fi in the hillside house less than speedy. Perhaps Bianca is using it out in her camper van? She hadn't asked Syd for the password, but maybe Curtis had shared it. It's fine. Syd can wait to scratch this ugly itch, to see the images and information already etched on her brain. She sips her coffee as the tiny wheel on-screen spins.

A list of Collette Jaspers appears, but none of them are her husband's lover. Sydney sits forward, peers at the screen. Has *the* Collette Jasper deleted her Facebook account? More likely, she's blocked Sydney. But why now? The affair ended over a year ago. Syd and Curtis have moved across the ocean. Why would Collette suddenly be worried about her privacy? It makes no sense.

Curtis would not have been in touch with Collette: It was discussed at length in therapy as the ultimate dealbreaker. Curtis had assured his wife that he'd felt no emotional connection to Collette, that he had no reason or desire for contact with his former lover. He'd quit his job and moved continents to prove the point! Plus, Sydney and Curtis are together practically 24/7. He'd given her the passwords for all his devices. She hasn't checked recently, but she could. Why would he risk it?

She tosses the laptop aside and drags herself out of bed. Despite the strong cup of coffee, her head feels fuzzy and muddled, likely from yesterday's drinks. She knows now isn't the time to spiral into doubts and trust issues. Slipping into a one-piece swimsuit, she searches for her cover-up, then remembers she left it on a pool chair to dry. Instead, she wraps Curtis's terry cloth robe around her and searches for her cigarettes.

As she sits smoking by the pool, Syd looks at the Westfalia broken down in the driveway. She wonders if Bianca is still asleep, or if she's meditating or journaling or doing some other healthy, spiritual activity that van-dwellers practice. Stubbing out the cigarette, she walks to the vehicle and knocks on the side door. Vinyl curtains cover the windows, but she hears rustling in response. Within moments, the door opens, and Bianca emerges, bright-eyed and perky.

"Good morning." She climbs out of the van, wearing a black bikini top, sweatpants hanging low on her hips. Bianca slides the van door closed behind her, but not before Syd's eyes flit to the interior. She doesn't mean to be nosy, but she's curious how this couple has been living so harmoniously in such close quarters. But all she can make out is a small countertop, the cupboards beneath it, and a rumpled, built-in bed.

"I was waiting for you to finish your cigarette," the Australian girl explains. She taps her chest. "Asthma."

"I just have one a day," Syd replies sheepishly. "I'm tapering off."

"Good." Bianca smiles at her. "I'm a nurse. I've seen too many people suffer and die from lung cancer and emphysema."

Syd changes the subject. "Have you heard from the guys?"

"No, nothing." Bianca's pretty face contorts. "I'm so sorry about all this."

"Let's make the best of it," Syd suggests. "There's coffee inside, and we can have a swim."

As Bianca stands at the pool's edge preparing for a shallow dive, Sydney treads water and tries not to feel bad about herself. Bianca is so young, so toned, so tanned. Sydney has always been tall, slim, and flat-chested: a model-esque figure. She looks good in clothes; Bianca looks good in this tiny swimsuit. It's juvenile, anti-feminist, and hard on the ego to be thinking this way, especially after she spent the morning comparing herself to Collette. Sydney dives under the water, kicks her way to the opposite end of the pool.

"Nothing better than a brisk morning swim," Bianca says when Syd surfaces. She's treading water in the middle of the pool now, her hair slicked back from her face. The girl is almost breathtakingly beautiful, but the bright sunlight illuminates faint acne scars on her cheeks, the slightest wrinkles around her eyes and mouth. She's human after all.

"Better than coffee." Syd swims to the edge, rests her arms on the concrete behind her.

Bianca swirls in place. "What kind of law did you practice back in New York?"

Sydney had mentioned her former job in passing yesterday, but she'd been intentionally vague. She knows the reaction her title can elicit. "I was a public defender."

"Seriously?" Bianca coughs. "You defended murderers and rapists?"

"I did," Sydney says, voice measured in the face of the woman's judgment. "The Sixth Amendment guarantees people accused of a crime the right to a lawyer, even if they can't afford one. That's how our legal system works. That's how we ensure everyone is treated fairly."

"But why choose that kind of law?" Bianca joins her at the side of the pool, her face scrunched with confusion. Or is it disdain? "Why not help good people instead of bad people?"

"Some of the people who use a public defender *are* good." Sydney climbs out of the pool, grabs a towel off a lawn chair, and dries herself as she talks. "Do you know how many low-income, marginalized people go to jail for crimes they didn't commit? Because they got railroaded by police or falsely accused by victims or witnesses? Or they just didn't have a decent lawyer?"

"No..." Bianca says, ascending the pool steps to join Syd. "I never really thought of it that way."

"There are nearly four thousand people on the National Registry of Exonerations. Most of them lived in poverty or with addiction or suffered racism. Many of them didn't have decent legal representation. I provided that."

"So, some of the people you represented were innocent," Bianca says thoughtfully as they lay their towels on lawn chairs and stretch out to dry off.

"Some," Syd says, though that isn't really the point.

"I think a lot of lawyers just care about money," Bianca says, "but you were making a difference."

"I tried to." Syd smiles.

Bianca turns to her, her eyes hidden by large dark sunglasses. "Aren't there acts that are unforgivable, though? Things so awful that they're indefensible?"

Bianca is talking about murder, abduction, rape, and torture. Why does Syd's mind go to Curtis's one-night stand?

"Everyone deserves due process," she says. "Everyone deserves to be heard."

"Even monsters?"

Just then, the rumble of a car, the crunch of tires on the rutted drive, saves Syd from diving into the moral and ethical complexities.

"Sounds like the guys are back." She gets up and heads inside.

Sydney Cleary and Curtis Lowe, Couples' Counseling Session
Ellen Dwyer, Psychologist, PsyD
July 1

TRANSCRIPT 2.

Ellen:
Curtis, do you feel comfortable telling me how the infidelity happened?

Curtis:
I work in property management. Commercial leasing. I don't normally handle clients, but we were short-staffed. And this was a big deal. It was a lot of money. So, I was spending a lot of time with this woman—

Sydney:
Her name is Collette. You can say it.

Curtis:
We'd finally closed on a location, and we cracked a bottle of bubbly to celebrate. Collette had some party drugs. MDMA, I think. I don't normally partake, but I'd been under so much stress. It just sort of... happened after that.

Ellen:
Was it an emotional affair?

Curtis:
God, no. I felt nothing for her.

Sydney:
He seems to think that makes it better, but I think it makes it worse. If he had real feelings for Collette, maybe I could understand why he'd betray me. But this was just careless. And cruel.

Ellen:
It's not uncommon for men and women to view the emotional component of an affair differently. Men tend to feel that infidelity is more forgivable if there are no feelings involved. Women are more likely to feel it's justified if there are. Was the relationship ongoing, Curtis?

Curtis:
No. It was just one time. Just one huge mistake. I was drunk and high—I know that's not an excuse, but it feels like it wasn't even me in a way. I know what I did, and I take responsibility for it, but if I was *normal*, if I wasn't so fucked-up, I would never have risked my marriage. I love Sydney so much, and I could lose her.

Ellen:
You seem very committed to this relationship. How do you feel, Sydney?

Sydney:
I don't know... I don't know if I can ever forgive him.

8

"They can't stay here for *ten days*," Curtis tells Sydney, who's sitting cross-legged on their bed, wrapped in his terry cloth robe. They'd absconded to their bedroom, saying they needed to change clothes, but they're really here to discuss their stranded houseguests. "We can let them spend one more night, and then I'll drive them to Girona in the morning."

"They might prefer to stay in Cadaqués," Syd offers. "Then they're near the beach. And we could still meet them for lunch or dinner."

Curtis hadn't realized his wife was so starved for companionship. Back home, she'd been so introverted—at least for a New Yorker—preferring to spend evenings on the sofa instead of in restaurants or at the theater. But after a few months alone with him, she's suddenly a social butterfly, excited to eat meals with a couple of Australian kids. He can't help but take it personally.

"They'll have to tow the van to Girona," Curtis says. "They might want to stay close to it."

"That'll cost a fortune," Syd says. "And why do they need to stay close to their van? That makes no sense."

"Girona's a great city," Curtis counters, watching his wife pull on a pair of shorts under the robe. "There's so much history there. And maybe they're *Game of Thrones* fans?"

"Maybe."

"Look," Curtis says with finality, "they're a nice couple. It's been fun to hang out with them. But we've got work to do around the place. We don't have time to entertain guests."

Syd drops the robe from her shoulders and reaches for a bra. Curtis feels a stirring at the sight of her skin, her breasts—it's been so long—but she quickly pulls on a T-shirt. "What if they pitched in?" Syd suggests. "Damian could help you fix up that old shed. He seems to know a lot about building. And Bianca could help me paint downstairs."

"Do you really want houseguests for that long?" Curtis says. "You know the old saying about fish and guests. After three days they start to stink."

Sydney shrugs. "We've been alone together for months. And we'll be alone again when they move on."

Curtis feels his face getting warm. It's frustration. Loss of control. He keeps his delivery level. "In therapy, Ellen said we need to build a new relationship, like a second marriage. How can we do that with another couple hanging around?"

"Ellen also said we need to socialize and have fun." Sydney hangs the robe on a hook on the back of the door. "To do the things we used to enjoy before *your affair*."

The words slice him like a sword, likely what Syd intended, and he backs down. He has no choice. He'll do anything to keep her happy.

She moves toward him, her demeanor softening. "Hiding out here alone isn't going to fix us, Curtis," she says gently. "And you know we need help around the place."

"Fine." He nods. "We can run it by them, if that's what you want."

The travelers seem unsure at first. "When we turned up here, we didn't even expect you to let us in," Bianca says. "We certainly didn't expect to end up staying here."

"You can see we need help around the place," Syd says. "And we'll pay you in pool time and wine."

"We don't want to intrude..."

"You wouldn't be," Curtis insists, forcing enthusiasm. "We'd love the company. And the free labor."

Damian and Bianca consult each other with a look. "I think we could get that shed fixed up in no time," Damian says, turning to Curtis. "I'd be happy to help."

"It's settled, then," Curtis says, voice upbeat with only the slightest hint of a waver.

"Show us all the jobs you need done," Bianca offers.

"The lower floor is still a disaster," Syd says. "I'll take you down."

Curtis watches the three of them move to the stairs, but he doesn't follow. No one will find his absence odd. They'll assume he's gone to the bathroom or maybe to start lunch. And soon he will begin cooking. But he has something important to take care of first.

Slipping outside, he hustles to his car and fishes under the driver's seat. He'd deposited the burner phone there when they returned from Girona. He never brings it into the house; he can't risk Sydney finding it and asking questions. Withdrawing the device, he stuffs it in his pocket and walks briskly toward the old shed. The derelict building has been the perfect hiding place, but that'll have to change once they start renovating. Glancing over his shoulder, he pushes open the door and moves into the musty space.

For a second, Curtis feels blind and disoriented, then his eyes adjust to the dim interior. He makes out the familiar mess: scrap lumber, rusted cans, thick cobwebs. Dust motes float in the strips of sunshine filtering through the rotted boards, scattering as Curtis barges through them. He retrieves a rumpled rag tucked away in a back corner. Ensuring the phone is powered off, he wraps it in the cloth, places it behind a stack of warped shingles.

"Whatcha doing, mate?"

Curtis spins around, his heart hammering in his chest. Damian stands in the doorway, a look of dark amusement on his features. Why did the Aussie man follow him out here? Why was he so damn quiet? And what did he see?

"Just assessing how much junk I need to clear out," Curtis says chipperly. His voice is high-pitched, too cheerful, but Damian won't notice. The guy barely knows him.

"We can start now." Damian rubs his palms together, like he can't wait to get to work.

"I need to strategize where to put things," Curtis says quickly. "Besides, we've got lunch. And then siesta."

"How do the Spanish get anything done?" Damian chuckles as the pair head back toward the house.

"Slowly," Curtis replies. "But we're living the good life now."

Sydney Cleary and Curtis Lowe, Couples' Counseling Session
Ellen Dwyer, Psychologist, PsyD
July 1

THERAPY PROGRESS NOTES—SESSION 2.

Curtis tends to diminish his culpability for cheating (he was on drugs, stressed, drinking heavily). He's dismissive of the other woman and her emotions. This seems to be an attempt to reassure Sydney. Or he may be trying to minimize his transgression.

Sydney feels Curtis's betrayal of their commitment is cavalier. His lack of feeling toward the other woman is not reassuring to her.

9

Syd stuffs beach towels, sunscreen, and water bottles into a midsize backpack. She's excited to show Bianca and Damian around Cadaqués, to take them to her favorite beach and for lunch after. The plan had been decided last night, over a full fish stuffed with lemon and herbs. Work could wait, Curtis and Sydney insisted. Their guests hadn't even had a chance to check out the town, the restaurants, or the sea. They'd enjoy a day of swimming, food, and getting to know one another.

"But there's so much to do around here," Bianca had objected, but Sydney had shut her down.

"People in Spain take enjoying themselves seriously. We didn't move here to work all the time like we did back home."

"So, what prompted the move?" Damian asked, chewing his fish.

"Look around," Curtis said, waving a hand toward the view. "It's heaven."

"It is. But most people don't pack up their lives, quit their jobs, and leave everything behind without some sort of catalyst."

Syd felt her cheeks burning, and she couldn't look at her husband. She didn't want this happy couple to know the truth of her marriage. She wanted a clean slate, without judgment or pity. "We honeymooned here and fell in love with it," she said brightly. "New York gets more expensive every day. After my mom passed, it felt like the right time."

Bianca smiled. "It's really brave to follow your passions while you're so young."

"Smart, too," Damian said, scooping up some rice on his fork. "If this winery doesn't work out, you can always go back and pick up where you left off."

"It'll work out," Curtis said tightly. "We're devoted to this plan."

"We're here to help," Damian replied, but Curtis had jumped up to clear the dishes.

Her husband enters the bedroom now, wearing his sun hat, his face tinted white with sunscreen. "Ready?" There's something tense, even apprehensive in his tone.

"Yep." She smiles at him. She appreciates the effort he's making. She knows she's enjoying the company more than he is. "Let's go."

They take the Citroën, the Australians squeezed into the back seat, down the winding hill to a dusty parking lot outside the town center. "It's usually half empty," Curtis says as they roll over the silty surface, looking for a spot. The lot is packed with tiny European cars.

"All the Spaniards are out enjoying life," Bianca says, and Syd tosses a smile over her shoulder.

Finally, Curtis parks and they walk through narrow, winding streets toward the sea. Syd still gets lost in this little whitewashed town, but Curtis knows his way. They walk under a canopy of bright purple and red bougainvillea, passing cafés, boutique hotels, and shoe stores with racks of espadrilles out front. As they get closer to the bay, the shops sell beach towels, straw hats, and swimming shoes for the rocky coast. Restaurants with patios serve coffee or beer to locals and tourists, mostly from France or other parts of Spain. Soon, they emerge into the main square, the statue of famous resident Salvador Dalí standing sentry.

"Oh my God," Bianca marvels, taking in the fishing boats bobbing in the turquoise water, the pale buildings hugging the curve of the bay. "It's stunning!"

"Incredible," Damian adds, turning in circles to take it all in.

"It's the most beautiful town," Syd says proudly, as if she'd discovered it or built it. "And there's a great beach right in the center of it." But as they approach the main beach, they see that it's teeming with people. Families wrangle squealing toddlers. Teen boys splash and roughhouse while their girlfriends lounge and smoke hand-rolled cigarettes. Beautiful topless women tan or pose for Instagram photos taken by their slight, enamored boyfriends. Parasols and beach blankets stake their claim. There's no space for four people to put their towels down, barely room to move in the frothing sea.

"Shit," Syd mutters. She peers down the bay to the next beach and sees it's similarly packed.

"There's a secluded little cove just past Portlligat," Curtis suggests. "It's a bit of a hike, but we'll probably have it all to ourselves."

"Good thinking," Syd says. She knows the beach her husband is referring to. The walk is long but scenic, and the spot is a hidden gem.

"Let's do it," Bianca says, and Damian agrees.

They walk along the seaside path for a couple of miles until it takes them inland. They pass a development of modern houses, many set behind thick walls and ornate iron gates offering glimpses of manicured, irrigated lawns. Holiday homes for rich Europeans, Syd assumes, far more luxurious and expensive than their remote abode. A gentle hill slopes toward Portlligat where they stop to buy ice-cold lemon sodas, sipping them in the shade of a stone building.

Damian indicates a queue of people with his chin. "What's that about?"

"That's Salvador Dalí's house," Curtis says. "You can tour the house and garden, but you have to book in advance."

"It's worth doing," Sydney adds. "We loved it. He was so eccentric."

"I read a biography on him," Bianca adds. "About him and his wife, Gala. She was his muse."

"She died here," Curtis says. "Dalí couldn't bear to live here without her, so he moved to his castle in Púbol. He died a few years later." He glances over at Syd, his eyes soft. "Such a love story."

"Except Gala was married when they met." Bianca sips her cold drink. "In fact, she came here with her poet husband and their daughter and abandoned them both when she fell for Dalí. They had an open marriage, and some people think Dalí was a virgin his entire life. He was a voyeur and encouraged Gala to have a lot of affairs. Even with her ex-husband."

"That's weird," Syd says.

"I think they were ahead of their time," Bianca replies. "A lot of people are realizing that the Disney version of romance and monogamy isn't sustainable these days. It's not realistic."

Curtis lobs his empty bottle into a bin. It bangs loudly against the metal sides, and Syd winces. "Ready to hit the trail?" he asks.

They move on, traversing a narrow dirt path that runs along the hilltop and offers incredible sea views. It's getting hot, though, and the sugary drink has left Sydney's mouth parched and sticky. Her lungs feel heavy, and she vows, again, to quit smoking. She doesn't remember the beach being this far away, and she worries aloud that they've missed the turnoff.

"It's here," Curtis says, stopping at the top of a steep trailhead. He points down a winding goat track to a small cove, a patch of white sand, the sea varying shades of blue from azure to navy. As they'd hoped, it's deserted.

"Wow," Bianca says, heading down first. Curtis takes after her, then Sydney, with Damian bringing up the rear. The incline is intense, and as Syd hurries to keep up with her husband, her sneaker skids on some loose gravel. As she's about to fall on her butt, she feels Damian's strong hands catching her, lifting her.

"Careful," he says gently. "You okay?"

"I'm good. Thanks."

"Let them go ahead." He smiles down at her, his dark eyes warm. "We can take it slow."

She flushes, nods her thanks. God, it's hot out.

They continue down the path, Damian's hand brushing her lower back. He's being gallant, ready if she slips again, but his fingertips touching her waistband feel intimate. She's heard that Australian men can be chivalrous, a quality sometimes construed as chauvinism. Syd's always been fiercely independent, but she likes this. Damian's attentiveness makes her feel distinctly feminine.

When they reach the bottom, Curtis and Bianca are staring into the water. The cove is teeming with small purplish jellyfish that had been invisible from above.

"I've never seen these here before," Curtis says.

"Crap," Syd groans. "We came all this way." She'd planned a day of fun and frivolity, but everything seems to be going wrong.

"We have these little buggers back home," Bianca says quickly. "They're totally harmless."

"Are you sure?" Curtis asks as they watch the tiny mauve blobs floating on the gentle waves.

"They come in with certain tides," Damian explains. "They're slimy, but they don't sting."

"Okay," Curtis says, kicking off his shoes and pulling his T-shirt over his head. "I'm going in."

"Right behind you, mate!" Damian perches on a rock, begins to remove his shoes.

Curtis wades into the warm sea, the gelatinous creatures bobbing away on the current he creates. He plunges under the water, swims a few strokes below the surface. He pops up, turns back toward the shore, easily treading water in the buoyancy.

Syd's T-shirt is sticking to her back, and she peels it off. She's feeling a little lightheaded, and she needs to cool off.

"Are you going to swim?" Damian asks. "Those jellies are pretty disgusting."

"I'm so sweaty," Syd says, dropping her shorts to her ankles. She moves toward the respite of the sea.

And then Curtis screams.

10

The first sting is like a hot needle stabbing into Curtis's thigh. The next, near his ribs, is a bigger, hotter needle. "Fuck!" he screams, splashing fruitlessly, trying to push the jellyfish away, but they float back toward him on the rippling waves. Now his forearm gets it. Next his lower back. "They're stinging me!" he screams toward the beach.

"Come in, mate!" Damian is waving to him. "Swim in!"

Syd is standing in her bathing suit, her face etched with concern. "Swim, Curtis!" she cries, and he does, as fast as he can. Jellyfish stings can be deadly, he knows this, and he can feel the toxins seeping into his bloodstream. He staggers onto the shore, the stabbing now morphed into throbbing, itching, and burning. He feels dizzy, a little nauseated. He stands dripping and in pain as his companions surround him, unsure of how to help.

"Fuck," Damian says, eyes roaming over Curtis's body. Curtis looks down and sees the angry red welts on his torso, his leg, and his arm. He looks up at Damian.

"You said they didn't sting."

"The purple ones at home are harmless," Bianca jumps in. "These must be different."

"No shit," Curtis grumbles.

"What do we do?" Sydney asks. She reaches a comforting hand out to her husband, but she's afraid to touch him, afraid to make it worse.

"We need to get the tentacles out," Bianca says. "Grab your credit cards. We can scrape them off."

"Are you sure you know what you're doing?" Curtis asks as the three of them dig in their backpacks and wallets. The thought of *scraping* his wounds is highly unappealing. "Maybe we should call for help?"

"B.'s a nurse. And this isn't my first rodeo," Damian assures him as they set to work plucking and scraping. Curtis winces and swears, bites his lip to hold back tears. He doesn't want to be a pussy in front of their guests, but the scratching on his stings is torture! Finally, Bianca fills a water bottle with seawater and pours it over the welts. The pain is somewhat bearable now.

"Okay," Damian says, grabbing the top button of his shorts. "I'm going to have to piss on you."

"No, thanks." Curtis steps back.

"It'll neutralize the sting." Damian moves toward him. "Stand still."

"I—I don't want that!" Curtis's voice is a screech. He moves away, stumbling on a loose rock, wobbling before he rights himself. Bianca and Damian dissolve into laughter.

"I'm kidding, mate. Everyone knows that's a recipe for an infection."

"Hilarious," Curtis growls.

"We've got some hydrocortisone cream in the van," Bianca says, containing her giggles. "The pain should go away in a few days."

Curtis looks at Sydney, who's trying to hide her amusement but not doing a great job. "You okay to walk back?" she asks.

"Fine." Curtis is already struggling into his shoes.

At home, Curtis takes a long hot shower, then Sydney applies the steroid cream to his welts. "Gentle," he mutters from his perch on the closed toilet. They're squeezed into the small but charming bathroom with its original aqua-blue tiles. "It still stings."

"Hopefully this helps."

"Why would Bianca tell me those jellyfish didn't sting? Damian said it, too."

"They made a mistake," Syd says, moving to the sore on his lower back.

"He's a commercial diver. How could he not know they were stingers?"

"There are probably harmless purple jellyfish in Australia, and they got confused."

"Nothing's harmless in Australia. They have more dangerous creatures than the rest of the world combined."

"So you think they sent you into the water to get stung?" Syd puts the cap on the tube. "Why would they do that?"

She's right. They wouldn't. But he's itchy, and in pain, and in a pissy mood. Speaking of pissy...

"I didn't appreciate him pretending he was going to pee on me."

Syd smirks. "He was trying to lighten the mood."

Curtis grabs the clean T-shirt Syd has brought him, gingerly pulls it on. "If he ever gets hurt in my presence, I'll be sure to make some tasteless jokes."

"It wasn't very nice. But now he's out there emptying the shed and taking measurements for you."

"I'll go help," Curtis says, hurrying into his shorts.

He's not up to working in the afternoon heat, but the burner phone is hidden in that shed. Damian mustn't find it. He can't have the Australian asking why he has a secret phone. Or mentioning it to Bianca or, God forbid, Sydney. It would ruin all the trust he's built with her.

The grass outside the shed is littered with its former contents: scrap lumber, those dusty coffee cans, the stack of warped shingles. Where is the phone? He can hear Damian inside the building, the thump of his feet heavy on the wooden floorboards, the zip of the tape measure. Curtis peers through the tall grass and spots it. The phone is still wrapped in its rag, nestled between the shingles and a jagged board. Damian clearly put it there. Did he unwrap the bundle? Discover the secret device? Curtis hurries over to it, removes it from the fabric, shoves it into his front pocket.

His guest emerges then, shirt off, muscles covered in a sheen of sweat. Curtis stays fit; he looks pretty good, but Damian is a specimen. "Hey, mate. How are you feeling?"

"Good," he lies. "Better." This is Curtis's opportunity to address the burner, make up an excuse for having a phone hidden in his shed. But how could he ask a virtual stranger to keep his secret? And, if Damian *didn't* see the phone, Curtis doesn't want to draw attention to it. So he says nothing.

He takes a step toward the entrance. "Let's get to work."

11

"How's the patient?" Bianca asks when Sydney wanders into the kitchen.

"Crabby." Sydney smiles. "He's pretty uncomfortable, but he'll be fine."

"He should rest," Bianca says. "Damian can work on his own. He's a machine."

"I'm sure he is." Syd grabs a dishcloth, focuses on wiping the counter.

"We both feel so badly that we told Curtis it was safe to go in the water," Bianca apologizes. "Damian and I assumed the jellyfish were the same species we have back home. Clearly not."

"You didn't know," Syd replies. "Are you a diver, too?"

"I've got my open-water diving certificate, but I don't dive much. Damian spends so much time underwater at work that he prefers to have fun on dry land."

"Understandable."

"I'm just glad we knew how to treat the stings after," Bianca says. "It would have been a lot worse if we didn't get the stingers out."

"Thank God you were there," Sydney says. She's a city slicker, an indoor girl. She wouldn't have known how to handle her husband's injuries.

"Should we start on the painting?" Bianca offers. "Or at least the prep work?"

"I think I'm going to lie down for an hour," Syd says, a little sheepish. "I'm still getting used to this heat."

"It gets *a lot* hotter back home," Bianca chuckles. "You go rest. I'll start moving boxes and furniture away from the walls. If you've got a screwdriver, I'll take off the outlet panels."

"There's no rush," Syd says. "Go for a swim. Or have a siesta, too." But when Bianca insists, Sydney finds a flathead in the kitchen junk drawer and hands it to her. Bianca rumbles down the stairs, seemingly eager to attack the chaos.

Retreating to her bedroom, Syd closes the door and climbs into the queen-size bed. She wonders if Curtis will join her there. He shouldn't be working in this heat, especially when he's in pain and not feeling well. But Curtis has never listened to her when he's in one of his moods. And she can tell he feels competitive with the physically bigger, stronger, more alpha male in their home. Curtis is smart, fit, and attractive in his bookish way. Damian is Thor.

As she nestles under the silk duvet, her body relaxes and her mind drifts. In the cocoon of privacy her thoughts slip back to the hike, that moment when she'd nearly fallen on the trail. Damian's hands, strong yet gentle, had caught her. They'd continued down the path, his hand hovering at the small of her back. Curtis had been so intent on getting to the bottom, he hadn't even noticed she'd stumbled.

Let them go ahead. We can take it slow.

She'd felt something then—a tremor, a tingle, a warmth—and she feels it now. She'd ignored it, shunted it away as they joined their partners on the beach, but it revisits her. It's a harmless little... *nothing*. She's lonely, that's all. There's such a distance between Sydney and her husband. Maybe she's even a little *horny*. It's not like Syd and Curtis are having sex... well, once, when they were tipsy, and it had not gone well. Curtis had seemed so hungry for her, so full of passion and desire. But ultimately, he couldn't get aroused. He'd blamed the pressure of the moment, but Sydney worried that wasn't the truth. She wasn't as hot or sexy as Collette. She was comfortable and boring, and Curtis couldn't perform.

Sleepily, she allows her hand to travel between her thighs as she imagines Damian's strong body, his undeniable manliness. She feels his rough hands on her, moving over her skin, through her hair. Guilt flickers around the edges, but she doesn't need to feel badly about this. This is just a fantasy. She would never act on it. She's not like Curtis.

Her husband appears in her imagination then, his features contorted with passion and desire. Sydney has always found Curtis sexy, and she eases into the familiarity of him. Suddenly, his lover Collette enters the scene, those long earrings dangling as she snakes her way up Curtis's body. Sydney had avoided the details of their liaison, but her imagination fills in the blanks. And her body shuts down, any trace of arousal snuffed out by the mental image of the affair. Annoyed, she rolls over and eventually falls asleep.

Her phone buzzes about an hour later. Afternoon naps have become routine, but she often wakes groggy and confused, lingering in that liminal space between her old life and her new one. Is she in New York or Spain? Is it day or night? Did her husband cheat on her, or is their marriage solid and happy? She reaches for the phone, thinking it's her alarm, but she never sets it anymore. Why would she? She has nothing to do, nowhere to be. And the ringtone is different. It's a phone call. They're rare these days. It will be her brother, Reid, or maybe one of her girlfriends back in New York.

Propping herself up on an elbow, she reads the name on the display: Brian Hale. He was a colleague from the public defender's office. They'd been pals—not exactly close, but there was an undeniable camaraderie. They didn't socialize outside of work, but they'd regularly grab a gyro on the sidewalk or go for a drink after a day in court. Brian was one of the good ones. Like Sydney, he'd been lured to the PD's office because he truly wanted to help the disadvantaged. The loan forgiveness inherent in a public service job didn't hurt either.

"Hey, Syd," Brian says. "How's life in Spain?"

"It's good. Great." Brian doesn't know about the troubles in her marriage. He'd assumed, like most people, that Syd had simply burned out on the intense workload. "How are things in the office?"

"Nuts. Crazy. Same old."

Sydney reads the news from back home, monitors the cases that will require a public defender. She knows how hectic Brian's life must be. "Sorry to abandon you."

"Every man for himself." He chuckles, then his jovial tone darkens. "There's something I thought you should know." He clears his throat. "It's about Jameson Drew."

A damp coldness prickles Sydney's skin at the sound of the name. Drew was her last client before she left the PD's office and fled to Spain. After her mom died, while her marriage was falling apart, she'd been tasked with one of the most violent cases of her career. Jameson Drew had murdered his lover, choking him to death with his bare hands. The two men had met on a dating app, had spent several days together drinking, doing drugs, and having sex. And then something had gone wrong.

Jameson Drew claimed his victim had attacked him in a drug-fueled rage, that he'd killed him in self-defense. He'd panicked. There were illegal drugs and a corpse in his apartment! He knew how it would look to the police. So Drew had wrapped the body in plastic, driven to a forested area in New Jersey, and buried it.

It had not been Sydney's job to decide guilt or innocence. Her role was to represent her client at arraignment, to ensure he understood his legal options. When the DA offered a plea deal—twenty years to life—she counseled Drew to take it. There was no way he'd win at trial. The crime was too violent. The video footage of Drew dragging the lifeless body to his car too chilling. The DA would fight for first degree, make her client out to be a cold-blooded killer, a predator. If a jury bought it, Drew would get life without parole. He'd never be free again. Jameson Drew had wept like a child when he was sentenced, but it was the right choice. Sydney stood by it.

"What about him?" Syd asks.

"He's dead."

"Oh no," Syd says, but she isn't surprised. Prison often has a shortening effect on a life.

"There's more, Sydney..." Brian says, and his tone is solemn. "It's about you."

Syd's chest tightens, narrowing her airway. She struggles to get a deep breath, her anxiety raising its ugly head.

Because she knows, even dead, Jameson Drew can hurt her.

12

Curtis pours chilled Spanish vermouth into glass tumblers with orange peel and olives, the Catalonian way. They'd had two bottles of red with dinner, and they're all a little tipsy, talking too loudly, laughing too easily. All except Sydney. She's quiet, her eyes glassy, a little unfocused. Bianca and Damian are discussing Australian politics, so it's not like they as Americans have much to add, but Syd is so obviously checked out. Curtis clears his throat, attempts to draw her into the conversation.

"I guess we'll have to educate ourselves on the Spanish government," Curtis says, looking directly at Sydney. "With our visa, we can become citizens in ten years. Right, hon?"

Syd snaps to, reorienting herself in the moment. "Yeah," she mumbles. She looks to Bianca, abruptly changes the subject. "You two should sleep inside. In the guest room."

"We're fine in the van," the younger woman says, sipping her drink and making a face at its strong flavor.

"It may look cramped, but you'd be surprised how comfortable it is," Damian adds.

"We have a perfectly good guest room," Sydney insists. "And you're our first guests. It'd be a shame not to use it."

Curtis keeps his tone light. "They said they're fine in the van, babe." He's enjoying their guests' company for the most part, and he appreciates Damian's hard work, but he doesn't need them sleeping down the hall. He doesn't want to hear them snoring, using the bathroom, or, God forbid, having sex a few feet away.

Syd ignores him. "It's safer if you're inside. We like to lock the doors at night, and you might need the bathroom."

"I can go in the bushes," Damian says.

"Speak for yourself," Bianca says. "There are snakes!"

"We can leave a door unlocked," Curtis placates. "It's perfectly safe. And we have the cameras."

"Those old cameras don't even work," Syd counters. "And they're not much of a deterrent if someone really wants to get in here."

"Who would want to get in here?" Curtis chuckles awkwardly. "We don't have many valuables."

"You never know when some psycho could be passing by." Damian swirls the liquor in his glass. "But you're Americans. You probably have a gun."

"We're from New York," Sydney retorts, and Curtis feels a flicker of satisfaction. He hasn't been blind to the dynamic between his wife and their macho guest. Damian's been attentive, even solicitous toward Syd. In his cloud of testosterone, she has been acting demure and girlish. But she's annoyed by his assumption, and Curtis finds it satisfying.

"No offense," Bianca says, attempting to smooth things over. "It's the media. They make it seem like every person in America is packing."

"If I lived all alone out here, I'd have a weapon," Damian says, eyes meeting Curtis's. "That's all I'm saying."

"We don't have a gun," Curtis says, and Damian nods with a slight knowing smirk. The Australian likely knows about the secret phone. Does he assume Curtis has a secret firearm, too?

Bianca smiles at Sydney. "I think it would be nice to sleep inside for a few nights. Thank you."

"It's settled, then." Syd's chair scrapes across the tile. "I'll make up the bed."

By the time Curtis and Sydney head to their room, his eyes feel gritty, and there's a mild pounding between his eyebrows from the drinks.

He unbuttons his linen shirt, glancing over his shoulder at his wife. Her back is to him as she hurriedly undresses. God forbid he get a glimpse of her naked body. He's always thought Syd was beautiful and sexy. But since his affair, she acts shy around him, almost ashamed, which makes no sense. She pulls a tank top over her bare torso and turns toward him.

"Do you remember Jameson Drew?"

"Should I?" Curtis climbs into bed wearing his boxers.

"I was representing him when you cheated on me," she says, that familiar edge to her voice.

"Right. Sorry. The murderer."

"Self-defense, according to him." Sydney pulls back the sheet, crawls in next to him "He's dead."

Curtis doesn't know how to respond. Is this sad? A man who got caught up in a bad situation gone too soon? Or is it good news? One less killer out there living off the public dime.

"He died by suicide," Syd says. "He sliced his wrists open with a sharpened toothbrush."

"Damn."

Syd turns over on her hip, faces him. "He left a suicide note. He said he couldn't take prison anymore. He said he was innocent, and he blamed me for not allowing him to go to trial."

"Criminals always blame their lawyers." Curtis places a comforting hand on her bare shoulder. "You know that."

Syd's eyes are shiny in the pale lamplight. "I was so distracted, Curtis. My heart was broken. My life was falling apart. I couldn't think straight. Maybe I fucked up?"

"You were an excellent lawyer, Syd."

"Maybe I could have—*should* have—done more. Maybe I should have gone to trial and fought for him, but I was too devastated."

"This isn't about you. This is about a man who killed someone and couldn't live with the consequences."

"Drew's father called the office looking for me. He threatened me."

"Legally? They can't prove you did anything wrong."

"He threatened to *make me pay*." Syd's voice trembles. "He thinks I killed his only son."

Back in New York, Curtis had sometimes worried about his wife's safety. She represented dangerous people, angry people. It would have been so easy for one of them to find Sydney and harm her. But not now.

"Does this guy know where you live?"

"I don't think so. But I'm sure he could find out."

"Even if he did, I doubt he has the resources to get to Spain. I mean, they used a public defender. Clearly they don't have a ton of cash."

"You're probably right."

"Is that why you want the Aussies to sleep inside?"

"I don't know. I just feel unnerved. Anxious."

"Are you taking your medication?"

"Of course," she snaps. "I think it's perfectly normal to sleep better with the doors locked when you've had a threat against your life."

"I agree. It's a good idea." He strokes her arm gently. "You're safe, babe. I'm here. I won't let anything hurt you."

"Thanks." Her body softens under his touch, head easing into the pillow. She looks up at him under heavy lids, and her eyes are warm, receptive. His hand moves up, strokes her cheek, moves through her hair. Desire wells up in him, and he inches his body closer to her. Slowly, he moves in for a kiss that he hopes will segue into something more. Their lips meet for a brief, tentative moment.

And then Sydney rolls over and goes to sleep.

13

Syd sits in the designated smoking corner, having her morning cigarette. She's groggy, a little hungover. She shouldn't drink vermut. It's stronger than wine, and she always pays for it the next morning. Recently, she's been drinking too much alcohol, grasping onto the frivolity and joie de vivre of their young guests. But last night was different. Last night, she'd been trying to blunt her fear and anxiety.

Taking a drag, Syd rubs at a sandy eye. She hadn't slept well, her phone conversation with Brian Hale replaying in her mind. A man was dead. His family thought it was her fault. Of course she was upset. How could Curtis dismiss it so easily, blame it on her medication? He may as well have asked if she was on her period.

Brian had been circumspect as he recounted the call from Jameson's father, Teddy Drew. "He was angry. He called you some nasty names and made some vague threats."

"Like what?"

"He wants to *make you pay* for what happened to Jameson, but he didn't mean it. But we recorded the threats just in case."

"Am I in danger, Brian?" Sydney's voice sounded thick.

Her friend sighed down the line. "If you still lived in the city, I might suggest a restraining order, but Teddy Drew is probably all talk. And he has no way to find you in Spain. He doesn't strike me as a big international traveler."

"I hope not."

"Since you're no longer practicing, you should check that your professional liability insurance has a tail that covers you. Just in case Teddy can find someone to represent him."

"He's going to sue me now? For what?" But she knew. For negligence. For being so broken by her mom's death, her husband's betrayal, that she sent a man to prison who may have had a case for self-defense.

Stubbing out her cigarette, Sydney stands, prepares for her morning dip. Hopefully the chilly water will perk her up, but she's doubtful. If they didn't have guests, she'd crawl back into bed, but she doesn't want to appear indulgent or lazy. Last night, she'd tried the guided imagery exercises Ellen the therapist had recommended to calm her racing thoughts.

"Change the channel," Ellen had advised, like the traumatized brain was nothing more than a TV. Finally, she'd been able to push Teddy Drew from her mind and drift off, only to be woken by muffled sounds in the house. It had scared her at first, until she remembered Bianca and Damian were just down the hall.

Eyes open in the darkness, Syd had listened to their gentle murmuring. A soft feminine gasp, a deep guttural groan. Her guests were making love. She felt both awkward and a little aroused. Syd had glanced over at her husband to see if he heard it too, but Curtis was asleep, mouth open wide, snoring wetly. She felt a swell of disdain at the sight (and sound) of the man she'd married, though she knew it wasn't fair. She nudged him with an elbow, and he rolled over with a muttered "Sorry."

As she wades into the cool water, Syd's breath catches, and her pulse begins to race. Her thick head clears a little. She's waist-deep, about to go under, when Bianca wanders onto the deck.

"Morning," the woman says, stretching tanned arms over her tousled honey head. She looks tired and puffy, but on her it's sexy, devil may care. Bianca's wearing a large T-shirt, the one Syd remembers Damian had on yesterday. The sounds of their lovemaking revisit her, and she feels her cheeks warming.

"Morning." Syd dips under the surface, swims a few strokes, allowing the cold water to bring her back to life. She emerges just as Bianca strips off the T-shirt to reveal tiny bikini bottoms and nothing else. Casually, the Australian lowers herself to the edge of the pool, dunking her feet into the water.

"Remind me not to drink that red cough syrup stuff," she says, shielding her eyes with her hand. "What's it called?"

"Spanish vermouth," Syd replies, averting her gaze. She's in Europe. Boobs are everywhere. Why does she feel so uncomfortable? "I feel a little rough myself."

"Who's ready for breakfast?" Curtis walks out on deck, stops short at the sight of Bianca's bare C cups.

The blonde leans back on her hands, perfect breasts thrusting toward the sky. "I'm not sure I can eat," she says. "That vermouth did a number on me."

Curtis seems mildly stunned by the sight of their topless guest, his eyes darting around her perimeter, but he composes himself. "I made ham and eggs. A greasy breakfast should settle your stomach." He turns to Sydney. "You ready to eat, babe?"

"Sure. I'll be in in a minute."

"Okay." He turns back to Bianca. "Do you want me to make you some plain toast?"

"I don't want you to go to any trouble."

"It's no trouble. I've got granola, too."

"Ugh." She makes a face.

Curtis chuckles. "Vermut is kind of strong. And it has a lot of sugar. Recipe for a brutal hangover."

"*Now* you tell me?"

As Syd watches her husband chat and joke with their nearly naked roommate, she feels something dark and ugly sprouting in the pit of her stomach. It's jealousy, a toxic blend of insecurity, fear, and anger. She doesn't want to make a scene, doesn't want to lose her temper, but how can Curtis not see that his casual banter with Bianca's tits is wildly inappropriate after what he did? She breathes deeply through flared nostrils, trying to calm her ire. How would Ellen suggest she handle this issue?

As though he senses his wife's upset, Curtis turns to face her. "I'd better get back in the kitchen," he says with a sheepish smile. "Come on in before the food gets cold."

And then he scurries away.

When Syd enters through the French doors, the aroma of coffee and Spanish bacon is enticing, but her stomach is tight and queasy. Damian sits at the table, eating a massive plate of food. "Morning!" he calls, half standing as she enters. He's in a tank top, sinewy muscles on full display, but Syd barely notices.

"Morning." She tosses the word in his direction, approaches her husband. "Can we talk for a sec?"

"Eat first." He grabs the frying pan. "The eggs will be rubbery."

"This won't take long." Her frosty delivery stops him short. He sets down the pan and follows her to the bedroom.

"What's up?" he says when the door is closed behind them.

Sydney knows how this will sound—pathetic and petty—but she has to articulate her feelings. Open communication is essential if they're going to rebuild their trust. "I'm not comfortable with you hanging out and chatting with Bianca when she's practically naked."

Curtis snorts. "I asked her if she wanted breakfast, Syd."

"You were flirting and laughing with her. And her breasts."

"I was not flirting with her," he says, calm and indignant. "I offered her food, and then I made small talk. She's our guest."

Syd's cheeks are getting hot, but she employs the language she learned in therapy. "I've been working very hard to trust you again." Her voice tightens as she goes off script. "Maybe you could respect the fact that I'm still feeling less than secure in our marriage after you had sex with your client."

Curtis's response is a low rumble. "Of course I respect that.

Everything I've done for the past year has been to make you feel more secure."

"Then stop ogling Bianca's tits and laughing about her hangover!" Sydney whisper-shrieks.

"*You* invited her to stay here," Curtis says through gritted teeth. "Why don't *you* tell her to put a shirt on if it makes you uncomfortable?" He storms back to the kitchen.

14

Heat shimmers off the black highway, an apt reflection of Curtis's mood. He steps on the gas, the Citroën lunging forward with a satisfying roar. Soon, he'll have to gear down for another roundabout, but for now he enjoys the swell of power, the reckless surge of speed. His passenger will be impressed with the way he handles the car. Not a lot of Americans can drive stick anymore. It takes skill and finesse, makes him feel both suave and masculine. Like Ayrton Senna...before he died in a tragic crash, obviously.

Curtis and Damian are going to Girona to order lumber and supplies for the shed renovation. Damian will check in at the garage, and Curtis has a private call to make. But mostly he needs to get away from his wife and her ridiculous accusations. He's been bending over backward to make her happy, to win back her trust, and the suggestion that he's been perving at their houseguest is beyond insulting. Especially when Syd's been acting like an eighth grader with a crush on Damian since he arrived.

If Sydney is still so insecure, why did she invite a beautiful younger woman to stay with them? Curtis hadn't even wanted guests, but he's been a perfect goddamn host: cooking, mixing drinks, keeping the house tidy. His welts are still itchy and irritating, and he'd slept fitfully last night. But he'd gotten up, made breakfast, and offered it to the women lounging by the pool like a couple of socialites. If his eyes *drifted* to Bianca's perfect tits for a split second, it was only natural. He's a red-blooded human male who's been deprived of sex for months.

Damian's voice shakes him from his reverie. "So, how did you and Sydney meet?"

"The old-fashioned way." Curtis smirks. "Plenty of Fish."

"Her profile must have blown you away. Sexy. Smart. Great job."

Curtis glances over at him—his words sound almost besotted—but Damian's face is turned away, taking in the scenery out the passenger window. The Aussie and his pretty partner seem solid, but Damian wouldn't be the first guy infatuated by Sydney's cool, aspirational beauty.

"Yeah, it did," Curtis replies. "And then I met her, and we just clicked." The remembrance warms him, and Curtis feels a smile play on his lips. "We talked for hours, and when we finally said goodbye, I knew I'd found my person." He chuckles softly. "It took about three years to convince Sydney, but she got there."

There's silence from Damian, so Curtis asks, "How'd you meet Bianca?"

"B. and I have been together since senior year." Damian glances over at him. "We basically grew up together."

"Wow. Long time."

"I first saw her when I was eighteen, and I was done for."

Curtis has to ask. "So you've never been with another woman?"

"I never said that." Damian cocks an eyebrow. "We're very understanding of each other's needs, if you get my drift."

"Right." Curtis feels a trickle of sweat run down his back. "Whatever works for you."

"Communication and respect are key," Damian continues, like he's some expert on relationships. "Monogamy isn't our natural state, but that doesn't mean commitment can't work."

Okay, Salvador Dalí. But Curtis doesn't say it out loud. "I had plenty of women before I got married," he says instead, wondering if six women would qualify as "plenty" in Damian's mind. "And now I'm with the love of my life, so I'm good."

Damian snorts. "You've never had a bit of action on the side?"

The question is rude, intrusive, and a little suspicious. Did Sydney tell Damian that Curtis cheated? Have they been having secret heart-to-hearts? He doesn't want the Aussies to know what he did, doesn't want them judging him, casting him as the villain, Sydney as the woman scorned and betrayed. The woman in need of comfort and understanding.

"Nope," Curtis replies, because one mistake does not make him a cheater. One fucked-up night that he'll regret forever does not define him. He gears down and takes the Girona exit.

Curtis is relieved to ditch Damian once they're in the city. His passenger's probing questions in the car added to Curtis's foul mood, so he's happy to leave the Aussie at the garage chasing down his fuel pump in novice Spanish. Curtis has some paperwork he needs to mail to his immigration lawyer in Barcelona, so he heads to the post office. He'll meet Damian at the hardware store later.

As Curtis walks, he pulls out his burner phone and dials a New York number. His stomach is loose as he listens to the distant ring. It's early in America, but Simon will be up. His friend and former business partner is a workaholic. It's why their property management company was so successful. It's also why Simon's marriage fell apart, why he only sees his two boys every other weekend and for a month during the summer. Simon is driven and ambitious, willing to do what it takes to get ahead. But when Curtis needed out of the company, Simon had done the right thing.

"I fucked up," Curtis had told his best friend, his eyes brimming with emotion. They were in a swanky hotel bar, about a block from their office. "I—I slept with a client."

"You fucking idiot," Simon muttered, taking a drink of his Scotch. "That's so unprofessional." But Simon was in no position to point fingers. He'd dipped his pen in the company ink more than once. They'd even paid a significant settlement after a young member of the sales team brought a harassment suit against him.

"Does Syd know?" Simon asks.

"Yeah... I told her."

"Why the fuck did you do that?" Simon scoffed.

"I had to! She knew I was hiding something. I couldn't keep lying to her." Curtis drained his drink, signaled for another. "I just... I just broke down."

"Did she leave you?"

"We've been going to counseling, trying to work it out. But... we need to make a change."

That was when he'd told Simon his Spain plan. It had taken some convincing (and some begging), but eventually Simon had agreed to buy Curtis out. For a fucking song. Curtis's half of the company was worth more than Simon was willing to pay, but Curtis was in a weak negotiating position. He needed out. Out of the business and out of New York. It would be expensive, time-consuming, and stressful but it was the only way to keep his marriage intact. And it was only a matter of time before Simon found out what else Curtis was hiding.

Curtis had tried to call Simon the first time he'd brought Damian to Girona, but then he'd been interrupted. Since then, he'd blocked Simon's calls to his regular phone and deleted his emails. Saving his marriage was his top priority; he couldn't afford to be distracted by business matters. But he couldn't avoid it forever. It was time to face the music.

His friend answers then. "Hello?" Simon doesn't recognize the number of this recent burner phone.

"It's me."

"Curtis," Simon says, and there's no warmth in his old friend's voice. "What the fuck have you done to me?"

15

Sydney's thumbs are slippery on the phone's keyboard as she types Jameson Drew's name into the search bar. She finds numerous articles detailing his arrest and conviction but no coverage of his recent death. The media reports on suicides carefully. And sparingly. Research shows that sensational coverage can be triggering to high-risk people. Plus, a prisoner dying while incarcerated is so common that it's rarely newsworthy.

A thump travels up from the floor below. Bianca is downstairs, shifting boxes, throwing drop cloths, preparing to paint the plaster in the future games room. Sydney is going to help, of course. She only came into her bedroom to change into painting clothes and got distracted by her phone. But she needs to check one more thing. Has Curtis's lover blocked her on Facebook? Or was her last fruitless internet search for Collette an anomaly?

Seeing Collette's image only fuels her jealousies and insecurities, but Sydney can't stop herself. It's like picking at a scab, poking a wound. She has the screenshotted photos for those dark moments when she feels the need to fuel her hurt and anger. But still, she types the woman's name into the Facebook search bar. The same list of Collettes appears, women around the world who did not sleep with her husband.

"Where the fuck did you go, Collette?" Sydney mutters into the silence. "Why did you block me?"

Closing the Facebook app, she types the name of Collette's business into the internet browser: Anderson Technologies. The uninspiring name is matched by the basic splash page.

Coming soon!

No dates. No details. Just the downtown address. Why would this company lease significant and expensive space and then take months to move in? It makes no business sense.

Shaking off her questions, she jumps into a pair of jean shorts and one of Curtis's old T-shirts and hurries down the stairs. "I'm here," she says, joining Bianca. The Aussie woman has already covered the storage boxes and mismatched furniture with plastic sheeting, poured primer into a paint tray. She hands Sydney a roller. "I'll cut in the edges, and you do the rolling."

"Sounds good," Syd says, dipping the roller into the stark white priming paint. She presses the microfiber to the wall, hears the satisfying squelch of the viscous liquid. "Sorry I took so long," she says, moving the roller back and forth across the wall. "I stupidly glanced at my social media. You know how addictive it is."

"Not really," Bianca responds, dabbing paint around the doorframe.

"Seriously?" Syd glances over at her. "I thought everyone who traveled around in a van did it for Instagram?"

"We don't have social media," Bianca replies, eyes on her work. "We're not performative like that."

"You're a gorgeous couple in a cute van in Spain. You could get tons of followers and all sorts of free swag."

"Probably," Bianca says. "But we're private people. We don't like to put on a show."

The words feel like an opening. Syd swallows her nerves, keeps her gaze forward. "I don't want to sound like a prude, but when Curtis is here, would you mind wearing your bikini top?"

Bianca laughs, as if Syd's just asked her to wear lederhosen. She pauses her painting, turns toward Syd. "Are you serious?"

Sydney lowers her roller. "Curtis grew up in a really conservative family." It's an exaggeration, not an outright lie. His mother was a devout woman who considered sex and the body shameful. Curtis has worked through his issues, but his uptight background provides a good excuse. Because Sydney doesn't want to admit that she's insecure. That she still doesn't trust her husband.

"He seemed totally comfortable this morning," Bianca says, eyes narrowed. "Did he say something to you?"

"I just know him," Syd says, her cheeks getting warm. "I mean, Damian would probably feel awkward if I was topless, too."

"No, he wouldn't."

"Well, Curtis does, so..."

Bianca snorts. "You talk like you're *so* European, but you're still so puritanical."

The insult makes Syd's temper flare. "This is our home, and we want to feel comfortable here. I hope you can respect that."

Bianca sets the brush on the paint can. "Is this about Curtis? Or about you?"

"Me?" Syd chuckles awkwardly, roller still in hand. "What do you mean?" But she knows what Bianca sees in her. A weak, jealous woman, afraid her husband will stray if he sees a pair of breasts other than her own.

Bianca's tone softens. "There's something between us, isn't there? A bit of a spark?"

The suggestion is a surprise. While Sydney finds Bianca beautiful and compelling, she's not bisexual. There was some experimentation in college—as one does—but it had felt somewhat forced and performative for her. She's undeniably attracted to Damian, but not to his partner. Is she?

"You're gorgeous, Bianca," Syd manages. "But I'm married. And I'm not—"

"It's okay." The Aussie woman holds up her hand. "I've got a bit of a crush on you, but if it's one-sided, I won't pursue it."

"But...you're with Damian."

"Damian knows I love women." Bianca moves closer, and Sydney can smell her shampoo, a sweet almond scent. Beneath it, a slight, not unpleasant, tang of sweat. "I'm open and honest about my needs, and Damian respects that."

Shame settles on Sydney's skin like mist. Her marriage is built on secrets, lies, and a lack of respect. No amount of therapy will change that.

"I believe in love and consent and exploring my sexuality," Bianca says. "But I won't pressure you if you're not into it."

Suddenly, Syd's conflicted. Bianca and Damian's relationship sounds so mature and evolved compared to her own. *Is* she attracted to this undeniably sexy woman standing so close to her? Is that the real reason she didn't want Bianca topless by the pool? Has Syd been so conditioned by her upbringing and her traditional marriage that she's shut down that part of herself? Maybe she could be happy with a woman? *Happier.*

Bianca's gaze is intense, magnetic. "I don't think your husband appreciates how amazing you are."

"Yes, he does," Sydney croaks. Because Curtis wouldn't have sold his company and moved them across the ocean if he didn't.

"Okay..." Bianca steps back, returns to her paintbrush. "If you're happy, then that's great." But there's pity in her tone, a whiff of judgment.

"I am," Sydney says. "We are." It sounds hollow and desperate, even to herself.

Bianca smiles. "And I don't want to make Curtis—or anyone—uncomfortable. I'll keep my top on. I promise."

She dips the brush into the paint and returns to the wall.

Sydney Cleary and Curtis Lowe, Couples' Counseling Session
Ellen Dwyer, Psychologist, PsyD
July 8

TRANSCRIPT 3.

Ellen:
How is your sex life now? After the affair?

Sydney:
It's nonexistent. I'm not interested, and neither is he.

Curtis:
That's not true, Syd. I'm trying to respect what you want.

Sydney:
You never touch me. You never even try.

Curtis:
I want to. But...I'm scared.

Ellen:
Does it feel okay to share some of what you're afraid of?

Curtis:
I'm afraid I won't be able to perform. That Sydney will think I'm not attracted to her anymore. And if I *can* do the deed, I'm afraid Sydney will assume I'm thinking about Collette.

Ellen:
Do you miss being physically close with Sydney?

Curtis:
Of course I do. I've always been attracted to her, and I still am.

Ellen:
And what about you, Sydney?

Sydney:

I miss being close to him. And I miss sex. But I don't want to have sex with Curtis anymore. It's too risky.

Curtis:

I used protection with Collette. I told you.

Sydney:

You had this incredible night of passion while you were drunk and high, but you expect me to believe that Collette had a condom in her purse, and you used it?

Curtis:

Yes, I do. I was honest enough to tell you about a meaningless one-night stand. Why would I lie about *this*? I've been tested for STDs. I got the all-clear.

Ellen:

STDs are a valid concern, but I think Sydney is wondering how you could put her physical and emotional well-being at risk for something so meaningless?

Sydney:

That's exactly what I'm wondering.

Curtis:

I fucked up! I know that. But does this mean we're never having sex again, Syd? We're just going to be roommates because I made one horrible mistake?

Sydney:

A *mistake* is forgetting to buy milk. Or losing your wallet in the back of a cab. You cheated on me! You broke my heart! You can't *guilt me* into making love to you.

Ellen:

Let's work on rebuilding emotional safety for now. On touching each other in intimate but nonsexual ways. This will help you find your way back to each other physically.

Curtis:

I hope so.

16

Curtis is at the sink, roughly washing a mixing bowl and banging it onto the drying rack. The lumber will not arrive for two days. The irritation Curtis feels at the delay highlights the fact that he's still a New Yorker, still wants shit done in a timely manner. This means he'll have Damian's help on the shed renovation for only a couple of days before their van is fixed and they move on. He's looking forward to their departure, though he'd hoped Damian would have gotten more accomplished before he left.

"There's plenty of prep work we can do," Damian says cheerfully, wolfing down the pancakes Curtis made. "I'll get up on the roof and tear off the rotted shingles. You can rip the old boards off the frame."

"Sure," Curtis mutters, drying his hands. He can't seem to shake this bad mood. It started yesterday with Syd's ridiculous accusations about ogling Bianca's breasts, was exacerbated by the lumber delivery delay, and cemented by the ugly phone call with his friend Simon. Ex-friend Simon. Yes, Curtis fucked him over, but he'd had no choice. It was a matter of survival. Simon—*anyone*—would have done the same.

Curtis moves the stack of pancakes to the table. "Breakfast!" he shouts in the general direction of the pool. He knows Syd's out there having her morning cigarette, but he's not about to approach. If Bianca is tanning her boobs, he's not going anywhere near them.

Syd stumbles into the kitchen, her hair mussed, her expression far away. He puts two pancakes onto a plate and hands it to her. "If your friend wants to eat, tell her it's ready."

"I don't know where she is," Syd mumbles, moving toward her seat.

"I'll find her." Damian stands up, leaves his sticky plate on the table. As he passes behind Syd, he gives her shoulders an affectionate squeeze. Syd's smile is small, but she clearly appreciates his touch, his attention. Curtis's back teeth grind together, but he doesn't comment. He addresses his wife.

"I'm going to get to work on the shed. Can you clean up after breakfast?"

"Of course." Her eyes are fixated on her plate.

Curtis hurries out to the dilapidated building, beating Damian there. His guest must be looking for Bianca, or maybe he's found her. She's probably in the van. Even though the pair has moved into the house at night, Bianca sequesters herself in the caravan periodically. She must have some clothing and personal items in there. And she likely needs a break from the group dynamic once in a while. Has Bianca noticed the flirtation between Damian and Sydney? For all Bianca's open-mindedness, she must be feeling some of the same irritation as Curtis.

Entering the musty shed, Curtis moves to the corner where he hides his burner phone. He does a quick check for spiders and snakes before shoving his hand under the pile of boards and retrieving the device. Unwrapping it from the protective rag, he shoves it deep into his pocket. This hiding place is fast becoming untenable, but what are his options? He'd considered the basement, but Sydney and Bianca are painting, shifting furniture and boxes. It's far too risky.

He'll keep it in the car, under the driver's seat. Sydney rarely drives, uncomfortable with the stick shift and the aggressive Spaniards on the road. About a month ago, she'd taken a solo trip into Cadaqués, asserting her independence. But when she returned, she was shaken by a near miss on a blind corner and she hasn't gone anywhere on her own since. If he parks the vehicle in the shade and turns off the device, the phone will be safe there. He steps back toward the door.

And then it happens: a splintering snap from above, a violent crunch. His arms instinctively fly up to protect his head as the roof comes crashing down on him. The sound of the wood striking his skull is deafening, but there's no pain. Not yet. It's too shocking. His nervous system needs time to catch up. There's another noise too, a high-pitched screech. He doesn't recognize the sound of his own scream.

Damian barrels into the small shed. "Jesus Christ! Are you okay?"

Curtis tries to gather his bearings, tries to form a sentence through the dull throb building in his cranium. "What happened?" he finally manages.

"I stomped some rotted shingles through a hole in the roof," the Aussie explains. "You weren't supposed to be in here. You can't skulk around on a construction site."

"I wasn't *skulking*," Curtis snaps, but he was.

"You're bleeding," Damian says, indicating the deep scratches on Curtis's forearm. "Let's get you into the light."

They move outside, and Damian looks Curtis over. "You might need some iodine on those scratches."

"Sure." Curtis touches his head gingerly.

"You're not concussed, are you?" Damian asks. "Close your eyes and stand on one leg."

"I'm fine," Curtis grumbles, feeling mocked. Again.

"Do you want to go in? Get some ice and have a lie down?"

The condescension is subtle, but it's there. Damian thinks Curtis is soft and weak. "I'll be fine."

"Good." Damian cocks an eyebrow at him. "You were supposed to be tearing off the rotted boards. What were you doing inside?"

"I—I came in to check..." But he trails off. "We should get back to work."

"Uh...yeah." Damian pulls off his cap, scratches his head through his thick hair. "I don't want to be a snitch, but there's something you should know."

Dread presses down on Curtis's chest. What is Damian about to tell him? Has Syd propositioned him? Have they done something? He feels lightheaded and nauseated. Maybe he does have a concussion. "What is it?" he groans.

"Follow me."

Curtis trails Damian around the shed, through the scrub toward the back fence. "I came back here for a slash," Damian explains as they walk. Curtis assumes he means a piss. "That's when I saw them."

"Saw what?"

Damian moves behind a huge evergreen oak throwing its shade on a good portion of the hillside. At the base, a few wild mushrooms grow. They're poisonous, and as Damian crouches down, Curtis considers warning him about them. But Damian points to a cluster of half a dozen cigarette butts on the ground. "Your missus shouldn't be smoking back here. It's tinder dry. The whole hillside could catch fire and we'd be goners."

He's right. Sydney's behavior is dangerous and reckless, not to mention sneaky. But Curtis is buoyant with relief. He'd expected something far worse than surreptitious cigarettes. He manages a stern tone. "I'm going to go talk to her," he says. "This has to stop."

As he moves toward the house, Curtis's relief morphs into a perverse sense of anticipation. Sydney has been so self-righteous, casting him so firmly in the role of the bad guy. And now he's caught her sneaking cigarettes, smoking in the bone-dry tall grass. It's reckless. It's dangerous. And it's deceitful. Obviously it pales in comparison to adultery, but he'll enjoy putting her in her place for a change. He can almost forget the pounding between his eyebrows, the sting of his forearm.

Damian calls after him. "Ice that head while you're in there, mate. Come back out when you're feeling steady."

Curtis doesn't turn around.

17

Sydney busies herself at the sink while Bianca enjoys her pancakes at the table. They haven't discussed yesterday's awkward conversation. Obviously Syd didn't want to bring it up with Curtis and Damian around, but it's been playing on her mind. She had tossed and turned last night, slipping in and out of disturbing dreams. It wasn't Bianca's stated feelings that kept her up: Sydney's flattered by her interest, maybe even a little titillated. It was another comment that has her troubled.

Bianca brings her empty plate to the sink. "Delicious," she says, touching Syd's waist. They do this, Syd's noticed. Both Bianca and Damian are tactile and affectionate—with each other and with her. She doesn't mind it; maybe she even likes it. But she wonders if Curtis has noticed. If he has, does it bother him?

"Ready to do another coat downstairs?" Bianca asks, sipping the last of her coffee.

"Sure," Syd replies, rinsing the frying pan and setting it in the draining rack. She turns as she dries her hands on a tea towel. "Can I ask you something?"

"Of course." Bianca sets her mug on the counter.

"Yesterday, you said that Curtis doesn't appreciate me. What makes you think that?"

"It's just a vibe I pick up from him," Bianca says breezily. "I'm an intuitive person. I always have been."

"So Curtis hasn't said anything?" Syd presses. "Or *done* anything?"

"Not really..." But it's practically an affirmation.

"Not really? Or no?" Syd's chest feels weighted, and she struggles for a breath. It's anxiety, that familiar tightness in her lungs. "Tell me, Bianca."

The Australian sighs, rakes her nails through her long hair. "It's nothing overt. But Curtis gives off a certain *energy* when we interact. It's hard to put a finger on it."

"What kind of energy?"

Bianca's gaze is steady. "I guess I'd say an *available* energy."

Syd swallows dryly. Curtis has been coming on to Bianca, subtly, even unconsciously. If she confronted her husband, he would laugh, tell her it's a bunch of woo-woo nonsense. But Syd believes in women's intuition... doesn't she? And yet, Bianca may have an ulterior motive. If she's got a crush on Sydney, maybe she's trying to cause problems between her and Curtis? Syd's mind swirls, but there's a dark pit of knowing in her belly. Because all Curtis's promises, and all their therapy, cannot erase the fact that he betrayed her. That he was willing to cross that line, to break her heart. She can't even be sure that Collette was the first time he did it. And she can't be sure that he wouldn't do it again, right here in their home.

Bianca's eyes flit to the side door then, and Sydney turns toward it. Curtis walks in, his hair dusty, bloody scratches on his arm.

"You're bleeding." Syd steps toward him. "What happened?"

"Damian was on the roof. He kicked some shingles down on me."

"What?"

"It was an accident. I'm fine."

"I'll get our first aid kit from the van," Bianca offers.

"It's nothing," Curtis calls after her, but she's already gone.

"I'll get a cloth," Syd says. "We should wash the dust out of the wounds."

"Later," Curtis says brusquely. "I need to show you something first."

"What is it?" Sydney asks as she follows him outside and up the hill. They're heading toward the shed the guys have been renovating, but there's no sign of Damian. He must have gone to retrieve something from the van or to cool off in the pool.

"You'll see," Curtis mutters.

Her husband's vague response frustrates her. She understands that Curtis is miserable. He's still got the jellyfish welts bothering him at night, and now he's had shingles dropped on his head. But Syd's in no mood for the steep walk in the already oppressive heat, and she doesn't appreciate his surly demeanor. Bianca's insinuations have her conflicted and on edge. "Just tell me, Curtis," she insists, stopping in her tracks.

But Curtis keeps moving through the brush, circling the massive oak at the back of the property. He points at the ground. "You can't smoke out here, Syd."

"What are you talking about?" She joins him, sees the scattering of cigarette butts on the ground next to a cluster of wild mushrooms.

"If the grass caught fire, this whole hillside would ignite." He sounds sanctimonious, even smug. "We could lose our house. We could even be killed."

Syd crouches down, peers at the butts. "These aren't mine."

"You don't need to lie," Curtis says. "If you're having trouble quitting, I get that. I know things have been stressful."

"I'm not lying." Sydney stands. "I smoke Chesterfields. The filter is yellow. These filters are white."

Her husband glances down to confirm. "Maybe Bianca's been smoking back here."

"She has asthma. It must have been Damian. He can't smoke around her, so he's been hiding out behind the tree."

"But Damian found these," Curtis explains. "He thought they were yours."

"It must have been kids then," Sydney mutters, peering around in the grass.

"What kids? There are no kids for miles."

"Jesus Christ," Sydney gasps, dropping down onto her haunches.

Her hands riffle through the tall grass, parting it. "Look." Curtis hurries to join her.

There, nestled in the dry weeds, is a pair of slim leather work gloves.

And a machete.

18

Curtis can see the panic in his wife's eyes, can see her struggling to take a deep breath. He doesn't want her going off the deep end over this. There has to be an innocent explanation, and he says so.

"Like what?" Sydney asks.

"A hobo," he says, though he's pretty sure that's no longer a politically correct term. "Or an itinerant worker passing through."

"Why would they leave their machete here? And their gloves?"

"They must have forgotten them."

"So they sat here and smoked six cigarettes? Why?"

Curtis scrambles to come up with a logical explanation, but he's flailing. "Maybe they stopped here six times. It's a nice spot for a smoke."

"Or maybe they've been watching us. Just waiting for a chance to break in and kill us all in our sleep."

"Don't go off the deep end," Curtis says gently. "We're perfectly safe."

"We can't just brush this off." Syd's voice is tight, brows knit together. "Could this have something to do with Collette?"

Curtis laughs. It's ridiculous. "You think Collette flew all the way to Spain to stand behind our tree smoking cigarettes? With a machete?"

"Does she smoke?"

"No. I mean, not that I know of."

"Does she have a jealous boyfriend? Or a husband?"

"She said she was divorced."

"She blocked me on Facebook, Curtis. Why would she do that?"

"You've been checking her out online? You know what Ellen said in therapy."

"Yeah, I do. And Ellen was right. Every time I look at Collette's photo, I feel sick. And angry. But I can't stop myself." Syd's voice is getting louder. "And her biotech firm hasn't even opened. How can they afford the lease?"

"I have no idea!" he says, his face burning. "That's Simon's problem now. I sold my half of the company for you, remember?" He needs to steer this conversation away from his affair. "What about Teddy Drew?" Curtis suggests. "You sent his son to jail. He's already made threats against you."

Syd chews a knuckle. "I'll call Brian at the office. Maybe he can find out if Drew's left the country."

They stand in silence for a moment, lost in their own speculation. Curtis becomes aware of the throbbing in his head, the tension pressing against his temples. His plan to remove them from all the ugliness in New York had seemed foolproof. What are the odds that trouble would follow them across the ocean? It seems implausible. But there's a tightness in his chest, acid in his throat. Because if it did...

A thought occurs to him then. "What if this has something to do with Damian and Bianca?"

Syd meets his gaze. "How?"

"Maybe someone's after *them*?"

"You think someone followed them from Australia?" Sydney rolls her eyes. "Now who's being over-the-top."

"What if they've got enemies in Europe?" he suggests. "They just showed up here out of nowhere. What do we know about them?"

"They're a couple of Aussie travelers whose van broke down."

"Did it, though? I mean, they could have *made* the van break down."

Syd shakes her head. "Why would they do that?"

"I don't know. That's my point." Curtis crosses his arms. "You invited two complete strangers to move in with us."

"*We* invited them," Syd retorts.

"Well, maybe it's time they leave."

"If someone is lurking around our property, I feel safer with Damian here," Syd counters.

"You're *my* wife. *I* can keep you safe." It comes out more caveman than Curtis intended, and he sees Syd bristle. But he's sick of being emasculated by the big loud Aussie, tired of him acting like Sir Lancelot while Sydney swoons like a damsel. He softens his tone. "I'll fix the security cameras."

"Why? So we can watch a replay of our murders?"

"Let's not get hysterical." Curtis keeps his voice calm. "I'm sure there's a reasonable..." But he trails off, because he hears something. It's coming from the house, faint but unmistakable: an argument.

"Did you hear that?" Curtis asks.

"What?" Syd says, and they both listen. But it's all quiet now.

"Damian and Bianca were fighting," Curtis says. "I wonder what about?"

"Can you imagine if we'd been cooped up in a van together?" Syd says. "We'd be..." But she trails off, because the Australian couple are now moving up the hill toward them.

"How ya going out here?" Damian calls.

"Not good," Syd mutters as the pair joins them. "These aren't my cigarettes. And we found these." She points at the gloves and the machete, still nestled in the tall grass.

"Oh..." Bianca bends over, peers at the items. "That's creepy."

"Not really," Damian says confidently. "It's probably the guy from the next farm checking his fence line. He must have stopped for a few smokes. No big deal."

"With a machete?" Syd asks.

"For clearing away brush," Damian responds. He crouches, picks up a glove. "This leather is good for working with barbed wire."

"Go to the next farm, Curtis," Sydney demands. "Take the machete and gloves back to the farmer. Make sure they're his."

Curtis scoffs. "I don't even know him. And I barely speak Spanish. I can't just walk onto their property carrying a machete."

"So we do nothing?" Syd snaps. "We're just going to *wonder* if some psycho has been out here watching us?"

"There's no psycho, Sydney," Curtis says, enunciating each word, but he's suddenly unsure. His head swims, and he feels confused, unmoored. The intensity of the sun, the knock on the head, and this creepy discovery are all overwhelming him. A clammy cold settles on him, and he wobbles on his feet.

Bianca touches his elbow. "Let's get you inside. I've got the first aid kit in the kitchen. We should treat those scratches, so they don't get infected."

He looks down at his arm, at the dried blood, the remnants of the jellyfish stings. He's going to need a couple of painkillers for his head, too. He's a wreck. And now, someone could be watching them. Maybe even planning to hurt them. Could it be someone from Curtis's past? If it is, he'll be no match for them in his current state. He won't be able to protect his wife or himself.

"Okay," he says hoarsely, because he doesn't know what else to do. He and Bianca start toward the house. They've gone a few yards when Curtis realizes his wife and Damian aren't following.

Looking over his shoulder, he sees them standing close, heads bent in conversation. Damian is talking in a low voice while Syd nods receptively. What the hell is he saying to her? Is he reassuring her? Offering to keep her safe from the cigarette-smoking bogeyman because her husband is so weak and pathetic? Curtis stops abruptly. "Coming?" he asks pointedly.

Syd and Damian look up, their expressions sheepish. Slowly, they move to join him.

Sydney Cleary and Curtis Lowe, Couples' Counseling Session
Ellen Dwyer, Psychologist, PsyD
July 8

THERAPY PROGRESS NOTES—SESSION 3.

There has been no sex in the marriage since the affair. Sydney's fear of getting an STD may be an excuse to avoid sex because she's not ready to be vulnerable with her husband. She could be worried she can't measure up to his former lover, that sex within the marriage won't be as exciting as sex with a new, illicit partner. Or she may be unconsciously withholding sex from her husband as punishment.

Curtis longs for sex with Sydney but is concerned about his ability to perform. He craves physical intimacy but fears Sydney's rejection and disdain. Curtis will need to be patient as they work on building emotional safety and strengthening their connection in a nonthreatening way.

19

As she smokes a Chesterfield next to the pool, Sydney calls her former colleague Brian, who promises to look into Teddy Drew's whereabouts. She doesn't mention the mysterious gloves, the machete, or the cigarettes. She doesn't want to sound paranoid. And she doesn't want to admit that her idyllic life in Spain is full of darkness and uncertainty. When Syd hangs up, she drops her butt into the jam jar and heads inside. She can hear Bianca moving around downstairs. The walls are primed and ready for their first coat of paint, and Syd needs to help. Bianca and Damian have been doing more than their fair share of work around the place. Sydney hurries to the bedroom to don her painting clothes.

She finds Curtis on the bed, a hand thrown over his eyes, his breath soft and steady. How can he sleep when they've just found evidence of a lurker out back? Not to mention a deadly weapon and leather gloves? Sydney looks at his scrapes and bruises, the faded welts on his tanned skin. Curtis's mouth hangs open, and he looks so vulnerable. Even pitiful. Her husband is injured, overheated, exhausted. As she slips into her spattered clothes, she recalls Damian's whispered promise.

"I'll go to the farm," Damian had assured her. "I'll make sure the gloves and machete belong to the farmer."

"And if they don't?"

"If someone is after Curtis, I've got his back. You don't need to be afraid."

"Why do you think someone's after Curtis?" she'd asked. "Do you know something?"

"Process of elimination." He'd shrugged. "No one's after B. and me. And I can't imagine anyone having anything against you." His tone was complimentary, even enamored, but she was too uneasy to feel flattered.

"Coming?" Curtis had snapped, and the conversation was over.

The women paint the basement walls a carefully selected shade of white: *Chantilly cream*. Their conversation is stilted as they work, their minds embroiled in the nefarious possibilities surrounding their recent discovery. At least Sydney's is. Bianca seems less concerned, but she's quiet, trapped in her own thoughts.

"We'll cook tonight," Bianca offers, out of the blue. "Curtis needs to rest."

"I can cook," Syd offers weakly, but she's terrible in the kitchen. She can make a simple pasta dish, and she's good at salad dressings, but Curtis has always taken care of the meals. She feels intimidated cooking for guests, while Curtis enjoys it.

"Damian and I love cooking together." Bianca smiles. "We've missed not having a proper kitchen in the van."

Syd smiles through a twinge of envy. Even before the affair, she and Curtis would argue and bicker when she tried to help in the kitchen. Now, she rarely sets foot in there as Curtis attempts to win her forgiveness through food. "Sounds great. Thanks."

"Damian should be back soon. We'll see what's in the fridge and come up with something."

On cue, the front door bangs. Damian has returned from the neighboring farm. The women drop their painting implements and hurry up the stairs. Curtis has woken, too. He stands in the living room, looking groggy and disheveled. Damian appears remarkably fresh despite a walk in the afternoon heat. His demeanor is upbeat.

"I returned the gloves and machete to the farmer," he tells them. "Manuel was happy to get them back."

Syd presses a hand to her chest in relief.

"Good to hear," Curtis says, turning to Sydney. "See? There's nothing to worry about."

"Thank God." Bianca moves to her boyfriend, slips under his strong arm. "I'm so glad that's sorted out."

"Why was the farmer smoking on our property?" Sydney asks Damian.

"Enjoying the view, I guess." Damian shrugs.

"It just seems weird that he'd climb through a barbed wire fence onto our land," Syd continues. "He could see the view from his side just as well."

"The language barrier was a challenge," Damian says. "I didn't ask for an explanation."

Bianca looks up at her partner. "We're cooking tonight, babe." She addresses her hosts. "Any dietary restrictions?"

Syd answers, "I'm allergic to mushrooms."

"She's not allergic," Curtis teases. "She just hates them."

"No one listens unless you tell them you'll go into anaphylactic shock!"

Bianca laughs. "I'm deathly allergic to green peppers, then."

"Message received." Damian takes her hand. "Let's see what they've got in the pantry."

Dinner is a saffron risotto with squid that Curtis had in the freezer. Damian opens a bottle of crisp white wine, and they eat heartily. All except Curtis. Sydney notices him picking at the calamari rings, taking small bites of rice.

"This is delicious," she says, to compensate for her husband's lack of appetite.

"It's Damian's specialty," Bianca offers. "He adds the stock so precisely."

"Timing is the key," Damian says with pride.

"Well done." Sydney smiles at him. "And thanks again for going to the farm today. I feel so much better. It would have been awful to be left wondering why there was a potentially deadly weapon hidden on our property."

"My pleasure." Damian's eyes meet hers over his wineglass. "I didn't want you to worry."

Curtis tosses his napkin on the table. "I'm going to hit the hay."

"Are you okay?" Syd asks. "Could you have a concussion?"

"He's not concussed," Bianca says confidently. "He'd be throwing up. He'd be dizzy."

"I played Aussie Rules football," Damian elaborates, shoveling rice into his mouth. "I know what a concussion looks like. He's fine. He's just not used to manual labor."

Curtis's jaw visibly clenches. "Thanks for dinner." His posture is stiff and tense as he leaves the table.

Sydney finishes her meal quietly as the Australians have a lively conversation about food, their favorite cuisines (Italian for Damian, Thai for Bianca), and the restaurants they miss back home. She helps Damian clean the kitchen, then decides to join her husband in bed. The stress of the day has been exhausting. When she climbs between the cool sheets, she feels almost weak with fatigue. As she drifts away, she's comforted by the sounds of her guests preparing for bed, talking in low voices. It's the safety she felt in her childhood bedroom, knowing her parents were still up, on guard for monsters and bogeymen. Thanks to Damian, she knows monsters aren't real.

But when she stirs hours later, the house is dark and silent. Curtis breathes evenly beside her. Syd rolls over and checks her phone. There's a message from Brian; he must have sent it yesterday evening, New York time.

Teddy Drew is here. You're safe.

She lets out a sigh of reassurance, plumps her pillow, and tries to get back to sleep. But another thought seeps into her mind, tickling the back of her brain. Bianca's suggestion that Curtis had been flirting with her had been eclipsed by the discovery of the gloves and the machete. But it revisits Syd now, leaving an unpleasant bitterness in her mouth.

Sydney is pragmatic; she deals in facts, not intuition. Bianca doesn't know Curtis, so how can she pick up on his so-called *energy*? Her husband hadn't wanted the Australians to stay in the first place, but is that because he can't trust himself around their beautiful female guest? Is he afraid he won't remain faithful unless Sydney is the only woman in his orbit?

Syd dozes fitfully until dawn turns the sky golden, and the morning brings improved clarity. And a concrete plan. The four of them have been working in gendered silos—the women painting, the men tearing apart the shed. Today, Sydney will suggest a day of rest, of fun, of togetherness. And she'll observe the dynamic between Curtis and Bianca.

Next to her, Curtis stretches and yawns. "How are you feeling?" she asks as his eyes flicker open.

"Better, I think. I'll know once I have a coffee."

"I'll make it," she offers, sitting up. He looks at her, bemused. It's unlike her to be so solicitous these days. "We've all been working hard," she says. "Let's take a day off. Take Damian and Bianca to Aiguablava for a swim. Have lunch at the old hotel."

Curtis scratches his neck, considers it. "There's not much we can do on the shed until the lumber arrives tomorrow."

"Perfect," Sydney says. She leans over and kisses his cheek. It's performative—she feels nothing—but Curtis smiles. She needs him to act natural, to drop his guard. He mustn't suspect that she's watching him. She climbs out of bed and heads to the kitchen. She's eager to tell the guests the plan.

And she's eager to learn if her husband can be trusted.

20

The Australians are on board for a day at the remarkable beach; of course they are. Sydney had done a great job pitching the outing.

"Aiguablava means blue water," she'd said, over a simple breakfast of toast and jam. "It's so beautiful there. And all the glamorous old movie stars hung out at the hotel."

"It's a really special place," Curtis added.

But after he washes the dishes, Curtis finds his wife stuffing a canvas bag with beach towels and holds a hand to his belly. "I'm not feeling great," he says. "I think I'd better stick around home."

"What's wrong?" Syd moves toward him, face scrunched with concern. "Do you need to see a doctor?"

"No. Damian's risotto didn't agree with me."

"You barely ate any." Syd's eyes are narrowed. "And the rest of us feel fine."

"It's something else, then," Curtis responds. "I just think I should stay cool. And close to the bathroom."

"I'm not going to leave you if you're sick."

"I'm not sick." He lowers his voice. "I need some alone time, babe. Damian is kind of a lot."

This seems to sink in. Syd can't be oblivious to how loud and obnoxious their guest is. "Okay," she says grudgingly. "We'll be home in time for dinner. I'll pick something up."

* * *

Alone in the house, Curtis makes a cup of coffee and sips it by the pool. Caffeine might be a mistake; his heart is already racing with nerves and anticipation, but he needs to kill some time. He needs to wait at least half an hour, to ensure the trio has gone too far to turn around and come back. And then he'll get busy. Because something isn't right about the Australian couple, and he's going to find out what.

He'd pushed away his niggling concerns because Syd was enjoying their company, but he can't ignore them any longer. Last night, as he lay in bed listening to Damian hold court about food like he was Anthony fucking Bourdain, Curtis realized it was more than the big man's bluster and bravado getting on his nerves. There's something malicious about Damian, even malignant. But if Curtis asks the pair to leave, he'll look jealous and insecure. What he needs is a reason.

It's more than just bad vibes he feels for his Australian guests. There are too many coincidences. What are the odds that their van would break down right outside Syd and Curtis's house? That Damian just happens to have a background in construction? That he showed up armed with bright ideas for the shed renovation? It's too calculated. Too premeditated. Syd was so starved for company that she couldn't see it. But Curtis is not so blind.

There are handyman scams all over the internet, supposed builders who show up and pressure the homeowner into using their services. Of course, Damian hasn't asked for any payment—yet—but if Curtis's suspicions are correct, he will. At the end of their stay, he'll present a bill for services rendered, demand payment or they won't leave. He might even tear down all the work he did. It's not a new grift, and Curtis is embarrassed he fell for it.

There's another possibility, far darker and far more dangerous. Taking his last sip of coffee, Curtis tries to push it away, but it buzzes in the back of his brain like an insect. Could Damian and Bianca know Sydney and Curtis from their old life? Could they have crossed paths back in New York? The Australian couple claim they've never left *Freo*, as they call Fremantle, but they could be lying. What if they came to Spain looking for Curtis and Sydney? Curtis is confident he's never laid eyes on the pair, but what about Sydney? Could there be some connection? It's unlikely but not impossible. And after what Curtis has done, he can't be too careful.

Getting up, Curtis takes his empty mug to the kitchen and heads toward the guest room. He's practically tiptoeing down the tiled hallway even though he's alone, his pulse audible in his ears. As he pushes open the door, the hinges creak loudly in the empty house. For a moment, he lingers in the entryway, taking in the hastily made bed, the clothes strewn on the floor, the two half-emptied duffel bags. Is he really going to invade his guests' privacy and rifle through their personal belongings? He is. It's the only way.

The double bed is pressed against the wall, one bedside table next to it. On the wooden surface, there's a bottle of sunscreen, some lip balm, and a mug half full of cold coffee. Behind it, in a tidy little pile, there's a necklace. He picks up the delicate gold chain, examines the oval-shaped locket. He hasn't noticed Bianca wearing it, but that doesn't mean she hasn't been. Ever since the topless encounter, Curtis has kept his eyes far from her collarbone. He pries open the tiny gold oval, takes in the photo of a blond girl with an unfortunate haircut who is missing a front tooth. The picture is faded, the girl's outfit dated. It must be Bianca as a child. Turning it over, he sees the initials engraved in the back.

L.B.

The letters mean nothing to him. He doesn't even know his guests' last names. As he carefully places the necklace back in its spot, he remembers that Bianca's mother passed recently. This must have been her pendant with a photo of her daughter inside. It's completely innocent.

Curtis opens the two drawers in the bedside table. A pen rolls around in the top one, a frilly sachet of dried lavender in the bottom.

Otherwise, they're empty. He moves to the piles of clothing at the foot of the bed, sifts through them. Picking up a pair of Damian's shorts, he finds a crumpled slip of paper in a pocket. His fingers feel damp as he smooths it open, eagerly reads it. But it's only a receipt from their recent trip to the hardware store. He's still not familiar with the Catalonian language, but the items appear to be tools or building supplies. The total is less than fifty euros. If Damian asks for reimbursement, it's not going to break the bank.

Gingerly, Curtis rifles through the rest of the clothing, moving on to Bianca's bag. He feels like a creep digging through her belongings, and when he finds her birth control pills and a box of tampons, he abandons the task. Moving to the dresser, he opens all four drawers but finds them empty. There is nothing helpful to be found in this room: no personal documents, no passports or ID, no invoices of any kind.

Those items must be locked inside the van. Curtis needs the keys, but they're not in the room. He lifts the mattress, checks under the bed, tips out a few pairs of shoes. No keys. Damian must have taken them with him, but why? Because he doesn't want Curtis to get inside his vehicle. Because he's hiding something in there.

Curtis hurries to the closet and grabs a wire hanger. When he was a kid, his dad locked the keys in their older-model car and opened the door this way. Curtis was small, but he remembers it. He untwists the wire and creates a hook at one end. Moving outside, he goes to the passenger door of the van, slides the wire down inside the window well. In the middle of the door, there will be a locking mechanism. He needs to grab hold of it with the hook and pull. He moves the wire around searching for it, but it won't catch.

"Fuck," he mutters. He draws the wire out, notes the scratches in the paint near the window. Will Damian notice that the door has been tampered with? Curtis will deny it, say the marks must have been there before or blame a tree branch or a stray dog. Moving to the driver's side, he inserts the wire again, but still no luck. He can't waste this opportunity. He needs to know what's in there.

Cupping his hands, he peers through the side window. The interior is dark, most of the windows covered by heavy vinyl privacy screens. Curtis's eyes scan the cab, peering between the seats for any personal items, roving over the dashboard, the glove box, the ignition. In the back, he can just make out the bed, some closed cupboards, a few plastic bins full of camping supplies. Peeking out from under the stackable boxes, he sees a wooden handle.

It's the machete.

His heart thuds in his chest, his pulse rushing through his ears. Damian never returned it to the neighboring farmer. Was it Damian's all along? It's normal to have a tool like this when camping, but then why had he lied about it? Why stash it in the tall grass? Panic washes over Curtis, a sheen of cold sweat. Why would Damian hide this weapon from them?

A thought occurs to him then, a brilliantly simple idea. All this snooping around has been overkill. There's an easy way to get proof of the Australians' true intentions. Why hadn't he thought of it before? If this works, he'll have evidence that the pair are disingenuous, even shady. Sydney will agree that they need to leave before they can cause any damage: financial, emotional, or physical.

Dropping the wire hanger in the outside trash bin, he hurries back into the house.

21

Sydney has never been a confident driver. The unease may stem from her father's sudden death in a traffic accident when she was a child. They'd lived upstate then, and her dad commuted to work just fifteen minutes by car. That short drive was enough time for him to get T-boned by a pickup truck driven by a joyrider high on cocaine. Their little family had been devastated. One minute, they were complete, with a father and a husband. The next, they were shattered, a priceless vase they hadn't realized was so delicate.

Syd's mom had insisted that trauma would not keep her children from gaining a valuable life skill. When Reid and Sydney turned sixteen, they were forced to get their driver's licenses. Syd had taken all the defensive-driving classes, had passed her test, but she's never felt comfortable behind the wheel. In New York, she'd preferred to take the subway or a cab. When she did take the Range Rover, she usually inched through city traffic, so she's unaccustomed to the quick and confident Spaniards on the road here. Curtis told her to take her time, not to succumb to the pressure of more aggressive motorists, but she's aware of a line of cars forming behind her.

"Did Curtis eat something funny?" Bianca asks from the passenger seat. "It can't be related to his knock on the head."

Syd keeps her eyes on the steep winding road. "He's okay." There's a smile in her voice. "I think he just needs a quiet day to himself."

"Fair," Damian says from the back seat. Syd glances in the rearview mirror, but Damian doesn't meet her eyes. In fact, he's looking over his shoulder, likely noting the frustrated procession behind her. "How long is the drive?" he asks.

"Hour and a half," she says, though it'll take longer at this pace. "I just need to get some fuel, and then we'll head up to the main highway."

Her passengers are quiet as she navigates the twisting road toward town. There are gas stations along the major artery, but Sydney's still adjusting to the car's manual transmission, is uncomfortable pulling off the busy road at high speed. She's familiar with the small station on the outskirts of Cadaqués, even if it adds some time to their journey.

She pulls up to the pump without stalling: a small victory. Syd turns off the ignition and climbs out of the car. As she moves around to the hose, Damian clambers out of the back seat. Syd's capable of pumping her own fuel, obviously, but she appreciates his chivalry.

"Bianca and I are going to head to the grocery store and get some snacks for the road," Damian says, opening the passenger door. "Come on, B."

"Good thinking," Syd says to cover her surprise. "I'll pick you up out front."

"Thanks," Bianca calls over her shoulder as the pair hurries away.

Syd swipes her credit card and inserts the hose into the car. As the fuel chugs into the tank, she watches her guests in the distance. They're walking briskly, hand in hand, headed to the main grocery store where she and Curtis shop. Well, Curtis does most of the shopping on his own, but sometimes Sydney tags along. She knows where to collect them.

When the tank is full, Syd gets in and drives down the narrow street, grateful for their tiny European car. The Range Rover was so huge and unwieldy, even on Manhattan's wider avenues. She does a loop of the block, slowly passing the storefront, but her passengers haven't emerged. She does a second and then a third loop. It must be busy inside the store. On her fourth trip around the block, she wonders if she's missed them somehow, until she spots Bianca standing alone on the sidewalk, hugging a bag of groceries. When she spies the Citroën, her face lights up. She smiles and waves.

"It's going to be a girls' trip," Bianca says, climbing into the front seat.

"Where's Damian?"

"He met this guy in the grocery line who does fishing charters. He had a cancellation on his next trip and invited Damian to go."

"Really?" Syd tentatively eases back into traffic. "This all happened in the grocery line?"

"You know how friendly Damian is. The guy heard him speaking English and they started chatting."

Syd shifts into second. "That'll be fun for him."

"And for us," Bianca says. "We deserve a break from all the testosterone flying around at the house."

Syd smiles over at her. "Yeah, we do."

The beach at Aiguablava is breathtaking, and Bianca is suitably impressed. She marvels at the turquoise waters, the fine golden sand, and the pine-covered cliffs. Though Bianca lives near the world's most beautiful beaches (according to Damian), she's full of accolades for this spectacular cove. Syd appreciates the enthusiasm. It validates her decision to give up everything and start over in this beautiful country.

Dropping their beach bags and their clothes, the women run into the waves. Despite Syd's affinity for a cold plunge, she's grateful for the ease of the warm waters. The pair swim out—it's nearly effortless in the buoyant ocean—and Syd savors the feeling of stretching her limbs and engaging her muscles. When they're a fair distance from shore, they pause, turn back to take in the golden beach dotted with sunbathers and brightly colored umbrellas.

As Bianca treads water beside her, Syd lays back, feeling suspended, almost cradled by the waters. For a moment, she's like a fetus: without thought, or care, or jealousy. Her worries about her husband, her marriage, and Bianca wash away with the gentle current. But the meditative state doesn't last long.

"Shit," Bianca mutters next to her. "I've got a cramp in my calf. I'd better head back."

"I'll be in soon," Syd says. She wants to extend this carefree moment, drifting in the amniotic suspension, but the spell is broken. Thoughts and concerns soon meander their way into her mind. She rights herself and swims back to shore, where Bianca sits on a beach towel, massaging her calf.

"How's your leg?" Syd asks, patting herself dry with the striped towel Bianca passes to her.

"It's okay. I should probably eat a banana."

"I'm not sure they serve bananas at the restaurant." Syd lays her towel on the sand, lowers herself onto it. "Banana daquiri maybe?"

Bianca forces a chuckle, stops her massage. "I have to tell you something."

Syd swallows a small sense of dread. "Okay."

"Damian didn't go fishing. We got into a fight in the store."

"Oh no," Syd says, but she's perversely pleased. Her houseguests' harmonious relationship has been a constant reminder that her own marriage is cracked and broken. Curtis had overheard the other couple arguing, but Sydney had dismissed it as normal tension and bickering. Perhaps things are not so peachy between the Aussies after all. This shouldn't buoy her, but it does.

"Do you want to talk about it?" she asks gently. Syd's eager for more details. She can't help herself.

"I don't want to upset you."

Syd sits up. "Upset *me*?"

Bianca twists her body to face Syd. "I told you how Curtis has been acting toward me. The energy he's been giving off."

There's a bitter taste in Syd's mouth. "Yeah."

"Damian noticed it, too. He accused me of enjoying it. Encouraging it, even."

A bubble of sick lodges in Sydney's throat, and she struggles to swallow. She'd dismissed Bianca's vague accusations, at least doubted them. But if Damian sensed Curtis's intentions too, then it must be real. How had Sydney been so blind? So trusting?

"I don't enjoy it, Syd," Bianca says. "I would never encourage him, I promise."

Sydney believes her. Because she has no reason not to trust Bianca. And every reason not to trust her own husband. There's a dull, ugly pressure on her sternum, making it hard to breathe, but she pushes out the words.

"Curtis cheated on me. That's why we're in Spain."

"Oh my God." Bianca reaches for Sydney's hand, grips it. "I'm so sorry."

"We went to therapy last year. I thought I could forgive him. We were going to rebuild our relationship, but... I don't know if I can."

"You don't have to, Sydney. You deserve to be cherished, not betrayed. Not made a fool of."

A fool. That's what Sydney's been. "I've given up everything: my career, my friends, my apartment. I made a commitment to this marriage. To Curtis."

"You can rebuild a better life," Bianca says. "Start over somewhere else. Do you have your own money?"

"Some," Syd says. While she and Curtis have a joint account for mortgage payments and bills, she still has her inheritance. Most of it. It wasn't substantial to begin with, so Curtis had promised not to touch it. But when the renovations had gone over budget, she'd offered. There was no other choice.

"When we get our van fixed, we'll drive you wherever you want to go," Bianca says. "And Curtis doesn't have to know. You can just... disappear."

Sydney considers the possibility of a new life alone. Where would she go? Home to New York? Or would she stay in Spain? Find herself a small apartment in Valencia or Seville. She could start life over as a single woman. But would that make her happy?

She's spent fifteen years with Curtis, her best friend, her lover. In all that time, he's made only one mistake, and then he fell on his sword, begged her forgiveness. Curtis had pleaded with her to rebuild their marriage, had agreed to go to counseling, had even left his job to make her feel more secure. Would Syd really leave him for *flirting* with Bianca? Are she and Damian blowing Curtis's behavior out of proportion? Or is it just a matter of time until Curtis finds another opportunity to cheat on his wife? And this time, she'd be alone in Spain, with no family, no friends, no support system. A deep choking sob erupts inside her.

"Oh, babe," Bianca says, leaning forward and gathering Sydney into her arms. Syd melts into the hug, tears slipping from her eyes, mixing with the seawater in Bianca's hair. It's been so long since Syd's felt comforted, cared for, and held. Since before her mother died, she thinks, which makes the tears come harder. She's vaguely aware of Bianca's hand running over her back, cupping her head, an effort to soothe her. Their faces are pressed together, and Sydney can smell their mingled feminine scents: sunscreen, a touch of makeup, Bianca's almond shampoo. Gradually, a feeling other than comfort stirs inside her. It's a connection. Or is it something more?

Tentatively, her fingers trace the length of Bianca's back, her skin soft and hot from the sun. They tangle into her long damp hair, move up under the veil toward her neck. Syd can hear her own breath pressed against Bianca's cheek getting heavier. She's aroused. There's no denying the pull she feels toward this beautiful woman. Could she explore this attraction to Bianca? Forget about her husband and all the pain he's caused her?

Bianca pulls back gently, wipes Sydney's tears with a thumb. Their faces are close, eyes connected. The beachgoers surrounding them fade away, and there is nothing but this moment. Is Bianca going to kiss her? Is Sydney ready for what this could mean?

But then the Australian girl speaks.

"I think we could both use a good strong drink."

She gets up, leaving Sydney breathless and confused in the sand.

Sydney Cleary and Curtis Lowe, Couples' Counseling Session
Ellen Dwyer, Psychologist, PsyD
July 15

татTRANSCRIPT 4.

Ellen:
Curtis, tell me about your parents. What was their marriage like?

Curtis:
It was toxic. They stayed married until my dad passed away a few years ago, but they were never happy. My mom was a hard woman.

Ellen:
Hard in what way?

Curtis:
She was extremely devout. She was very judgmental and basically impossible to please.

Ellen:
How did your father deal with that?

Curtis:
He went along with whatever she wanted. But he kept a stack of porno mags and a beer fridge hidden in the back shed.

Ellen:
So he hid his true self for the sake of harmony with your mom. What about your relationship with her?

Curtis:
I played the perfect son, but I got up to plenty. I just never got caught... That's why I had to be honest with Sydney. I don't want our marriage to be based on lies like theirs was.

Ellen:
And, Sydney? What was your parents' marriage like?

Sydney:
They were mostly happy, I think, but my dad died when I was young. In a car accident. My mom dated a bit, but she never remarried.

Ellen:
That's a devastating loss for a child. I wouldn't be surprised if it made you feel fearful of loss in other relationships, too.

Sydney:
Yes. And Curtis's infidelity hurt more because I know my parents didn't choose to abandon me. Curtis did.

Curtis:
I didn't abandon you, Syd. I *chose* you. I came clean to save our marriage. To save *us*.

Sydney:
My whole life, I've been guarded in relationships. I've always protected my heart. But when I married you, Curtis, I gave you everything. I let my walls down and I opened up to you. And you broke me.

Curtis:
I never wanted to hurt you. And I never will again. I promise, Sydney.

Sydney:
I'm trying to believe you. But it's really fucking hard.

22

Curtis clears his throat as he holds the phone to his ear. Even with the help of Google Translate, he's not confident in his word choice or pronunciation. What he's trying to express is not simple, even in English.

"Did my friend come in about a week ago and try to order a fuel pump for his van? Or is he a liar and a fake?"

A man answers on the fourth ring, his Spanish so quick and fluid that Curtis doesn't even recognize the name of the garage. It's the second place he's called. The first mechanic had no memory of an Aussie trying to order a part—or at least that's what it sounded like to Curtis. Maybe the man didn't understand Curtis's convoluted query? Or his terrible accent? It's possible that the mechanic he spoke to wasn't working that day, that someone else assisted Damian. Or maybe Damian was never there. Because his van is perfectly fine.

"Hola," Curtis begins. *"Tengo una pregunta..."* I have a question. Curtis reads the translation he'd jotted down on the pad of paper resting on the kitchen counter. He's not confident in the Catalonian translation, so he uses basic Spanish, enunciates carefully. *"Hizo mi amigo Australiano..."* Did my Australian friend...

The mechanic cuts him off in his rapid language, sounding frustrated, even annoyed. He calls out in Spanish, hopefully summoning someone who speaks English. Curtis waits, listening to the banter in the background. He strains to recognize a single word in their discourse, but he gets nothing. They could have forgotten he's on hold, could be discussing what they're having for lunch for all he knows. And then he hears a noise outside.

Curtis pulls the phone away from his ear and listens. It's quiet now, but it was there, he's sure of it. A scuffling on the gravel, a rock displaced. It could have been an animal; they've seen deer in the area and have heard there are mountain goats. There are smaller creatures too, like marmots. It's nothing to worry about. He returns to the call, the distant debating in Spanish.

"¡Hola!" he calls into the device, hoping to recapture some attention.

"Hola." The response comes from inside the house.

Curtis bursts from the kitchen, heading for the front door. Damian stands in the hallway drenched in sweat. His smile is bright but cold, and Curtis's chest tightens. His eyes dart to the big man's hands for the machete, but they're empty. If Damian is armed, he's hiding it well.

"What are you doing back here?" Curtis's voice is high-pitched. He tries to act cool, but his hand trembles as he hangs up the call, shoves the phone into his pocket.

"I was worried about you," Damian says, moving into the living room. "How are you feeling?"

"I'm fine. Better. Where are the girls?"

"They went swimming." Damian flops on the sofa, puts his feet on the ottoman. "Who were you talking to?"

"No one. A friend back home." He changes the subject. "How did you get here?"

"I hiked up the trail from town. It's a bloody workout. I could use a beer."

"Sure." Curtis moves into the kitchen, grabs two bottles and removes the caps. He returns, hands his guest a beer, then perches on the ottoman facing him.

Damian takes a long swallow before he speaks. "I lied to you," he says. "About the farmer."

"Oh?"

"He'd never seen the machete or gloves before. I just didn't want the girls to freak out."

Curtis raises his eyebrows in feigned surprise. He can't let on that he's been peering inside the van, that he spotted the handle under the stack of bins. He takes a drink. The liquid is bitter but cold. "That's strange." His voice sounds almost normal now. "I wonder who they belong to?"

"I don't know." Damian shrugs his muscled shoulders. "I wouldn't worry about it, though. I hid the machete in the van."

Curtis nods tightly. The weapon in Damian's possession does not put him at ease.

"If someone's after you, mate, they'll never get through both of us."

"After *me*?" Curtis scoffs, but his face feels hot, and he drinks more beer. "Why would someone be after me?"

Damian ignores the question, his eyes penetrating. "I came back here because you and I need to talk."

Curtis grew up keeping secrets from a cold, punishing mother. He knows that responding could lead to self-incrimination, so he says nothing. He presses his molars together, keeps his expression placid, and waits.

"I'm sure you've noticed there's something brewing between the women."

"*Brewing?*"

"Bianca and Sydney are getting closer. I think there are some real feelings developing there." Damian picks at the label on his bottle. "Romantic feelings."

Curtis is bemused. "Sydney isn't gay. She's not bi either."

"Bianca has a way of opening a girl's mind." He sounds almost proud. "I've seen it in action."

"What do you care? I thought you two had an open relationship?"

"We do. But this feels different. More serious."

"Are you worried they're going to run off together?" Curtis laughs, but it rings hollow.

"I hope not." Damian drains his bottle. "I can't believe you haven't noticed."

Curtis had been concerned about the chemistry between Syd and Damian. He'd been intent on not appearing to flirt with Bianca. Had he been blind to what was building between the two women? Is Bianca the reason Sydney cringes from his touch?

"I need another beer," Damian says, dragging himself up off the sofa. "Want one?"

"Why not?" Curtis still has half a bottle, but he suddenly craves the release of the alcohol. He takes a big drink, hoping the booze will ease the anxious feeling brought on by Damian's suggestion. His marriage hasn't felt solid since his infidelity. But could he really lose Sydney to a woman who lives in a van?

The Aussie returns moments later with two cold bottles in one hand. In the other, the notepad Curtis had left on the counter.

Fuck.

"What does this say?" Damian asks.

"I was checking on the lumber delivery," Curtis says smoothly. "Making sure it's still arriving tomorrow."

"It says 'Australiano' here," Damian presses. "Were you talking about me?"

Curtis can feel the sweat prickling his hairline, but he keeps his cool. "I mentioned that I came in with you. I thought they might remember you because of your Australian accent."

"You have an accent, too."

"That's true." He shrugs. "I don't know what I was thinking."

"As long as you're not talking behind my back." Damian's expression is dark, his tone almost threatening. But Curtis keeps his response light.

"What would I be talking about? I barely know you."

"Just kidding, mate." Damian hands him the beer. "Let's drink these by the pool. I might go for a dip."

"Good plan," Curtis says, taking the frosty bottle. Bullet dodged, he follows the big Aussie outside.

23

Sydney and Bianca are in Cadaqués, sitting out front of the bar and casino. Syd drove them back here, parked the Citroën in an overnight lot so she doesn't need to worry about driving. She can enjoy the goblet of gin and tonic before her, and they can walk up the hill to the house later. The path is steep and could be difficult to navigate in the dark, but she's not thinking about that now. She's fully cemented in the present moment.

This is where the locals go for cheap drinks, their tables plunked on the sandy beach, the surf tickling their bare feet. She takes a sip of her boozy beverage, soaks in the collegial atmosphere. Around them, people drink, laugh, even argue, but Syd feels envious of their camaraderie, their joie de vivre. It's so distinctly European, and it can't be faked, no matter how hard she tries.

"You drink too slow," Bianca cajoles, hoisting her heavy glass. Obediently, Syd drinks, enjoying the effects of the gin. She's beginning to feel bleary and relaxed, the awkwardness of that intimate moment on the beach becoming smudgy and indistinct. She looks at Bianca, smiling and carefree. Sydney doesn't need to feel uncomfortable about what happened. Or didn't happen. Bianca makes everything feel okay.

"Let's go to a club tonight," Bianca suggests. "We deserve to get fucked-up."

"There's a club here?" Syd asks.

"Of course there is," Bianca teases. "This is a holiday town in Spain. Do you think everyone goes to bed at ten just because you do?"

Syd takes a giddy sip. "I haven't been to a club in years."

"Why not? Because your husband won't let you?"

"No," Syd answers honestly. "I was never really into that scene. And I guess I feel like I've outgrown it."

"You're still young," Bianca gushes. "And you're so elegant and beautiful. You'll have guys all over you." Her eyebrow arches slyly. "Maybe you could even the score with Curtis?"

Syd shakes her head and laughs, because it's a joke. It must be. "That wouldn't solve anything."

"It might be fun, though."

She forces a game smile, though hooking up with a random stranger in a bar does not sound fun to Syd. It sounds tawdry, and gross, and possibly dangerous. But the sexual thoughts she's entertained about both Damian and Bianca are not without risks either.

Bianca stands. "I'll get us another round." She moves toward the bar before Syd can object. This will be their third drink. They're too sweet and too strong, and Sydney didn't eat much at dinner. She's starting to feel slightly ill and more than a little unsteady. But the thought of getting drunk, of losing herself in a sea of hedonistic strangers in a steamy nightclub, is oddly appealing. And she can't go home to Curtis. Not right now.

Her eyes drift over the crowd of revelers. There are a range of ages, races, and she hears snippets of various languages: Spanish, of course; some French; and there's a loud older woman speaking English with a British accent. Syd feels a part of this scene and entirely outside of it. But she's comfortable, almost carefree in this moment. Or maybe she's just drunk.

And then she feels a prickle at the nape of her neck, the distinct sense that someone is watching her. She twists in her seat, and her eyes connect with a man's. He's leaning against a low rock wall, wearing shorts and a button-up linen shirt. He's about her age, lean and tanned. His eyes are dark and piercing as they bore into hers. He's a stranger, but there's something familiar about him. He raises a cigarette to his lips and takes a drag. It has a white filter.

A chill shudders through her, and the glass trembles in her hand. She sets it down, averts her gaze. Does she know this guy from somewhere? Or does he know *her*? Her mind scrambles to place his face. Does he resemble Jameson Drew, the man she sent to jail?

Bianca sets two more drinks on the table with a thunk, takes her seat. "Someone's got their eye on you."

"He's giving me the creeps," Syd whispers. "He's looking at me like he knows me."

"Those are come-fuck-me eyes," Bianca says with a laugh. "You need to relax."

Syd turns back toward the man, but he's lost interest in her now. She watches him sidle up to a small table where two attractive women share a bottle of wine. Relief washes over her, and embarrassment. "I need to get out more."

"You do, babe." Bianca hoists her heavy glass. "One more drink and then we hit the dance floor."

The nightclub smells dank and musty, the air thick with sweat and pheromones. Normally, Sydney would struggle to breathe in this close environment, but her anxiety has been obliterated by the effects of the gin. She knows it's a temporary fix, that tomorrow she'll likely feel more amped up than usual, but she's not thinking about that now. She's just absorbing the thud of the bass, the flashing of the lights, the electronic notes building to a crescendo. She's high on the energy of the young people gyrating around her. And she's comforted by the warmth of Bianca's hand in hers, pulling her toward the dance floor.

When they're immersed in the crush of bodies, Bianca turns to face her. She lifts her arms in the air, drops her head forward, and moves her body to the music. Syd watches her, rapt and envious. Bianca's movements are so free, so self-assured. At times, Syd still feels like the tallest girl in her grade, the one none of the boys would dance with. But tonight, nothing matters, no one cares. She lets herself go.

Her hair falls over her face, obscuring her surroundings. She's alone with the music and the energy and the heat. Sydney is sexy and free, unburdened by the doubt and pain that have been dragging her down. She needed this outlet, this night of alcohol and hedonism.

Bianca's mouth is close to her ear. "You're so hot." Her hands rest on Sydney's hips, and she feels that same tug of desire. Syd had been shy before, on the beach, but she's brave now, confident. She reaches out for Bianca, pulls her closer. And then she feels a hand run down her back, two fingers stroking the bare skin of her shoulder. She turns her head.

It's Damian.

"I found you," he says, not to Bianca but to her. His strong chest is pressed against her back; his big hands hold her waist. Electricity pulses from his fingertips, and Syd closes her eyes. It's wrong to feel this way. Syd is married. Damian is with Bianca. But their chemistry is so simple, so undeniable. She's powerless to stop what's about to happen.

Bianca watches them, eyes shining, a smile on her lips. She moves closer, hands reaching for Sydney, fingers tracing her cheek, cupping her chin. Bianca leans in and kisses her. *Finally.* Syd savors the softness of her lips, the sweetness of her breath. Damian's mouth is on her neck now, the stubble of his cheek against her delicate skin. The juxtaposition of masculine and feminine is confusing and exhilarating and *incredible.* She turns her body toward Damian, opens her eyes. And then she sees him.

At the edge of the dance floor, Curtis stands alone, watching their entanglement. His face is expressionless, but his eyes are so full of pain. Syd may have thought she wanted to hurt him just like he hurt her, but she can't do it. No matter what he did in the past. Even if he has been coming on to Bianca... She still cares about his feelings. She still loves him.

She tears herself away from the couple, stumbles toward her partner.

Sydney Cleary and Curtis Lowe, Couples' Counseling Session
Ellen Dwyer, Psychologist, PsyD
July 15

THERAPY PROGRESS NOTES—SESSION 4.

Curtis's parents clearly had a toxic marriage. Secrets were the norm for him growing up, and he likely became adept at presenting a facade to those close to him. While he's full of apologies and promises, is he being authentic with his wife? Are his emotions and regrets sincere?

The loss of Sydney's father when she was just a child has had long-lasting impacts on her. She's protective of her emotions, wary of being hurt again. She wants to trust Curtis, but she'll have to overcome significant trauma to be vulnerable with him. And should she?

Will Sydney be emotionally safe if she stays in the marriage?

24

Curtis watches his wife sleep, her head curled into her chest like a little bird, her breath shallow and uneven. Morning light sifts in through the blinds, but she doesn't stir. She's going to feel like shit when she wakes up. Syd's not a big drinker, despite their plans to get into the wine business. He's never seen her so out of control, even when they were younger. He wonders if Bianca had convinced Syd to take something last night, a party drug to make her drop her inhibitions. Or Bianca might have slipped it into Syd's drink without her knowledge. Will his partner even remember what she did at the nightclub? How close she came to ruining everything?

His mind drifts to Damian, his role in last night's debauchery. The two men had had a few beers, Curtis had grilled some steaks and veggies. They were getting along for once. Without the women to impress, Damian had dropped the annoying macho act. He'd been interested and interesting. Maybe he'd gotten the guy all wrong? And then Damian had checked his phone.

"The girls are having drinks in Cadaqués," he'd said, reading a text message. "They're heading to a club."

"Really?" Curtis had scoffed. "Sydney doesn't go clubbing."

"I told you Bianca's convincing." He'd taken a swig of beer. "Let's go meet them."

Curtis had retrieved his phone, but there was no message from Sydney and certainly no invitation. Would she welcome her husband's surprise appearance? Or did she want to be alone with Bianca?

But Damian had been insistent. "They're probably drunk," Damian continued. "They might need help getting home."

That argument won Curtis over. The car was parked somewhere in town. If Curtis stopped drinking now, he'd be able to drive them back up the hill, ensure everyone got home safely. Before anything regrettable happened. And so he'd agreed to hike down the darkened trail, using their phones as flashlights. Damian brought a beer for the journey, but Curtis was intent on sobering up.

When they'd reached the nightclub—dark, dank, and sweaty—Curtis had gone directly to the bar. *"Agua sin gas,"* he'd ordered, thirsty from the hike. He'd turned to see if Damian wanted a drink, but his companion had evaporated. With his bottle of water, Curtis had pushed his way through the throng, moving toward the dance floor. And that had been where he'd seen them.

He had no right to be angry at Sydney, not after what he'd done to her. In fact, he'd sometimes wondered if his wife leveling the playing field might allow them to move forward on more even footing. But last night, he'd watched Bianca kiss Sydney on the dance floor, pass her onto Damian like some kind of human present. Curtis had felt sick, angry, and jealous, but he'd pushed down those feelings, stayed motionless on the periphery. And that had been when Bianca's gaze had found him. And she'd smiled, a smug *fuck-you* grin. She wasn't falling in love with Sydney. She was getting off on hurting Curtis. Why?

When Sydney spotted him, she'd extricated herself from the threesome on the dance floor, had stumbled toward him. "Y-you're here," she'd stammered, collapsing into his arms. "I'm sorry."

"It's okay." He'd held her for a moment. She'd been trembling and sweaty—from adrenaline, drugs, or guilt, he didn't know. And then he'd led her through the press of bodies, out of the dank club. Somehow, he'd coaxed the location of the car from her, found the keys in her pocket. He'd driven her home, put her to bed, had lain awake simmering with anger and hatred for their houseguests, who were still out clubbing. They'd have to show up at some point: Their van and all their belongings were here. He would confront them then, tell them to pack their shit and leave, arrange a tow for their van. But eventually Curtis drifted off, exhausted from the mix of intense emotions. The Aussies must have crept in while he was asleep.

Sydney stirs then, rolls toward him. Her eyes flutter open, and he sees the blankness, even confusion in them. It takes a few moments for realization to dawn, the memory to revisit her. Her face crumples. "Oh, Curtis..."

"I'm not angry, Syd. I know I have no right to be."

"I didn't mean for that to happen," she says. "I was so drunk. Bianca said..." She trails off, pressing two fingers between her eyebrows. "It's all fuzzy."

"Go back to sleep."

She nods, drops her head back onto the pillow. He leans over, kisses her forehead, and slips from the room.

The house is silent except for the hum of the fridge, the wind rustling through the trees outside the windows. Curtis makes himself a coffee, drinks it standing at the kitchen counter, gathering his courage. The Aussie couple has worn out their welcome. They're too wild, too flirtatious, too promiscuous. And he can't forget the look on Bianca's face last night as she kissed his wife. She was fucking with him. She's a sadistic bitch.

Curtis strides down the hall to the guest room, knocks on the door. Silence. Tentatively, he pushes it open and peers inside. It's empty, and the bed hasn't been slept in. For a moment, he thinks the pair has taken off, left all their belongings behind. But it's wishful thinking. They wouldn't abandon all their clothing, a sentimental locket, birth control pills.

Outside, the midmorning heat is already stifling. As he moves down the driveway, he smells burned grass, baked soil. The van is still and silent, but they're in there. They must be. Curtis knocks on the panel door and waits. There's no response. He's about to knock again when the door slides open. Damian emerges, dressed in shorts and a T-shirt. Fresh and alert.

"Morning, mate." The greeting is without warmth. Subtly mocking.

"I need a word with you two," Curtis says.

"Bianca just headed to the pool," Damian says, sliding the panel door closed behind him. "But you can talk to me."

They will have this out, man-to-man. Curtis prefers it this way. He doesn't want Sydney to witness this conversation, and he doesn't need Bianca chiming in either.

"Last night was pretty fucked-up," Curtis begins.

"It was just a little fun. Relax, mate."

"I'm not your fucking *mate*," Curtis snarls. He's so sick of the idiom, and Damian's overuse of it. "I'd like you two to leave."

"Why? Because we danced with your wife?"

"I don't need to explain myself to you." Curtis's voice is shaky with repressed anger, but he pushes through. "This is my house, and I want you gone."

"But we're still waiting on our fuel pump."

"You can call a tow truck for the van. You can take the bus to Girona." The adrenaline rush of Curtis's rage is almost a high. "But you two need to get the fuck off my property."

For a moment, Damian is speechless. Bullies often respond this way when a target stands up to them. Curtis waits for him to cower and apologize, to admit that what happened last night crossed the line. But a slow smile takes over Damian's face, and his eyes narrow.

"We're not going anywhere, buddy."

There's no trace of an Australian accent.

DAMIAN AND BIANCA

25

Damian Walsh had never wanted to live in Butt Fuck, Indiana. He'd been happy living with his mom in Tacoma until he got kicked out of school. He hadn't started the fight that got him expelled, but he'd finished it by putting the other kid in the hospital with a fractured eye socket. His mom had totally overreacted, deemed him "out of control" and "dangerous." She didn't feel safe or comfortable with her own son anymore. So he was shipped off to live with his dad in a small town near the Michigan border.

His dad, Ron, was not happy to see him. "You may have controlled and manipulated your mother, but things are going to be different around here."

They weren't different—not for long, anyway. After getting his sixteen-year-old son a busboy job at his golf club, Ron soon got bored with his disciplinarian act. The curfew slipped away, and most of the chores were ignored. His dad was busy with his various investments and scams, juggling it all with a gambling habit and a few girlfriends. Damian was towing the line anyway. His grades were decent. He showed up at work on time. And when he charmed his boss at the golf club into promoting him to waiter, Ron was proud.

"These are the people you need to know," his dad told him. "They're the people who run this town."

Damian bit back a smirk. He didn't care who ran this ass-backward town. His dad may have been impressed by a bunch of mediocre rubes-done-good with their car dealerships, their farm equipment auction houses, or their Arby's franchises, but Damian wasn't. He was meant for more. He had plans. Still, he played along and kissed their asses to make his life easier.

It didn't take him long to figure out how to skim their credit cards. The good ol' boys were too arrogant to check their statements, their wives too tipsy from lunchtime martinis to remember if they'd ordered a designer scarf or a pair of gloves afterward. Cybersecurity was lax then. And he was careful with the purchases he made with the stolen numbers, never buying anything that would cause alarm. Most of it he resold, put the money into his "escape" fund. As soon as high school was over, he'd move to France or Italy or Greece. Somewhere with sunshine and beaches and sophisticated people.

He already looked the part. With the stolen credit cards, he ordered himself stylish clothes, designer sunglasses, and trendy sneakers. He was tall and good-looking, but his elevated style made him stand out. Damian liked foreign films, and he'd read all the Jason Bourne novels. Most of the guys in town thought he was stuck-up, or weird, or gay. They were jealous of his acquired class, his curated sophistication. Damian didn't care. He wasn't there to make friends. The town was just a pit stop.

He had his choice of girls, though. They were so easy to charm and manipulate. They brought him home-cooked food and expensive gifts; they did his homework for him and helped him cheat on tests. And yet, no matter the time spent nor the level of intimacy they reached, he never got emotionally attached to any of them.

Sometimes, Damian wondered about his lack of feelings. He felt no connection to his dad and only a nostalgic fondness for his mother. Was he even capable of love? He read a book about sociopaths and wondered, briefly, if he was one. But eventually he concluded that he was an exemplary human trapped in a mediocre world and any actions or behaviors that elevated him out of the mire were justified. When he stole money or cheated on a test, it was a means to an end.

If he felt no empathy or compassion for the people around him, it was because they were small-minded losers.

His senior year, he went to a fast-food place with a guy who caddied at the golf club. The girl behind the counter was pretty, even in her unflattering uniform, but she was aloof, bordering on rude.

"Hey, Samantha," he said, reading the badge sewn on her brown tunic. "I haven't seen you here before. Are you new?"

She rolled her eyes. "Do you want to add fries to make it a combo meal?"

"Lez," his buddy whispered, as if Damian was bruised by the rejection. He wasn't. He was intrigued. He went back to the chicken restaurant alone the next evening. The girl was there, but she either didn't remember him or pretended not to. He tried to be friendly, tried to flirt with her, but she was brusque and efficient. It took him three weeks (twelve chicken burgers, fifteen sides of fries, and twenty Cokes) to crack through her armor. Eventually, he learned that they were the same age, she was about to graduate from the high school across town, and that her parents were divorced. She hadn't seen her dad in years, her mom was a toxic narcissist, and her little sister, Lyric, was the only person she cared about. He also learned that her name wasn't Sam.

"It came with the uniform," she explained. "My name's Bianca."

"I like it." He grinned at her. "I'm Damian."

"I know," she said, spraying the counter with a bleach solution. "The fry cook goes to your school and has a huge crush on you."

"Oh my God!" the fry cook shrieked from the kitchen, and hurried into the back room.

"Do you want to go to prom with me, Bianca?" It just came out. He hadn't planned it.

"No thanks."

He was shocked. And stung. "Why not?"

"Because I don't want to celebrate graduating from an institution that taught me nothing but to embrace mediocrity. And I'm not interested in school-sponsored, forced fun. It's Americana bullshit."

If he had to pick a moment, that was when he fell in love with her.

It happened fast from there. They began to spend all their free time together when they weren't at school or working. The feelings Damian had thought he was incapable of bubbled out of him like lava. He was fiercely, ferociously in love with Bianca. He was lit up, inspired, and so cheerful that his dad asked if he was on drugs. This was the true stuff of life, not money, clothes, not even adventure. Suddenly, all the love songs made sense. The sappy romantic movies his mom watched on the sofa with a box of tissues had nailed it.

On prom night, they took his dad's car to a farmer's field half an hour from town. They climbed through the barbed wire fence, smoked a joint, then lay on their backs in the prickly grass, talking about their future. There were no games with Bianca, no playing indifferent or hard to get. They wanted to be together forever. It wasn't even a question.

"Let's get the fuck out of here," he said. "I've got enough money to get us to Greece. It's cheap to live there. I'll get a job at a bar or something."

"I can't leave."

"You hate this town." He rolled onto his side, looked at her perfect profile. "Your dad's not around. Your mom doesn't give a shit about you."

"My mother is poison. If I leave, she'll destroy my sister."

"Lyric will be fine," he tried, but he knew how much Bianca loved that kid. She was just seven, a cute little thing with a smattering of freckles and a homespun haircut. He rolled onto his back, disappointment seeping through the marijuana haze. "You can't sacrifice your own life for your sister," he muttered.

"If you want to go traveling, go." She turned toward him. "I'm not going to make you choose. I'm not going to stand in the way of your dreams."

It made him love her even more. "I'll wait for you," he said.

And he did. For almost eleven years, he stood by her, kept his promise. And then a shocking tragedy, an unthinkable nightmare, changed the course of their lives. As horrific as it had been, there had been a silver lining.

It finally set Damian free.

26

Life in that small Indiana town had been tough for Bianca. She grew up in a rundown house with little money and a mother who didn't love her. It was an indisputable fact, like her mom's green eyes flecked with gold or the slight gap between her front teeth that made her look like Lauren Bacall. (According to her mom. Bianca didn't even know who Lauren Bacall was.) Bianca was aware that her mother's indifference was unusual, that her upbringing would have been a lot more pleasant had Yvonne Richards been able to summon some maternal feelings, but Bianca didn't dwell on it. She knew it had made her strong. A survivor.

Her existence wasn't completely devoid of love. When Bianca was ten years old, her mom brought her baby sister home from the hospital. Bianca was full of excitement, jumping around with new-puppy exuberance. Yvonne laid the tiny bundle on the sofa, and Bianca knelt on the floor next to it. She stroked the downy head, gazed into the dark blue eyes. The baby's fingers were so small, her nails so tiny but so sharp. Bianca tickled her hand, and the baby gripped her pinky tightly.

"Hello, baby sister," Bianca whispered.

"Half sister," her mom corrected, sitting heavily on the end of the couch. "Her name's Lyric."

The baby and Bianca had different fathers. Lyric's dad, Darrel, was currently in the kitchen, heating up a lasagna that one of the neighbors had dropped off. Bianca's dad was in Texas. He'd gotten a job in the oil fields when Bianca was just three. He'd come home to Indiana twice a year for visits for a while. Bianca remembered the presents: Texas-branded T-shirts and key chains from the airport gift shop, packets of pretzels or cookies from the plane. And she remembered the fights. Screaming, yelling, bottles smashing on the floor or against the wall. Eventually, her father stopped coming.

Yvonne Richards was movie-star beautiful, but men treated her badly. They fell hard for her, but they didn't want to deal with the reality of life with her. And her kids. After Bianca's father left, there was a string of boyfriends and a second husband. None of them lasted. "It would be a lot easier if I'd never had you," Yvonne said. "If I'd known your dad was going to be such a deadbeat, I would've had an abortion."

Darrel and Yvonne weren't married, but with the baby here Bianca was sure Darrel would stick around. He'd fall deeply in love with Lyric. How could he not? She was so tiny and perfect. Even if they were only half sisters, Bianca felt a powerful, familial bond. And she liked Darrel well enough.

But when Lyric was four and Bianca fourteen, Darrel left. He took Lyric with him, storming out with his daughter on his hip. "Sorry, kid," he murmured as he passed Bianca. She was devastated to lose her sister, afraid to be left alone with her mom, but even then, she knew this would be better for Lyric. Darrel was a decent guy. He wasn't smart or hardworking or particularly stable, but he wasn't toxic and cruel like Yvonne. Darrel wouldn't taunt and control and manipulate his little girl.

"I'll get your sister back," Yvonne promised, "if I have to kill that motherfucker."

Bianca wasn't sure why Yvonne wanted custody of Lyric. She didn't have the time or energy for a small child. It was Darrel or Bianca who took the kid to daycare, who made her meals and gave her baths. But her mom liked to win.

Yvonne began dating a lawyer, and she asked him to help her get custody. Darrel had his own lawyer, who claimed Yvonne was dangerous, mentally unstable, and an abuser of substances. Darrel Bentley would go to court to protect his child if necessary. A trial would be time-consuming and expensive, and Yvonne didn't have the resources. She sobbed and wailed and drank herself into oblivion for a week or so. And then she stopped talking about Lyric. It was almost like she'd given up.

One night, Darrel was driving home from after-work beers when he apparently fell asleep at the wheel. His car veered off the road and down a steep embankment, crashing into a large tree at the bottom. He was killed instantly. No one was suspicious, no one questioned it, but Bianca knew better. Darrel Bentley was not just a drunk driver who got what he deserved. Yvonne was behind this. Lyric came home then. She was confused and traumatized, but Yvonne acted like it was a celebration. They had cake and presents. She played loud music and drank sparkling wine.

Bianca grew up knowing her mother was a killer, a person who would take what she wanted by any means necessary. It shaped Bianca, obviously, made her hard and cold and afraid to trust people. And it made her fiercely protective of Lyric. She didn't want her sister to be corrupted by their mom's malignant influence.

A couple of months before graduation, Damian Walsh came into the chicken shack where she worked. She basically ignored him. He'd hooked up with half the girls in town, and Bianca wasn't even sure she liked guys. She'd had a thing with a girl in eleventh grade, but they'd kept it private, hadn't labeled it.

But once Damian set his sights on her, he was relentless. He needled her into going out with him, and eventually she agreed, hoping it would get him off her back. One-on-one, he was different: sweet, open, and vulnerable. His troubled past almost rivaled her own (almost). He wormed his way under her protective shell, got her to talk about her dad's abandonment, Darrel's death, her mom's cruelty. It didn't take them long to recognize that they were two bright lights who'd found each other in their dark hole of a hometown.

Damian wasn't built for a traditional life, and neither was Bianca. The expected trajectory of college, marriage, children was so trite, so banal. They both craved adventure and new experiences that their hick town could never provide. Damian introduced her to foreign films. She shared her love of art and historical biographies. When school finished, Damian suggested they go to Europe. Bianca wanted to, but she couldn't abandon Lyric. Not until she was old enough to take care of herself. He agreed to wait for her.

But a decade passed, and they didn't leave. They got stuck in their routines, trapped by their circumstances. Bianca wonders if they'd have stayed in Indiana forever if not for the phone call that came in the dead of night. It had ripped her heart out, left a gaping hole in her chest, and it had sent them to Spain. When they arrived, that wound became infected—with rage, and hate, and a thirst for vengeance.

She was her mother's daughter after all.

27

The phony Australian accent had been Damian's idea. When they decided to come to Cadaqués to confront Curtis, he'd made the suggestion. Bianca and Damian had lived with an Aussie roommate for a couple of years. He had been from Fremantle, a port city near Perth, Western Australia. The Aussie had fallen for an American girl and followed her home. They'd broken up soon after, but he had chosen to stick around until his visa ran out. The guy had talked at length about his isolated hometown: the beaches, the creepy-crawlies, and his job as a commercial diver. Damian and Bianca had mimicked him often and easily for laughs. Damian was confident they could pull it off.

"Why do we need to use an accent?" Bianca had asked.

"It's disarming," he'd told her. "No one will suspect a couple of Aussie travelers. And if we're not from the States, they'll have no reason to think that we know who they really are."

"What if we slip up?" Bianca was biting the edge of her thumb, a sure sign she was feeling stressed. "What if they ask us questions about Australia that we can't answer?"

"We won't be there long enough for them to ask much. And we'll say we're from *Western* Australia," Damian advised. "No one goes there. It's too far. They'll have no way of knowing if what we say is true or not."

Bianca had acquiesced, and they'd practiced at home. It had seemed easy at first, even fun. But once they got to Spain, once it *counted*, it seemed less convincing. Damian could hear himself slipping into

British while Bianca leaned Kiwi. There were brief moments when they forgot to use it at all. He'd caught himself using Americanisms like "senior year" and heard Bianca say "green pepper" instead of "capsicum." Fortunately, Curtis and Sydney were too wrapped up in their own drama to notice the inconsistencies.

It feels surprisingly good to drop the accent now, for Damian to speak in his authentic American voice. Almost as good as watching the fear and confusion take over Curtis's features.

"Who are you?" Curtis asks, his voice a whispered growl.

"Let's just say we have a mutual friend." Damian smiles. "We thought we'd come see how your new life is taking shape. You've done well." He indicates their surroundings with a sweep of his hand. "But you didn't really think you could get away with what you did back in New York, did you?"

"What are you talking about?" Curtis is trying to sound impassive, but he's pale. Clammy. His eyes are wide and full of fear.

"Do you want me to spell it out for you? Your wife could walk out here any minute."

A pronounced vein throbs in Curtis's temple, and he speaks through gritted teeth. "What do you want?"

Damian could tell him, but he's enjoying watching Curtis squirm. While he's played the perfect host, cooking and mixing drinks, Curtis's condescension has always been there, just under the surface. He thinks Damian is less intelligent, less sophisticated, less worldly, but he's wrong. Because Damian knows what Curtis is hiding.

He wishes Bianca were here to watch this. She hadn't wanted to toy with Curtis for this long. In fact, she hadn't wanted to toy with him at all. They had come to the Costa Brava to find Curtis Lowe and make him pay for what he'd done. So they'd parked their van on the nearby hillside and Damian had pulled the fuel pump relay. When they knocked on the door, armed with their dead phones and cheerful accents, they'd planned to lure Curtis out to look at the van. They just needed access to him, to tell him what they knew and what they wanted. But then Sydney had invited them in, invited them to stay. And Damian saw an opportunity too good to miss.

"It's basically a free holiday," he'd told Bianca, out of earshot of their prospective hosts. "We're here, babe. We finally made it to Europe."

"I'm not going to spend my vacation with that piece of shit," Bianca had hissed.

"But it's the perfect opportunity to fuck with him before we go in for the kill," Damian had added. "To make him suffer before we destroy him."

Bianca had been unsure at first, but soon she saw the beauty in Damian's plan. She'd loved watching him taunt, torment, and emasculate their host, but so subtly that Curtis couldn't ask them to leave without sounding like a crybaby. A pussy. They'd both flirted with Sydney, luring her into a physical encounter last night that Curtis had been powerless to stop. Even the physical abuse they'd inflicted on their target was so indirect that they couldn't be accused.

Bianca had kicked it all off with the jellyfish. When she'd sent Curtis into the water teeming with invertebrates, Damian had thought the smaller man might be killed. He had no idea if the floating purple blobs were harmless or deadly, and neither did Bianca. How could they know? She's a graphic designer in landlocked Indiana, and Damian sells major appliances. At least, he did. He's never going back to that mundane career. When Curtis started screeching like a toddler, Damian was sure that was the end. But the stings were only mild, and his shrieks were just dramatics. Damian had seen the satisfaction flit across Bianca's features, though she'd quickly masked it with concern.

"We need to scrape out the stingers," Bianca had ordered, which was a nice touch. She'd told Curtis and Sydney she was a nurse (everyone loves a nurse), but she only knows the most basic first aid. And yet she'd sounded so legit that, for a second, Damian wondered if she was really trying to help Curtis. But it soon became clear that raking the plastic credit cards over those welts was torture. Almost as bad as the boards and shingles Damian had stomped down on Curtis's head. An involuntary smile of satisfaction curls his lips at the memory.

"If it's money you want, I don't have much," Curtis says.

Damian snorts as he takes in the house, the pool, the acres reserved for grapevines. "It looks like you're doing just fine from where I'm standing."

"Appearances can be deceiving," Curtis growls. "Most of my money's tied up."

"I suggest you untie it."

"Or what?"

Damian leans his back against the hot metal of the van. It's time. Finally. "A woman is dead because of you. And we'll tell Sydney all about it."

The color drains from Curtis's face, leaving him waxy and corpselike. He opens his mouth, but no words come. As Damian watches him gawp and splutter, he worries Curtis is having some kind of breakdown, even a stroke. But finally, Curtis finds his voice, low and raspy.

"What the fuck are you talking about? I've never killed anyone."

"Yes, you have. And we've got proof."

"What proof?" But he's grasping, his eyes wild and fearful. Because Curtis knows what he's done. He knows who he *was*, back in New York.

"We've got video evidence," Damian says with a cruel smile. "Let's just say you come off in a bad light. And if you don't pay us, Sydney will see it. We'll send it to all your contacts. Your wife, your family, and all your business associates will know who you really are."

"How do I know you have the video?" Curtis whispers, and Damian chokes back a smirk. They don't have the video, but they know it exists. And so, clearly, does Curtis.

"You don't. You'll have to trust us."

"Show it to me," Curtis demands on a surge of bravado, but his voice is reedy.

"Happy to." Damian glowers. "I'll post it on your Facebook wall. You can watch it there, along with Sydney and everyone else. The cops will find it interesting." He smirks. "A guy like you will be really popular in jail."

The other man's voice is low and defeated. "How much do you want?"

"Five million US in crypto," Damian replies. It's the number he and Bianca had come up with—a sum that Curtis could scrape together, but an amount that would leave him desperate, in debt, forced to sell his Spanish dream house. And it's enough money for Bianca and Damian to buy a place on a Greek island—finally—to retire, to do some traveling, to live the life they deserve.

"I don't have that kind of money lying around."

The response is expected. "You can get it, though," Damian says. "If not, we'll invite Sydney to our short film festival. I'm sure she'd love to see you in all your glory."

"Don't," Curtis snaps. "I'll need some time."

"You can have a week. If you deliver, we'll say the fuel pump has finally arrived and we'll be on our way. Your wife will never know what you really are."

Curtis nods slightly and walks away, headed toward the steep path that leads down the mountain toward town. Damian watches him go, high on the successful delivery of the message, the fruition of their plan. They'd plotted and strategized for over a year, and now it's in motion.

He can't wait to tell Bianca.

28

Bianca lounges on a deck chair, sips an iced coffee, and pretends to be hungover. Next to her, Sydney lolls in the shade, her skin pale, droplets of sweat on her forehead and upper lip. Syd had stumbled out to the pool a few minutes ago, had dropped onto the chair with a mumbled "Morning." Bianca can practically smell the alcohol in her perspiration, even from here. Bianca feels fine. She'd ordered plain tonic water for herself and double gins for Sydney. Last night was all by design.

The nightclub had been their grand finale, the ultimate step in Curtis Lowe's emotional torture. If Sydney hadn't been so wasted, they would have taken it further. Bianca isn't attracted to Syd—she's too meek, too much of a victim, not to mention too thin—but to hurt Curtis, Bianca would have seduced his wife, shared her with Damian to add salt to the wound.

Their make-out session last night was enough to make Curtis want them gone. He will ask them to leave today; Bianca's sure of it. She'd like nothing more than to get away from their poisonous host and his idiot wife, but their mission is not accomplished. Yet. Damian has stalled and delayed. Why? To extend the holiday? To avoid hurting Sydney? Bianca's not blind. She knows he's gone soft on the attorney. Now Damian's hand will be forced.

When she first found out what Curtis had done, Bianca had wanted to kill him. It would have been a crime of passion; a jury would have gone easy on her. Even if they hadn't, she was sure the satisfaction of ending Curtis Lowe's life would be worth any sentence. It was Damian who calmed her down, who convinced her to be more strategic.

"There are other ways to destroy a man," he'd counseled. "Ways that won't send you to prison."

"Like what?" she'd asked, unconvinced. Curtis Lowe deserved pain and torture, a slow, excruciating death.

"We hit him where it hurts," Damian suggested. "He's a rich, arrogant prick, so we'll ruin him financially and destroy his reputation. And then we'll find out what he cares about most and take it from him."

The idea was appealing. They would take everything from him, then force him to continue existing with the guilt, shame, and pain. So they'd begun their research. Curtis Lowe had sold his company, fled New York, and was living a private life with his wife in Spain. His social media presence was negligible, but his profile page included his alma mater. Posing as a writer for their alumni journal, Damian had contacted Curtis's old frat brothers. They'd happily reminisced about their debaucherous college days, but no one had heard from Curtis in years... except for Simon Waters. The pair had started a property management business together straight out of grad school. Damian had called the office, pretending to be a potential client, but Simon had abruptly ended the call when Curtis's name was mentioned. Clearly, there was bad blood there.

Curtis was an only child whose father had passed away six years earlier. He had no relationship with his mother, who'd sounded bitter and resentful when Bianca called pretending to be an old friend looking for his contact details. Curtis's most marked attribute was his fierce devotion to his wife. He had given up everything for her, stealing her off to Spain so she'd never find out the truth about him.

"The wife's a public defender," Damian said. "Her online bio says she's passionate about helping marginalized and low-income people get appropriate legal advice and representation."

"How noble," Bianca had sniped. "And yet she's married to that sick fuck."

"She's his good girl," Damian concluded. "She makes him feel like a decent human being by association."

"When we tell her what he's done, she'll leave him. And he'll be destroyed."

"Exactly," Damian said. "But first, we'll make him pay to keep us quiet."

Bianca didn't care about the money, but Damian convinced her it would kill two birds with one stone. They'd bankrupt Curtis and destroy his marriage (obviously they'd tell Sydney the truth once the funds were transferred). Her boyfriend had assured her that she would feel better once Curtis Lowe's life was in ruins, with no financial means to rebuild it. And a significant sum of money would go a long way to soothe her pain.

And then Damian had made a suggestion. "We should go to Spain," he'd said. "Confront Lowe in person."

Bianca had balked at the idea. Wasn't blackmail carried out through anonymous emails all the time? Or they could go old-school, send a note with letters cut from magazines. But Damian had insisted that messages could be traced, that Curtis had the money and resources to track the source of their missives. Or Curtis might panic, concoct a story for his wife, convince her to flee to some remote island. If they met Curtis in person, extorted him verbally, they could keep an eye on him. And there would be no proof. It would be Curtis's word against theirs.

"We've always wanted to travel," Damian cajoled her. "And finally, we can."

And so they'd booked this trip on credit, confident they could pay it off once Curtis gave them their money. They would only stay for a few days, just long enough to make Curtis twist and suffer, but Damian had fucked it all up. He'd had the perfect opportunity to tell Curtis what they wanted and what they knew when the two men drove to Girona to investigate fuel pumps. But when Damian returned, he'd pulled Bianca into the van.

"He's got a burner phone," Damian whispered. "He's hiding something."

"We already know what he's hiding," Bianca hissed. "That's why we're here."

"If he's still involved, there could be more leverage. And more money."

"This isn't about money for me," she snapped. "This is about destroying him."

"I know, babe, and we will. We'll make sure he loses everything he cares about. He'll never recover." He touched her cheek tenderly. "But if he's hurting people, we need to stop him."

The thought of what Curtis Lowe had done made Bianca's throat close, her eyes well. Even as she recalls it now, her vision mists behind her sunglasses and her chin wobbles. But she inhales through her nose, digs her nails into her palms. There is no room for emotion. She came here to destroy Curtis Lowe's life, and she will.

Sydney stirs next to her. "I'm too hot," she mutters. "I need to go in."

"Drink some water. And take some electrolytes if you have them," Bianca says sweetly. She has always been able to mask her true feelings, paste on a smile when she's hurt or angry. It's a skill she learned growing up in a home with a narcissistic mother and her revolving door of boyfriends. Bianca mastered the art of compliance, made herself small and benign. It was a survival mechanism that she employed until she finally escaped her mother's grip. It's proven useful.

Sydney drags herself out of the chair, then looks down at Bianca. "Do we need to talk?" Her cheeks are pink under her deathly pallor. "About last night?"

Bianca has been expecting this. "Nothing to talk about, babe." She grins, peers over the rim of her shades. "We got carried away. I'm sorry if we crossed the line."

Syd smiles, clearly relieved, but an undercurrent of concern flits across her brow. She's tormented by last night's passion, distressed by how close she came to infidelity. She's been trying to work on her marriage, and in one drunken moment, she'd nearly blown it all up. Syd considers herself so virtuous, so decent, but she's not. She's as morally weak as her husband. Sydney shuffles toward the house, looking frail and older than her years. Bianca could almost pity her.

But she doesn't. She hates her.

29

Damian finds Bianca alone by the pool, eyes hidden behind enormous shades. She's undeniably gorgeous in her red bikini, her skin tanned and glistening with sunscreen and sweat. But he can't ignore the hatred that seems to emanate from her being, the palpable aura of bitterness. It mutes her beauty, twists it. With just a nod, he indicates that she should join him in the van, that he has something to tell her. Obediently, she gets up and follows him. She already knows.

It's stifling hot inside the Westfalia, and Curtis turns on the battery-operated fan. It spins fruitlessly in the sluggish air, but at least it camouflages their voices. Sydney mustn't hear this. It would ruin everything.

"I've given Curtis a week to get the money together," Damian says, voice low. "He tried to say he didn't have it, but once I told him what we knew, he said he'd find a way."

"Was he terrified?" Bianca's voice is gleeful. "Did he cry?"

"He looked like he was going to puke," Damian says with a chuckle. "I wish you could have seen it."

"Me too," Bianca responds. "Where is he now?"

"Dunno. He took off down the hillside path."

She bites on a smile. "He'll spend the next week desperate and panicking. I can't wait to watch it." She shifts herself closer to him, touches his chest. "You were right."

"About what?"

"Coming to Spain." She kisses him gently. "I want to watch that bastard suffer."

Damian kisses her back, their hunger for each other rapidly escalating, as it always does. It's too warm for such close contact, the quarters are too cramped, but Bianca is already reaching for his zipper. They have sex in a sweaty, frenzied rush, Damian's hand over Bianca's mouth as she climaxes. When he comes, moments after she does, his mind is no longer in the van with Bianca. It's inside the house now. And it's with Sydney.

Bianca collapses on top of him, her forehead sweaty in the crook of his neck. He feels her heart rate slow, her body relaxing, becoming deadweight. He's suddenly claustrophobic in the airless space, hit with a strong urge to push her body off him. But he resists it. Thankfully, Bianca soon climbs off, pulls a T-shirt over her head.

"I've been thinking," Damian says, climbing back into his shorts. "About Sydney."

"What about her?" Bianca keeps dressing, doesn't meet his gaze.

He clears a clog in his throat. "She doesn't deserve to be destroyed like Curtis."

"Yes, she does." Bianca looks up, her eyes drilling into his. "She's too smart to be so blind. She had to know on some level what he was doing."

"I don't think so." He swallows, looks away. "She should at least be able to keep the money her mom left her."

"Curtis has probably already liquidated it." Bianca digs through a plastic storage bin, extracts a pack of cigarettes. "I need a smoke."

Damian sighs, leans back on his elbows. "Why did you start smoking again?"

"This trip has been a tad stressful," she retorts. "And everyone smokes in this country, including Sydney. I've had to smell her cigarettes every morning." Bianca shimmies into a pair of shorts. "I told her I had asthma so she wouldn't smoke around me, but it still triggered my cravings."

"You can't smoke behind that oak tree anymore."

"Obviously." Bianca smirks. "You scared the shit out of them when you found those butts."

"*You* did." Damian can't help but smile. "Who takes a machete to have a smoke?"

"There are snakes!" Bianca cries. "And your gloves kept my hands from smelling like cigarettes. I didn't need you lecturing me about lung cancer. Not right now."

"Sorry," he mutters. They'd argued when Bianca admitted she'd been smoking again, hiding behind the oak tree so Damian didn't catch her. But they'd pulled it together, gone outside to confess. And then Sydney had found the machete, the gloves, and she and Curtis began to make assumptions. Bianca was quick to play along, to stoke Syd's fear. There had been a dull ache in Damian's chest at the sight of Sydney so terrified, but by then, it was too late to come clean.

"Don't get caught," Damian says. "We still need Sydney to trust us for the next few days."

"I know," she replies, rolling her eyes. "If Syd catches me smoking, I'll talk my way out of it. She's basically in love with me now." Shoving a lighter into her pocket, Bianca climbs out of the van. Damian hears her feet crunching down the drive as she walks away.

The best liars know to stick as close to the truth as possible. Damian had learned that from his dad, who'd had a number of successful real estate scams before he'd been sued into bankruptcy. Despite their false Australian identities and their fake jobs, much of what he and Bianca have told their hosts is honest. They're high school sweethearts in an open relationship that allows Bianca to explore her bisexuality. This understanding has allowed them both to pursue Sydney. It didn't matter who seduced her. They were only doing it to hurt Curtis.

And then Damian began to feel things.

He's attracted to her, of course—Syd is a beautiful woman—but his emotions are more complex than that. It all started when he was researching her online, digging into Curtis's bride of twelve years. He'd been impressed by Syd's Ivy League education, her career choices, and the high-profile cases she'd defended. There were a handful of media clips where Sydney stood by a defendant she'd freed from a corrupt justice system. Sydney was so smart, so good, so passionate about righting wrongs. She was like an avenging angel.

But the Sydney Cleary he met in Spain was a faint shadow of the strong woman she'd been. She was thin and frail, self-medicating with alcohol and cigarettes. Syd had pharmaceutical support, too. Damian had seen the bottles of pills in the aqua blue bathroom. Bianca thinks Syd is stupid and blind, that she's nothing more than collateral damage. But to Damian, she's another victim of Curtis Lowe's toxic net. She doesn't deserve to suffer.

Slamming the van door, Damian walks toward the house. The air is still, eerily so. Bianca's gone off for a sneaky cigarette. Curtis has wandered toward town to freak out or make panicked phone calls to his bank and his rich friends. Where is Sydney? Despite their age difference, he feels an almost paternal need to check on her, to make sure she's okay.

Damian's loyalty is to Bianca, of course. He's loved her since they were kids. When he met her, she was emotionally shut down, damaged by her neglectful father, her poisonous mother. He'd burrowed under her protective shield, made her open up to him. They had connected on a soul level, the two of them against the world. Damian had felt like Bianca's savior, her personal Jesus.

But Bianca is different now. She's so full of seething hatred, so bent on revenge, that he can't reach her. At first, Damian had stoked her rage, used it to develop their blackmail plan, but now it's created a vast distance between them. Damian has to believe that once Curtis Lowe is destroyed, once he hands them a life-changing sum of money, Bianca will find her way back to him. They'll disappear to a beachside bungalow on a Greek island where they can finally live out their dream.

So why can't he stop worrying about what will happen to Syd in the aftermath?

Inside, the house is silent. Sydney must have gone back to bed to sleep off her hangover. He's drawn toward her closed door as if it's a magnetic field... as if he's a creepy voyeur getting off on watching a woman sleep. But it's not like that. He just wants to make sure she's okay.

Gingerly, Damian presses open the door, just a crack. He spies Sydney's inert form in the bed, hears her steady breathing. He wants to slip into the room, stroke her hair, ask if she needs anything. Would she welcome his presence? Maybe even invite him to lay with her, to hold her? Or would she panic, call out to Curtis or even Bianca? No, she wouldn't. There's something between them—he hasn't imagined it. But their situation is so fucking complicated.

A distant rumble startles him, and he quickly closes the door. It will be the truck from Girona delivering the lumber. It's a waste of wood. Curtis and Sydney's winery will never happen. Because this house, that dream, will have to be sold. Everything liquidated. Curtis will be destitute. And Damian and Bianca will be rich. That's what matters. Not Sydney Cleary.

Silently, he closes the bedroom door.

30

A flatbed truck loaded with lumber rumbles past Bianca as she walks along the side of the road. It's hot, and the vehicle leaves exhaust fumes in its wake, but she sucks gratefully on her cigarette. She wishes she wasn't wearing these ridiculous gloves in the midday heat. She wishes she was lying by the pool, enjoying a leisurely smoke, instead of hiding her habit from Sydney. Bianca would love to drop the silly accent that Damian had suggested, too. But they can't. Not yet. They still have to play along.

She's not sure if it's the effects of the nicotine, the intense sex, or the progress of their plan, but Bianca feels jittery and on edge. In a few days, the game will be over. Curtis will have lost everything: his dream house, all his money, his perfect lawyer wife... Bianca had nearly laughed when Sydney confessed that Curtis had cheated on her. His infidelity is the tip of the iceberg. If Sydney only knew what he'd really done, she'd be horrified. Repulsed. She'll find out soon enough. If Damian doesn't fuck everything up.

Flicking ash into the gravel, Bianca reflects on her partner's concern for Sydney. Damian's taken to his role as strong, protective he-man with relish. But the lines of reality and role-play seem to be blurring. She's watched Damian soften toward Syd, treating her with a tenderness unusual for him. Last night at the club, she'd observed the way he touched her, the way he kissed her. Damian has some kind of mommy-figure crush on the older woman. He's falling for her victim act. But Sydney Cleary is not a casualty of her evil husband. She's a moron. A pathetic, weak woman trapped under the spell of a monster. She's an enabler who allowed a predator to get away with murder. If Damian tells Sydney to run, to save herself, she'll go straight to Curtis. Bianca has no doubt. But she won't let that happen.

Stubbing out the cigarette with her heel, Bianca turns back toward the house. Her jaw is tight with tension, so she opens her mouth wide, stretches out her tongue. It sends a throbbing through her temples, a sweep of dizziness, and she stops, drops her head between her knees. The pressure of keeping up the sweet and stupid facade is crushing her. One more week, she tells herself. It will all be over, one way or another.

Damian is intent on the blackmail scenario, and Bianca wants it to work out, too. Five million dollars will go a long way to healing her pain; she believes that. And leaving Curtis broke, in debt, and with no way to pick up the pieces of his shattered existence has always been her goal. But she's not sure she can trust her partner anymore. If Damian betrays her, chooses Sydney over Bianca, she will have nothing. And no one. Bianca's life will be meaningless. And that means she's got nothing to lose. The thought is strangely freeing.

She strolls back toward the van, pulling the leather gloves off finger by finger. Her machete is in there now, concealed beneath the storage bins. She'd first discovered it rummaging through the clutter clogging the basement rooms. While Sydney napped or surfed the internet, Bianca had gone downstairs under the auspices of painting prep. She'd dug through boxes filled with books, old photographs, and Christmas decorations. Sifting through the remnants of Curtis and Sydney's privileged New York life had fueled her loathing. And her determination.

There were other miscellaneous items strewn about, likely remnants of previous owners: tangles of dusty cables, rusted tools, monitoring equipment for the broken security system. Buried under a pile of fraying ropes was the machete. It was a manageable size, meant for clearing brush. Bianca had touched the blade, found it surprisingly sharp given its obvious neglect. It could be useful.

She'd slipped outside with the machete, hidden it in the tall grass behind the oak tree. She had no concrete plans to use it then—unless a snake came along—but she felt better knowing it was there, that she was the only one in the household with access to a deadly weapon. As she smoked behind that oak tree, she assessed what she'd be willing to do to exact her revenge. She'd have to take Curtis out while he slept. Sydney would wake up, of course, but she'd be easily overpowered. Bianca wouldn't hesitate to put her out of her misery.

But then Sydney found the machete and gloves and freaked out. Bianca had savored the woman's fear and unease until Damian had stepped in to assuage it. He'd pretended to return the items to a neighboring farmer, said their presence was totally benign. The weapon is now secure in the van, but Bianca needs to move it. Hide it. Somewhere only she can get to it.

It's not that she thinks Damian would use the machete against her. She trusts her partner in that regard. He can be shady, manipulative, driven by greed, but he'd never hurt a woman. In fact, Damian is softening before her eyes, weakening. If he becomes a liability, she'll have no choice but to rid herself of him. If he backs out of their plan, she'll do what needs to be done.

The lumber truck is parked in the driveway. Damian and the driver are unloading the boards meant to build Curtis's dream winery. Curtis is nowhere to be seen, of course. He and Sydney are so lazy and entitled. Bianca clocks the resentful scowl on her boyfriend's face, but he's focused on the task at hand. He doesn't notice her drifting down the path toward the van.

Slipping around the side of the vehicle, Bianca opens the panel door and climbs inside. First, she mists herself with perfume to camouflage the smell of smoke. Then she drops to her knees and pulls the machete out from its hiding place. Her hands are shaky as she holds it, feels its heft and its potential. Where can she put it? She needs a spot where no one else can find it but where she'll have easy access if she needs to use it. If she needs to attack.

A dizzying wave sweeps over her, and she steadies herself with a hand pressed to the low ceiling. How did she get to this place where she can conceive of pulling a Lizzie Borden? She thinks of the blood, the bone, the gore, and she feels ill, lightheaded. Bianca has always known she's harder, tougher than the average person. She's had to be. But she's only resorted to violence once, and that was justified, practically self-defense. Curtis Lowe has turned her into this. He's made her a cold-blooded monster.

A sob bubbles out of her when she thinks about Damian. She loves him. At least, she loved him. She knows that what they had was real. But he has his own agenda now. She's watched him grow increasingly selfish, focusing on his own wants and desires. If he gets in her way, he'll have to be sacrificed. Just like Sydney Cleary. She presses a fist to her lips to block her pathetic blubbering. There is no room for emotion and sentimentality. Hatred is all she's allowed to feel; revenge is her sole mission. Sentimentality is for the weak.

Wrapping the machete in Damian's dark blue sweatshirt, she climbs out of the van. Her boyfriend is engaged with the delivery driver, a frustrating conversation about payment, no doubt. Bianca hugs the bundle to her chest and moves around the side of the house past the pool. No Sydney. No Curtis. She keeps walking downhill, away from her smoking spot toward the lower fence line. The grass is tall and wild here. The trees are old and gnarled. Ensuring no one is watching, she hides the machete next to a rotted log.

With a casual gait, she moves back toward the pool. When will Damian notice the weapon has been moved? What will he think? Will her partner confront her? Assume she's double-crossing him? Bianca's not an idiot. Of course she wants the money. She knows it will make her life exponentially better. But most of all, she needs Curtis Lowe to suffer. She needs his entire life to crumble.

Or she'll have to snuff it out.

31

Damian is soaked with sweat after helping the driver unload the lumber, and there's a tight knot under his left shoulder blade. (Curtis hadn't returned to help, probably worried he'd get a sliver.) Damian had considered rejecting the delivery—the winery dream is dead now—but that might alarm Sydney. So he'd stacked the boards next to the driveway. The driver had asked Damian for a credit card, but obviously he wasn't about to give him his. They'd debated in broken English and even more broken Spanish. Finally, Damian convinced him that Curtis had already paid at the store. He doesn't know if that's true, and he doesn't care. The boards will sit there and rot.

Hot and irritable, Damian heads to the pool. He's done too much physical labor around the property already, while soft pasty Curtis stood by or made up an excuse. Damian's done being the hired help. His quads ache from yesterday's sprint up the mountain path, but he'd had no choice. Sydney had suggested a relaxing beach day, but Curtis had opted out at the last minute. Curtis said he was sick, but he wasn't. He was suspicious. But Damian was too quick for him.

While he doubted Curtis had the street smarts or engineering know-how to break into their van, there was too much evidence in there. If Curtis found proof that Bianca and Damian were liars, he'd present it to Sydney, and she'd dismiss them before they could blackmail her husband. So Damian had suggested Sydney stop in Cadaqués for road snacks. Inside the store, he told Bianca his plan.

"I'll hike up the mountain path. I can do it in about forty-five minutes if I push it."

"What do I tell Sydney?"

"Make something up."

He'd pushed it, done it in forty. As soon as he'd reached the property, he'd gone to the van. There were scratches near the passenger window, evidence that Curtis had at least tried to break in. But inside, everything seemed to be undisturbed: Their US passports and IDs were still hidden deep under the mattress. The machete was still under the stackable bins. Their secrets were safe. But it was time to tell Curtis why they had come.

Damian had needed a few beers for courage first. And when Curtis offered to barbecue some steaks, he couldn't say no. He was starving after the hill climb. While Curtis grilled, Damian drank and made small talk. He knew a lot about Curtis Lowe's life already, but he played dumb, fished for more information.

"So, what did you do for fun back home?"

"Syd and I worked a lot," Curtis said, turning the meat. "We kept late hours and got up early. That didn't leave a lot of time for extracurriculars."

He was lying, the sick bastard. Curtis had made time for his debaucherous hobbies. "Come on," Damian cajoled, "you must have gotten up to no good once in a while?"

Curtis had given him a look then, and Damian knew to pull back. There was a fine line between interested and probing.

They'd eaten their meal outside beside the pool. Curtis had cooked the steaks to perfection, and Damian allowed himself to savor the food, the cold beer, and the moment of camaraderie. It almost felt normal, like Damian belonged in this hillside oasis, like he and Curtis were buddies. If Bianca had been there, he'd have had to resume his antagonist role. She would've been incensed to see the two men hanging out in relative harmony.

Damian washed the dishes and brought out two more beers. They drank them by the pool, shooting the shit as the stars twinkled in the night sky. "Tell me about New York," Damian said. "It's like a foreign country to me."

"It *is* a foreign country to you."

Shit. Damian had momentarily forgotten he was Australian. Taking in Curtis's bemused expression, he realized it was time. He had to do it now before Curtis grew suspicious. Damian narrowed his eyes, opened his mouth to speak, then his phone buzzed in his pocket. Bianca.

Syd's totally fucked up.

Meet us at the club in Cadaques.

Bring Curtis.

A feeling of dread had clutched his insides. Bianca hated Sydney so much. If he and Curtis didn't get there soon, she'd leave Syd passed out in the gutter. Let some drunk Eurotrash take her back to their Airbnb. So he convinced Curtis to take the steep path into town, and they'd gone to the nightclub. While Curtis ordered a drink, Damian had sifted through the crowd and found the two women. Syd was wasted; it was obvious in the way she was moving, hair in her face, arms in the air. Bianca was whispering in Syd's ear, touching her, seducing her. He'd felt a stab of something sharp, ugly, and unfamiliar. It was jealousy. It wasn't an emotion present in his relationship with Bianca. They were open and secure. This was about Sydney.

He'd crept up behind Syd and touched her shoulder. She'd turned her face to his and smiled, her eyes bleary but happy. He pressed his body against hers, felt her receptiveness as she tipped her head back onto his shoulder, opened herself up to him. Bianca's eyes were on them both, shining with perverse pleasure. What he'd seen on his partner's face wasn't desire or arousal: It was malicious delight. A cruel child tearing the wings off a fly.

Damian has reached the pool now, and he pulls off his shirt, tosses it on a lawn chair. He spies Bianca walking up the hill toward him, her expression distant and dark. He observes her unnoticed for a moment.

She'd been so excited when he said their plan was finally in motion, but now she looks troubled. His sweatshirt is wrapped around her shoulders despite the heat. Is she unwell? She looks up and meets his eyes, but he can't read her. He's never been able to.

"Where were you?" he asks, moving in her direction.

"Looking for Curtis," she says. "I thought I might hear him screaming and crying on the trail to town."

Damian indicates the pool with a sweep of his hand. "Sydney's in a hangover coma. Curtis is off sobbing or maybe begging for cash. Let's enjoy ourselves."

"I like the way you think." She smiles. "I'll go put my swimsuit on."

"Why?" His eyes twinkle at her as he drops his shorts. "This is our place now. We don't need bathing suits."

She laughs, a welcome sound. She's his girl again: damaged, calloused, but not evil. Not obsessed with revenge, forsaking all else. He still loves her. He just needs to focus on that.

"Want a drink?" she asks.

"Read my mind."

"Two beers coming up." Bianca moves inside. Damian dives into the refreshing water.

32

The beer slides down Bianca's throat: cold, fizzy, alcoholic. She feels content, relaxed, a little buzzed. Her doubts about Damian melt away with the sun that's baking her naked skin. She glances at her partner, his golden physique sprawled on the lawn chair next to her, and she feels a swell of fondness. They're a team. They always have been. The stress of recent events, this fraught situation, had made her stressed and paranoid, but she can trust her partner. And if not, she's got her hidden weapon.

Damian put some music on the outdoor speakers, and she worries it's too loud. If Sydney wakes up and finds her guests in the buff, she'll be traumatized. Or maybe she'll be turned on... Who cares? Syd's probably taken something from her pharmacy of pills and will be unconscious until morning. Bianca takes another sip and smiles to herself. Their plan is finally in motion, mission nearly accomplished. There's nothing to do now but wait, enjoy themselves, and apply more sun protection to their vulnerable bits.

"Pass the sunscreen," she says, and Damian lifts his head. He reaches for the plastic bottle, turns over on his stomach. "Do my back?"

Bianca pours lotion into her hand, rubs it across his hot tanned skin. At home, Damian hit the gym religiously, and the manual labor here has kept his muscles strong and taut. His shoulders are broad, narrowing to his waist in a V. Even after so many years, she feels a tug of desire as she touches him. She can't blame Sydney for lusting after

Damian. Curtis is technically attractive, but he's too cerebral, too soft. Even if Bianca didn't loathe him, she wouldn't be into him.

"You're done." She slaps Damian's ass cheek, and he flinches.

"Want me to do yours now?"

"I need another beer first. Want one?"

"Yeah."

Bianca gets up, pulls the blue sweatshirt over her head. It covers her bottom—just. Sydney will be scandalized if she finds Bianca in the house so scantily clad, but she can't accuse her of being naked. And if Curtis has slunk back inside, Bianca doesn't want him to see her body. She doesn't want to feel vulnerable or exposed. She has the power now. She can't forget that.

Her damp feet leave marks on the tile as she strolls into the kitchen. It's cool in the house, the air-conditioning on blast for Sydney's nausea. Bianca digs in the fridge for two more frosty bottles, flips the caps off. As she turns back toward the pool, she hears the front door open, then close with a soft click. It's Curtis. It has to be. Her jaw tightens, and her stomach clenches. She sets the bottles on the counter and waits.

Curtis hurries into the kitchen, his phone gripped in his hand. He's pale, his hair damp with sweat. His shirt is soaked at the collar and underarms. As always, his presence prompts a visceral surge of loathing. She doesn't have to hide it anymore.

He stops short, clearly surprised to see Bianca wearing only a sweatshirt in his kitchen. "Where's Sydney?"

"Asleep."

"And Damian?"

"By the pool."

"Can we talk?" Curtis tentatively closes the space between them. "Just the two of us?"

"There's nothing to talk about." She sneers at him. "Damian told you what we want. And what we know."

"But he didn't," Curtis pleads in a low voice. "If I know what you're talking about, or *who* you're talking about, maybe I can explain."

Curtis thinks he can talk his way out of this mess, explain away his vile behavior. He assumes she's soft and weak, that he can manipulate her feminine sympathies. His hubris is expected, but that makes it no less revolting. "If you really don't remember what you did, that makes you even more disgusting than I thought," she growls.

"Do I know you?" He's staring at her like they've just met, like she hasn't been living in his house for days.

"No, but I know you."

"Did I...do something to someone you care about?" His voice wobbles with desperation. He's grasping, confused, on the verge of tears. She finds it satisfying.

"Getting warmer." She reaches for her beer and takes a drink.

Curtis looks around the kitchen to ensure they're still alone. Then he clears his throat and starts. "Back in New York, I worked with some people who were into some shady stuff. I regret that I got wrapped up in it. But I never hurt anyone. I certainly never killed anyone."

"Yes, you did," she snaps. "And we have proof."

"Keep your voice down." He grabs her by the arm, pulls her toward the back door. She's about to scream, to hit him, but that will bring Damian and Sydney running. Everything will come out then, and Sydney will leave. Curtis will be hurt but not destroyed. That means Bianca will have to kill him.

They step outside, between the house and the skeletal remains of the shed. Curtis closes the glass door behind them. "Who is L.B.?" he demands.

Her hand moves to her chest, touches her locket. How has Curtis seen the inscription on the back? She took the pendant off both times they went to the beach and left it on the nightstand. Curtis has been in their room, searching for information. Of course he has.

"Was that your mom? Did she lease property from my company or something?"

Bianca laughs in his face. "You think we'd do all this over a property lease? You think this is about a business transaction gone wrong?"

"I don't know what else it could be! I've never hurt anyone!"

The intensity of Bianca's rage is blinding, deafening. For a moment, she sees a blank whiteness, hears a shrill hum. Her body vibrates as every cell screams at her to attack, to smash the beer bottle over his head, to claw, to scratch, to strangle him. But she can't. Not yet.

So she spits in his face.

Curtis doesn't flinch, doesn't wipe it away. Because deep down he knows he deserves her vitriol. He knows what he's done, even if his arrogance won't allow him to admit it.

"Get the money," she growls, "or Sydney will know what a piece of shit you really are." She heads back inside.

33

Damian feels the sun baking his naked skin, soothing his tired muscles, drying the pool water in his damp hair. He's vaguely thirsty, and he wonders where Bianca is with his beer, but he's too relaxed to look for her, too content. This is the life he's always wanted. It's the life he's always deserved. He slips into the fantasy that this is *his* house, that he and Bianca are alone in the hillside haven. It feels comfortable and right. Soon, their reality will rival the dream.

It's not that their life back in the States was terrible; it was just mundane. They had decent jobs. They rented a cute little house. A lot of people would be satisfied with what they had, but not Damian. He's known since childhood that he was destined for more, a bigger, bolder existence. And then he fell in love. He put his partner first. He's been patient and devoted. He'd kept the promise he'd made to Bianca in that field on prom night, and he'd waited.

After high school, Damian attended community college. Tech was where the money was, so he studied computer programming. It didn't take him long to realize that he wasn't cut out for it, so he switched to a psychology major, worked at a big-box appliance store part-time. He moved into a house with a bunch of guys he'd found in an online rental group. It was filthy, rowdy, fun.

Bianca still lived at home then. She was going to design school, running interference between her mom and her little sister. Bianca stayed with him on weekends, and sometimes Lyric came, too. She was a cute kid then, silly and goofy. He didn't mind playing grown-up for a few hours a week, but he worried about Lyric. His roommates regularly came home wasted, smoked grass on the back deck, and brought various sex partners home. It was no place for a kid, and he told Bianca that.

"It's fine," she said. "It's still a healthier environment than my mom's house."

One day, shortly after he'd finished college, he went to pick Bianca up at her mom's battered bungalow. He rang the bell, but no one answered. He knocked loudly, but no one came. A crash came from inside, followed by a screech. The door was locked, but he rattled the handle, banged on it with his fist. Finally, Bianca opened it. Her face was flushed, and she had a duffel bag over her shoulder.

"Lyric and I are moving in with you," she stated, only the slightest tremble in her voice. "She's packing her stuff."

"Uh...okay." He wasn't sure how that was going to work, but it didn't appear up for debate.

Yvonne staggered into view then. She was clearly drunk or on drugs, perhaps both. She wore a silky robe and nothing else, her thigh slipping through the fabric. "Damian, why are you with this little whore?" She slinked toward him. "You could do so much better."

"Leave him out of this, Mom," Bianca growled.

Yvonne was close now. He could smell booze on her breath. "If you ever want to be with a real woman, you know where to find me."

It turned his stomach, made his skin crawl. Damian's parenting bar was fairly low, but Yvonne Richards was on another level.

"Lyric, hurry up!" Bianca cried.

"She's not going with you." Yvonne's smile was triumphant. "She loves her momma. You can't turn her against me."

"I'm not going to let you destroy her," Bianca said. "Lyric, come on!"

The girl appeared then. She was about thirteen at the time, and while her heavy makeup made her look twenty, her coltish body and the innocence shining in her eyes betrayed her real age. "I—I can't go," she stammered. "All my stuff is here."

"See?" Yvonne crowed, eyes on Bianca. "She doesn't love you either."

"Lyric, come with us," Bianca pleaded. "You know it's not safe here."

"I'll be fine," the younger girl said. "I promise."

Yvonne moved to Lyric, draped an arm around her shoulders. "Get the fuck out, Bianca. You're not welcome here anymore."

So they left. Bianca never talked about it, never shed a tear, but it hurt her. Her emotional callus thickened even more.

Soon Damian and Bianca moved out of the party house and into a decent modular home. It had two spare rooms, and they rented one to help with costs, kept the other for Lyric. At first, she came around often, but Lyric was growing up, changing. Damian had been fond of her when she was a kid, but she'd become a pain in the ass. She had attitude in spades, not that he could blame her. He knew what Yvonne was like. He knew what it took to survive in that house. But Lyric could be rude and condescending to Bianca, treated her like an annoyance instead of a savior. The kid didn't want rules and boundaries. She wanted the freedom of Yvonne's indifference.

Damian and Bianca were busy. They worked their nine-to-five jobs; they had a network of like-minded friends who were open-minded, sex-positive, and uninhibited. There were parties, blurry nights when he'd wake up next to another woman, find Bianca in a different room with another lover. He was okay with it, most of the time, but sometimes he'd feel insecure, and they'd argue. But they always pulled it together, provided a wholesome environment for Lyric, who came over every Sunday.

One weekend, they waited for Lyric to arrive. When she didn't show up, Bianca texted her, but the message wasn't delivered. She tried calling, but it went straight to voicemail. "Something's wrong," she said to Damian.

"Your sister's seventeen. She'll be off with her friends. Or maybe her phone died."

"No," Bianca insisted. "Something's not right. I can feel it."

She couldn't call her mom. Yvonne had blocked Bianca's number years ago. There was no option but to go to the house. Damian had offered to go alone—Bianca would not be welcome—but she was adamant that she accompany him. She stood behind Damian as he rang the bell.

Yvonne was dressed and appeared sober when she answered. "If you're here to see Lyric, you're too late."

"What do you mean *too late*?" Bianca pressed forward, pushed her way past her mother and through the front door.

"She's gone," Yvonne said as Bianca peered around the cluttered house.

"Gone where?"

"She moved. To New York City."

Damian had snorted in disbelief. Lyric was a teenager, a small-town kid. How could she pick up and move to the biggest city in America? He'd had big dreams at her age too, but reality had set in, had kept him here. Bianca wasn't laughing.

"She's seventeen," she said. "She hasn't even finished high school."

Yvonne rolled her eyes. "Who cares? She wasn't exactly academic."

"What will she do there?" Bianca asked. "How will she support herself?"

"Not my problem," Yvonne sniffed. "Lyric thinks she's something special, but she'll end up a whore or dead in the gutter."

Bianca hit her mother square in the face with a closed fist. Damian heard the crunch of bone and cartilage, saw the blood spurt from Yvonne's nose. Yvonne bent double, hands covering her face. Blood seeped between her fingers and dripped onto the floor.

"You fucking cunt!" she screeched. "I'll call the police! I'll have you charged with assault!"

Bianca launched herself at Yvonne, and they tumbled to the floor. Bianca straddled her mother, grabbed her by the throat, and squeezed. If Damian hadn't been there, if he hadn't ripped her off, dragged her kicking and screaming out to the car, Bianca would have killed her. He saw the cold determination in her. He saw the rage and the hatred.

"This is bad," Bianca said, nursing her bruised knuckles as he drove them home. "Lyric is a naïve kid. How could my mom let her move to New York?"

"Lyric's wise in a lot of ways," he tried to assure her. "She's a pretty girl. She'll be fine."

But she wouldn't be fine. Because she was about to meet Curtis Lowe.

34

Bianca is rattled by the confrontation with Curtis, shaken by his denials, his feigned ignorance, his attempts at manipulation. Spitting in his face had been a weak expression of her hatred, just a drop in the bucket of her loathing. She needs to calm down, to compose herself and process his words. She hurries out of the house, to the privacy of the van. It's hot and stuffy, but she's shivering, cold all over. The strength of her disgust has chilled her to her core.

She hears Curtis's car start and back quickly out of the driveway. Part of her hopes he's gone in search of the money; part of her hopes he's planning to drive his little car off a cliff. How can Curtis live with what he did? Does he really not remember his vile, immoral behavior? Perhaps he'd blocked it out to combat his guilt. Or were his depraved actions normalized by his cohort of entitled narcissists? People with so much money that they think the rules don't apply to them, that they can indulge their sickest fantasies with no repercussions. Either way, Curtis's innocence is a delusion.

Just for a breath, she lets herself consider his denials. Did Bianca somehow get it wrong? She wasn't there. She hasn't seen the video evidence, though she knows it exists. But Bianca has always trusted her gut instinct, her inherent ability to sort good people from bad. What happened in New York is likely worse than Bianca could imagine. She only knows what Lyric told her, but that's enough.

It was a Sunday in October when Bianca found her sister. It hadn't been that difficult: Lyric wasn't hiding, exactly. After a couple of weeks of silence, she responded to Bianca's barrage of concerned texts. Lyric had assured her older sister that she was safe, happy, even thriving in New York City, but she was short on details. She had an apartment, but she didn't say where. She was working at a restaurant but wouldn't say which one. Lyric claimed to be loving life in the Big Apple, but she didn't mention museums or the theater or even nightclubs. It was all too vague for Bianca's comfort.

"I need to go see her," Bianca told Damian. "Something feels off."

"I'm sure she's fine," he'd said dismissively. Damian cared for Lyric, but he was not her family. And more than once he'd complained about her teenage presence: the mess, the attitude, the sense of entitlement. "Go if it'll make you feel better."

When Bianca told her little sister she was coming to visit, Lyric was quick to inform her that she shared a one-bedroom apartment with two other girls, that her "room" was a futon behind a cheap paper screen. There was no space for guests. Bianca booked a relatively cheap hotel in Midtown for two nights and a flight with a budget airline. Her younger sibling agreed to meet her at a nearby Pret A Manger. They'd grab coffees and spend the day together exploring the city.

Lyric arrived a little late, but not concerningly so. She wasn't wearing her sophisticated makeup, and she looked beautiful in an easy, unassuming way. Her long wavy hair was still damp from the shower, and Bianca noticed a couple of pimples on her chin that she'd tried unsuccessfully to conceal. She looked young, sweet, and wholesome. Lyric dropped her too-cool attitude and ran to embrace her.

"I missed you." The girl's voice was muffled by Bianca's hair.

"Me too." Bianca savored her sister's closeness, the concrete knowledge that she was safe. Bianca had been right to come, to see that Lyric was okay with her own eyes. She felt a nearly jubilant sense of relief.

They made their way toward the park. Lyric lived downtown, didn't know her way around the chaos of Midtown, but they found their route, chatting breezily about her life in the city. Lyric was more open in person, discussing her roommates (a girl from Atlanta who was cool, and another from Chicago who she suspected had an undiagnosed personality disorder). Lyric had a job as a food runner at a chichi restaurant.

"But when I'm twenty-one, I can train to be a server."

Bianca didn't comment that four years was a long time to wait to become a waitress. She wanted their visit to be pleasant. Later, she'd bring up Lyric's high school diploma and some sort of career training.

"Do you make enough money?" Bianca asked. "New York is an expensive place to live."

"I get amazing tips," Lyric assured her. "All our customers are super rich. And really generous."

"Maybe I'll come in for dinner tonight?" Bianca suggested.

"Good luck," Lyric laughed. "You have to reserve months in advance unless you're a VIP." She scrunched up her nose. "And it's *really* expensive."

Lyric sounded impressed, thrilled to be serving New York's upper crust. Bianca was tempted to remind her who she was and where she came from, but now was not the time. She needed more details on her sister's life and couldn't risk her storming off in a huff.

They strolled the tree-lined promenade of Central Park, their arms linked. The fall weather was brisk, the sky a flat gray, but colorful leaves clung to the tree branches. Lyric asked about Damian, about their hometown, about Bianca's design job. Neither woman spoke to their mom anymore, and they both felt lighter for it. Healthier. There was no guilt. Yvonne had a new boyfriend; she wouldn't miss them.

"Are you hungry? Can I take you for lunch?" Bianca asked. She couldn't afford anywhere fancy, but she was still the big sister.

Lyric checked the time on her phone. "Sure. I've got a couple of hours before I have to get ready for work."

They walked back to Midtown, where Bianca had noticed a decent diner next to her hotel. Their conversation was full of giggles and reminiscences, and Bianca felt at ease. Her kid sister was on an adventure. She was young, and she would make mistakes, but there would be time for her to get back on track.

Over corned beef sandwiches and Diet Cokes, Bianca teased more information out of Lyric. She got the name and location of the fancy restaurant where Lyric worked, the venue where Bianca could *never hope* to get a table. She wrote down the address of her sister's Chinatown apartment, promising to send her some of the items she'd left behind in her haste to leave. And she insisted they meet for breakfast the next day.

"What time?" Lyric whined. "I work late, and sometimes we go out after."

Bianca sipped her Diet Coke. "Where do you go?"

"We get invited to clubs and we get VIP entrance." Lyric was lit from within. "Sometimes we go to private parties that are *insane*."

As her underage sister spoke about bottle service and velvet ropes, Bianca felt her comfort level plunge. She'd never been impressed by shallow displays of wealth, and she knew the narcissism that often came with money. Rich people played by their own rules. They took whatever they wanted.

"You have to be careful." It came out sounding distinctly maternal. "You can't trust these rich pricks. You're just a kid, and they'll take advantage of you."

"They're not like that," Lyric said, setting down her sandwich. "They're really nice people. Important people. And they have connections in finance. And Hollywood. And Silicon Valley. Something big is going to happen for me here, B. I can feel it."

Bianca looked at her bright-eyed sister, so young and pretty, and she wanted to believe her. But she couldn't. She knew the ugly side of human nature, the dark desires of powerful people. She wanted to tell Lyric to come home and finish school, to live with her and Damian, who could keep her safe. She could move back to New York when she was older, smarter, wiser. But Lyric wouldn't listen to her. She was wild and rebellious. She was a girl.

"I've flown a long way to see you," she said. "It won't kill you to go home early one night so you can get up and meet me for breakfast."

"Fine." Lyric rolled her eyes. "I'll be there."

35

When Bianca still hasn't returned half an hour later, Damian pulls on a pair of shorts and goes looking for her. The house is empty but for Sydney snoring softly behind her closed door. He grabs himself a beer and surveys the property. No Bianca. No Curtis. He heads out to the van. Pulling open the panel door, he finds his partner on the bed, curled into the fetal position. "What's wrong?" he asks, climbing inside and pulling the door closed behind him. He perches next to her, lays a hand on her shoulder.

"I ran into Curtis," she says, and he realizes she's trembling. "I hate him so fucking much."

"What did he do?" Damian demands, a rush of protectiveness tensing his muscles, balling his fists.

"He tried to tell me that I've got it all wrong. That he hasn't hurt anyone."

Damian lies next to her, presses himself against her small body. "He's gaslighting you, babe. He's desperate. And afraid."

"I know what I saw," she says, more to herself than to Damian. "I know what she told me."

"If Curtis was innocent, he wouldn't be trying to get the money." He strokes her hair. "He wouldn't even consider paying us if he had nothing to hide."

She twists in his embrace to face him. "I don't want to play this fucking game anymore. I just want him to pay for what he did."

"It's almost over." Damian tries to soothe her. He can't have her going rogue now, talking to Sydney and ruining everything. "I'll tell Curtis to stay the fuck away from you. I'll tell him he can only deal with me."

"He left," she says. "I heard the car drive off."

"When he gets back, I'll talk to him," Damian assures her. "Hang in there for a few more days. Curtis will get the money, and we can leave. We can have the life we've always wanted."

She looks up at him, her expression stormy. "And then we'll tell Sydney everything. And Curtis will be left with nothing."

"Exactly." He kisses her forehead.

"I'm so tired," she says. "I haven't been sleeping."

"Come inside. I'll get you one of Syd's pills to help you rest."

"I'd rather stay here," she mumbles, turning away from him again.

"Okay." He turns on the fan, the gentle breeze cooling Bianca's skin. "I'll be back." He lets himself out of the vehicle.

Inside the silent house, Damian moves straight to the bathroom. Opening the mirrored medicine cabinet, he sifts through Sydney's prescriptions. He finds one that will help Bianca relax and doze off. He shakes a couple of tiny pills into his palm, slips them into the pocket of his shorts. As he heads to the kitchen to get his partner a glass of water, he hears the coffee machine.

Sydney. It must be her. They're alone in the house, and he feels a childish flutter in his belly. He can't indulge this crush. He needs to keep his eyes on the prize. Calming himself, he strolls into the kitchen.

"How are you feeling?" he asks, resuming his Aussie accent and carefree manner.

"Not so bad now," she says, smiling weakly. "I drank way too much."

"It happens."

Sydney turns toward him, coffee mug in her hand. "I want to apologize to you and Bianca. For my behavior last night."

"You were fine," he assures her. "We were all having fun."

"I wasn't. I mean...I was." Her face flushes. "I was really drunk. And confused. But Curtis and I...we're monogamous. It was wrong for me to betray him like that."

Damian leans his forearms on the counter across from her. "Bianca said Curtis betrayed *you*."

Sydney takes a sip of coffee before she answers. "He did. But we went to therapy, and we agreed to rebuild our relationship. What I did last night was not okay."

She's blaming herself, and it makes him sick. She has no idea who she's married to. "You're an amazing woman, Sydney. You don't deserve to be with a liar and a cheat. I don't know how Curtis could ever have betrayed you like that."

"He made a mistake, but he came clean, and that means a lot." She sips her coffee, smiles tightly. "We have history. And we have a future. And that's worth fighting for."

"Are you sure you trust him?"

"Is this about Curtis flirting with Bianca?" Her expression darkens. "She told me about that. If you saw something, I'd like to know."

Well played, Bianca. But Damian breezes past it. "You need to look out for yourself. Emotionally and financially."

"*Financially?*" She sets her mug on the counter, crosses her arms. "What are you talking about?"

"You need to protect yourself." He glances at the door, to ensure they're still alone. "Your mom left you money, right? Make sure Curtis can't get to that."

"We're using that money for the winery," she says. "It's our dream. My mom would have wanted that."

"Curtis may have other plans. Other obligations. You should put that money somewhere safe."

"If you know something about his finances, tell me." She steps toward him, and he sees the confusion on her face, the concern in her eyes. He wants to tell her to run, to take all her money, all her assets, and flee. But saving Sydney would ruin everything.

"Just look out for yourself, that's all." He forces a casual tone. "Never trust a cheater, as we say back in Aus." Do they say that? He has no idea. "If a guy can break his marriage vows, he's capable of anything."

He heads to the sink and fills a glass with water. "Bianca's taking a nap in the van. I should go check on her."

"Sure," Syd mumbles, but he can see the wheels turning in her head. He's planted a seed of suspicion and doubt.

Mission accomplished.

36

Bianca wakes in the dead of night. The pills Damian gave her had helped her sleep, but now she feels wide awake. And slightly befuddled. For a moment, she doesn't know where she is. It's so dark, so quiet but for the constant hum of the small fan. Soon, she places herself inside the van, tucked into the double bed, all alone.

Damian must have slept in the house. She can't blame him for choosing the comfort of the guest bed over this thin foam mattress. The van is too warm, too stuffy, especially with two occupants. But her partner had handed her some strange medication, watched her take it, and then left her out here by herself. What if she'd had a reaction? She'd already had a couple of beers. What if she'd been sick? Did he even care?

She feels around for her phone and checks the time: 12:23 a.m. She'd gone to sleep so early that now she feels alert, rested. Her mouth tastes burnt, and her throat is parched. The glass of water Damian brought her is somewhere on the van floor, so she uses the light of her phone to find it. She drinks the rest of the tepid liquid, lies back down. Will she be able to go back to sleep? The medication must still be coursing through her system, the sedative effects lingering. But she really needs to pee.

At first, she tries to ignore it. She doesn't want to leave the safety and privacy of this tiny space. If she goes into the house, she risks running into Curtis again. Damian will have told him to leave her alone, but if Curtis wakes up, hears her enter, he might secretly confront her.

Attempt to manipulate and twist her mind again. Sydney slept most of the day, so she could be awake now. Bianca doesn't have the energy to resume her cheerful Aussie traveler facade. She could pee outside but... snakes.

Giving in to the building pressure in her bladder, she climbs out of bed and stumbles out of the van. She's unsteady on her feet from the lingering effects of the meds, so she picks her way gingerly through the darkness. Her phone flashlight illuminates about a foot in front of her, but this isn't safe. She could fall and hit her head, step on a deadly spider, or disturb a wild boar. And yet Damian abandoned her out here. He didn't care that she might wake up, might be frightened, might need to find her way into the house in a compromised state. He'd gone inside, and he'd spent the evening with their hosts. With Sydney.

Trying the front door, she finds it unlocked. At least her boyfriend cared enough about her to not lock her out. Bianca lets herself into the darkened house, picks her way down the hall to the blue bathroom. She pees but doesn't flush, doesn't want to risk waking anyone. She's about to head to the bedroom, to climb in next to her sleeping partner, when she hesitates. She won't get back to sleep now. And there's no point lying in bed wide awake.

Quietly, she opens the medicine cabinet and inspects the orange plastic bottles lining the shelves. They're prescriptions for Sydney, filled at a Spanish pharmacy, but the drug names remain the same or similar to what they would be in the States. All the medications are for anxiety and depression. No wonder. Being married to a monster would be a real downer. The thought of Sydney's willful blindness, her intentional stupidity, fills Bianca's mouth with bitterness. Why can't Damian see her for what she really is?

Slipping out into the hall, she tiptoes over the cool tiles toward the living room. She runs a hand along the wall for balance, but she feels steadier now, almost back to normal. Curtis's laptop and tablet sit on a corner shelf, and she wonders if she could access them. But his devices would obviously be password-protected. He has so much to hide.

As she nears the kitchen, she becomes aware of the hollowness in her belly. When did she eat last? She and Damian had a couple of beers, but she hasn't had any food since breakfast. Her wobbliness makes sense. Curtis, Sydney, and Damian must have eaten. Did all three of them sit down to dinner together? Or did Damian and Sydney dine alone? Either way, she hopes there are some leftovers. She's moving to the fridge when she hears it. A low mumble, a woman's voice. It must be Sydney. But who is she talking to?

Bianca's heart skitters with dread. Is she about to catch Damian and Sydney in an intimate moment? Is he telling Syd everything because he cares more about protecting her than he does Bianca's revenge? On stealthy feet, she moves toward the living room. The glass door is ajar, and Syd stands just outside it, wearing a short robe made of lilac silk. A thin wisp of smoke curls into the air, and Bianca notices the cigarette in Sydney's hand. In the other, she holds a phone to her ear. Creeping closer, Bianca can hear Syd's words.

"Anderson Technologies," she says. "On Franklin Street."

There's a pause while the other person talks, and Sydney takes a drag on her cigarette. It's late in Spain, but not in the States. And Sydney is speaking English. She must be phoning someone back home. Clearly, this is a call she doesn't want anyone to overhear.

"Try the client's name. Collette Jasper." There's another pause before Sydney says, "That's so strange. I appreciate you trying." She hangs up with a muttered "Shit..."

Bianca watches Syd exhale a plume of smoke into the night air. She could really use a cigarette herself, but that's not what she's thinking about right now. Why is Sydney sneaking around in the night? Who was she talking to? What is she hiding?

Perhaps Bianca should slip away, head to the kitchen, and pretend she hadn't been eavesdropping. But her thirst for information usurps her desire for discretion. She pushes open the glass door and walks outside.

"Jesus Christ!" Syd spins around, hand flying to her heart. "You scared me."

"Sorry." Bianca pastes on that pleasant smile. "What are you doing out here?"

"Sneaking a cigarette." Sydney butts her smoke out on the paving bricks. "Don't tell Curtis."

"Your secret's safe with me. I thought I heard you talking on the phone."

The possibility of denial flits across Sydney's features, but she ultimately decides against it. "I had some business to take care of back home."

"What kind of business?" It's rude and probing, but Bianca doesn't care.

"Work stuff."

"Who's Collette Jasper?"

"No one. An old client of mine."

"Why are you looking for her?"

Sydney narrows her eyes. "What happened to your accent, Bianca?"

Oops.

"I've been here too long," Bianca says, putting on the Aussie. "I think I've been picking up your American accent." She points a thumb back at the house. "I slept through dinner. Is it okay if I grab something to eat?"

"Help yourself."

"Do you want anything? I can make you some eggs?" She's being sweet, obsequious, but Sydney's expression remains hard. And suspicious.

"I'm good."

Bianca backs toward the house. "I'll be quiet. Good night, Syd."

"Night."

Her voice is ice-cold.

37

Sometime in the small hours of the morning, Damian feels Bianca slide into bed next to him. She smells vaguely of cigarette smoke, but he's too sleepy to care if she's been caught. He rolls away from her and tries to drift back to sleep, but there's a leaden pressure between his eyebrows, and his mouth feels dry and mossy. Clearly, he'd had one too many drinks this evening. But he'd felt so upbeat, even celebratory.

With Bianca resting in the van and Sydney sufficiently warned to look out for herself, Damian had felt a real sense of accomplishment. There was nothing left for him to do but relax, enjoy the house, the food, the pool... and fuck with Curtis some more. Damian's excited to leave, of course, to get the money and get on with their life, but he'll miss tormenting that asshole. That lying, manipulative piece of shit.

Curtis had made himself scarce most of the day. Damian imagined he'd gone somewhere private to freak out, to cry and wail about all he stood to lose. Then he would have pulled himself together and begun to strategize ways to get the money. He'd have called his Spanish bank and his New York wealth manager. And he would have reached out to whomever he contacts with that secret burner phone.

Alone in the house with Sydney, Damian had felt surprisingly nervous. He hadn't been so unsettled around a female since he was a kid, shy and awkward. Even in her hungover state, with her bloodshot eyes and her hair scraped back from her face, Sydney was still gorgeous, almost ethereal. Without the buffer of their partners, he didn't know how to act around her. So he grabbed another beer.

"Hair of the dog?" he offered, holding the bottle up to her.

Sydney was prone on the sofa with her laptop. She looked up and made a face. "God, no. I won't be drinking for a while."

"I could make you a fresh-squeezed orange juice?" he offered. "Or an iced tea? We could sit by the pool." He hated the pleading sound in his voice, like a lovestruck twelve-year-old.

"I've got some stuff to do," she said, eyes on her screen. "Go enjoy yourself. Curtis will be back soon to keep you company."

Damian had taken his beer outside, sunk into a deck chair, and tried not to feel dismissed. He knew Sydney was attracted to him. He'd felt her desire more than once. She was likely annoyed with him for not telling her all the dirt on Curtis. And part of him wanted to. He could be her hero, earn her gratitude, even devotion. But giving her that information would jeopardize their blackmail plan, and five million bucks was five million bucks, no matter how hot he was for Sydney.

He'd sipped his beer and scrolled through his phone until the sun began to dip behind the mountain and the air cooled. Heading into the warmth of the house he went to the living room to look for Syd, but she'd absconded to her bedroom again. Damian was hungry by then. The Spanish liked to eat late, but he'd never really gotten used to it. He was rifling through the fridge when he heard the front door open, then close. Curtis had finally returned.

Damian greeted him in his American accent. "Good timing. I'm starving."

"Help yourself." Curtis tossed his key fob on the counter.

"I thought you could whip up one of those frittatas."

"Seriously?" Curtis snorted. "You expect me to cook for you still?"

"Nah, it's okay." He cocked an eyebrow. "I think I'll go watch a video with Sydney."

Curtis's eyes narrowed, and he lowered his voice. "It's a lot of money. It's going to take some time."

"You have seven days."

"I don't know if I can get it all by then."

Damian shrugged. "Then you know what will happen."

Curtis moved to the fridge and wrenched open the door. He grabbed a beer and flipped off the cap. "You've got it all wrong, you know." He took a drink, wiped his mouth with the back of his hand. "I tried to tell Bianca, but she wouldn't listen. I'm innocent. I've never hurt anyone."

His manipulations wouldn't work on Damian. Bianca may have been shaken by Curtis's denials, but Damian was not so gullible. "We're not interested in your excuses. We know what you did."

"I did nothing! You're going to destroy an innocent man when there are still evil people out there doing evil things."

"You're not innocent, Curtis. Bianca saw you."

"If you'd just let me explain—"

"Sydney!" Damian called, cutting him off.

Curtis blanched, and his eyes widened. "What the fuck?" he whispered.

"I bet your wife would like to hear your explanation, too."

She strolled into the kitchen then, still pale and wan from last night's excesses. "Yeah?"

Curtis spoke before Damian could. "Damian suggested a frittata for dinner. Does that work for you?"

"Sure. Whatever." Her eyes flitted between the men, then she turned back toward her room. "Call me when it's ready."

Damian rolls over and fumbles for the glass of water on the nightstand. He drinks heartily, washing away the coating in his mouth. It had been a good night after that, worth the mild hangover he's now suffering. The three of them had eaten dinner together, had opened a bottle of red. Sydney hadn't partaken in the alcohol and ate quietly. But Curtis had been nervous, drinking his wine in gulps, almost ignoring his food.

"So, Sydney..." Damian began, as he topped up his glass. "As a public defender, you must've had to represent some real scumbags."

"Sometimes."

"Who's the worst person you defended?"

"She doesn't want to talk about that," Curtis interjected.

"Why not?" Damian asked him. "Sydney's comfortable around monsters. It was her job, after all."

"It's okay," Syd said. She fixed Damian with a steely glare. "I represented a father who killed his two children to punish their mother for leaving him," she said. "He's the worst person I was forced to defend."

"That's fucked-up," Damian said, his voice quieter. "I don't know how some men can do the things they do."

"Anyone for dessert?" Curtis offered. "Tea or coffee?"

"I could go for a vermouth," Damian suggested, and he'd smiled as Curtis jumped up to get it. He'd felt Sydney's eyes on him and turned to meet her gaze. Had she noticed her husband's obsequious behavior? His deferential manner? But Sydney's face was closed, and he couldn't read her. Soon after, she excused herself and went back to bed.

Damian's thoughts become fragmented as he drifts closer to sleep. In the morning, he'll tell Sydney he hurt his shoulder, so she doesn't wonder why he's not working on the winery. He and Bianca can have a day of relaxation. Maybe they'll borrow the Citroën and head to a beach. Or they can hang out by the pool and have Curtis bring them drinks. With that satisfying image in his mind, he drifts toward sleep.

It's only moments later that the slight vibration of the bed stirs him awake again. He already knows what's causing the subtle movement. Bianca is crying in silence, her body shaking with her grief. His partner has never shed a tear in front of him, not since the memorial service. Then, she'd let them slide down her cheeks untouched, but she hadn't made a sound. Bianca is always so stoic, so strong. But he knows the pain is there, silently eating her alive.

He closes his eyes again, but the pleasant thoughts and images are gone, expunged by Bianca's suffering. As much as he's been enjoying the process, he can't forget why they've come.

He can't forget that Curtis Lowe caused this.

38

On her last night in New York, Bianca decided to surprise her sister at work. She took the subway downtown to visit the fancy restaurant that Lyric had bragged about. Bianca didn't have a reservation, but she hoped she could talk her way inside. She'd flown hours to visit her kid sister. Surely, the hostess could find her a seat at the bar, where she could splurge on a cocktail and watch Lyric in action.

She got off the subway and let her phone direct her to the Meatpacking District. She'd dressed up a bit, but her clothes were a combination of bargain basement and thrift store, unlikely to fool the well-heeled crowd. Still, Bianca was an attractive woman, perfectly presentable. She was confident she'd be allowed inside.

The restaurant was as chic as Lyric had promised. Located in a distressed-brick building with massive latticed windows, it had a heated outdoor dining area where sleek customers ate oysters off beds of ice and drank flutes of champagne. Bianca walked up the steps and into the tiled entryway, jittery with nerves and anticipation. Lyric had done it. She'd come to this massive city as a naïve kid, and she'd landed a decent job in a reputable establishment. Bianca felt proud. And relieved.

She was greeted by the maître d', a thin man in a tailored blue suit.

"I don't have a reservation," Bianca explained, "but my sister works here. I flew in from Indiana to visit her."

"And who's your sister?"

"Lyric Bentley."

His expression tightened. "Lyric no longer works here."

"I saw her this morning," Bianca blurted. "She told me she did."

"Well, she doesn't."

"When did she leave? Did something happen?"

"She stopped showing up about a week ago." His eyes flicked past her to the patrons in the queue. "I'm going to have to ask you to step aside."

Bianca found a small bar with cheap drinks and sticky tables. Over a whisky and Coke, she processed the information she'd learned, her sister's lies and fabrications. She was vibrating with the need to call Lyric, to demand an explanation, but she knew what that would illicit: more denials, more manipulations. They'd both learned those skills from Yvonne. They knew how to twist the truth, to talk their way out of messes. And she didn't want her sister to get angry and go dark, to cut Bianca off. She needed to know the girl was safe in her new life. Lyric was her only family. She meant everything.

Over a second drink, she resolved to stay calm and handle the situation delicately. She'd meet Lyric for breakfast tomorrow and pretend she'd never gone to the restaurant. Then she'd gently tease out the truth by assuring her sister there was no need to be ashamed of feeling overwhelmed in such a high-stress environment, serving an elite clientele. Lyric was a kid from a small town who'd tragically lost her father, had survived a toxic mother. Bianca needed to go easy on her.

In the morning, Bianca packed her small suitcase and took the subway to the breakfast place they'd chosen. She ordered coffee and waited for her sister. And waited. As she sipped her third cup, she broke down and called. Bianca was irritated by then, but not angry. Lyric must have slept through her alarm. It was typical teenage behavior. But the call went straight to voicemail. The kid had turned off her phone or set it to Do Not Disturb.

Now she was pissed off. As she wheeled her suitcase through the streets toward Lyric's apartment, she simmered over the selfishness.

Bianca had spent a lot of money to come here, to check in on her sister. She was the only person who cared about the girl, and Lyric couldn't be bothered to get up and eat some fucking waffles with her. It was rude and inconsiderate.

Her sister's building was a squat three-story structure surrounded by bustling restaurants and delis. Bianca weaved through delivery trucks and marched up to the ancient intercom. She hit the button for Lyric's unit and plugged an ear against the background noise. There was no response at first, so she pressed the button again. And then again. Finally, a sleepy voice answered.

"Hello?"

It had to be one of Lyric's roommates. "Can you get Lyric? I'm her sister." It was a demand, not a question.

Bianca waited. A few moments later, the staticky voice returned. "She's not here."

"Where is she?"

"I don't know. Maybe she stayed at a friend's last night."

"So, she didn't come home last night? Has her bed been slept in?"

"No...I don't know."

"Where did she stay? Does she have a boyfriend?"

"I don't know. Maybe? Look, I worked late last night. I need to go back to sleep."

"Open the door. I need to come up."

There was a brief pause. "Who did you say you were again?"

"I'm her older sister!" Bianca realized she was yelling. "Let me in!"

There was silence. The girl had hung up.

A sickening sense of wrong churned the coffee in her stomach. In Indiana, she'd known something was off; that was why she'd come here. Lyric had tried to fool her, convince her that everything was fine, but it wasn't. Bianca felt the certainty in her marrow. She needed to get into that apartment, so she stabbed the buzzer again. And then again. The girl inside did not answer.

Panic made Bianca's breathing shallow. This apartment, that

roommate, were her only connections to her sister in this huge, anonymous city. She needed to know if Lyric had a boyfriend or a girlfriend, someone who kept her out all night. How was she making her money? How would she pay her rent? She buzzed again, and again, and again. She'd annoy Lyric's roommate so much that she'd have to let her in.

Aggressive honking at the end of the block caught Bianca's attention. She turned toward the eruption, saw a sleek black town car blocking the street. A burly man in a too-tight suit got out of the driver's seat and hurried around to the passenger side. He opened the door and dragged a girl out of the vehicle. She was stumbling, drunk or high, as the big guy half carried her toward the sidewalk. He set her down on the curb and hustled back to his vehicle. Bianca was already running before her mind had fully processed the scene. It was not just any girl; it was Lyric.

As she sprinted toward her sister, the sleek car sped past her. Bianca glanced inside, caught the briefest glimpse of the driver: shaved head, pockmarked skin, dark glasses. He was just some guy, a hired chauffeur, a man paid enough to dump a nearly unconscious teenager on a city sidewalk. She reached the crumpled form of her sister on the asphalt, her head bowed between her knees. Bianca knelt beside her, and Lyric lifted her head. Her eyes were blank, confused, and frightened.

"What happened to you?" Bianca demanded.

Lyric started to cry. "I—I don't know..."

"What do you mean, you don't know? What are you on? What did you take?"

"I...don't remember." She looked around her, terrified. "I don't know where I am." She gripped Bianca's arm. "You have to help me."

"I'm here. You're safe."

Bianca held her little sister as she trembled and cried.

39

In the morning, Damian has a slight hangover—from booze and from guilt. He glances at his partner, sleeping in after her emotional night, and climbs gently out of bed, trying not to disturb her. Bianca's silent grief stays with him as he dresses and slips out of the room. He's been having too much fun taunting Curtis, crushing on Sydney, focusing on the money and how it will change their future. It's not like he's forgotten what Curtis Lowe did, but he's been living in the moment. His partner is still living in the pain.

Bianca has played the part of carefree Aussie traveler to perfection. She's buried her grief under a perky facade, but she's still suffering. Destroying Curtis is part of Bianca's healing. He'd promised to help her do that, and he will. In return, Bianca has agreed to extort money out of Curtis Lowe and build a new life with Damian in Europe. A deal is a deal.

Even as a kid, Damian knew he was an extraordinary person trapped in a bland existence, biding his time until he could escape. He'd grifted, scammed, and manipulated to get enough money to leave. And then he'd fallen in love with Bianca, let her waylay his plans. He'd done it willingly. The relationship had provided a sense of peace and belonging he hadn't realized he was missing. He'd gotten comfortable and complacent. But as the years stretched out and he remained stuck in Indiana, he began to feel antsy. And resentful.

And then...tragedy. As devastating as it was, it was also a release. There was no reason to stay put anymore. Damian and Bianca had managed to combine their goals into a trip to Spain, but he's beginning to worry. If Curtis can't get the money together, if he backs out or double-crosses them, how will they stay here? They'd paid for this trip on credit; their savings have dwindled. Neither of them can legally work in the EU. Bianca would be content to ruin Curtis, then return to their shitty little town. But Damian has had a taste of the life he's always wanted. He's never going back.

As he brushes his teeth, he reflects on this new lease on life. Since they touched down in Barcelona, he's felt like a man emerged from a coma. They'd spent a few days in the city playing tourist: eating, drinking, checking out the Sagrada Familia and Park Güell. They bought the old van at a lot on the outskirts of the city, headed north toward Cadaqués. The drive was only a few hours, but they'd agreed to camp out along the way. It would make the van look more lived-in, make them more bedraggled and authentic. And it was a chance to practice their Australian personas before they met Curtis and Sydney.

They'd hung out with other campers, sharing their made-up stories about life Down Under. Bianca couldn't stand all the shaggy kids living in tiny vans, posting photos of their picnic lunches and beach yoga. She thought they were vapid and shallow, but Damian had enjoyed them. They'd spent their days swimming and hiking, their nights drinking beer and smoking joints. Of course he'd have preferred a suite at the Four Seasons, but this was a taste of the hedonism he'd always craved. Being in Spain, in Europe, is the beginning of a new chapter. It feels like he's finally arrived.

After splashing his face with water, Damian heads to the kitchen. Curtis and Sydney are seated at the dining table, drinking coffee in stony silence. He has the distinct impression he's interrupted an intense conversation, but he plays ignorant. "Morning," he says brightly, accent in place.

"Morning," Curtis mumbles, but Sydney is silent.

As Damian heads to the coffee machine, he rotates his arm and winces. "Buggered up my shoulder unloading those boards yesterday. I'm going to need to rest it for a few days."

A look flies between the couple at the table, but Curtis is quick to cover. "No problem. There are ice packs in the freezer if you need one."

Damian makes a coffee, takes it over to the table, but he doesn't sit. He hovers as he drinks it. "Since I'm no use around here, I thought I'd take Bianca to the beach. Can I borrow your car?"

He knows Curtis will say yes. He could ask him to strip naked and cluck like a chicken and he'd do it.

"Sure." Curtis stands obediently. "Can you drive a stick?"

"I'm a little rusty," Damian lies. He's not about to admit that his experience is limited to racing video games. "I could use a refresher."

The two men head out to the car in tense silence. It's not until they're alone in the driveway, several yards from the house, that Damian speaks. "Any updates on the money?"

"Not yet." Curtis scratches his stubbled jaw. "I told you this wouldn't be easy."

"It'd be a real shame for you to lose everything you've worked for."

"I'm going to make some more calls today. I—I'm still hopeful."

"I've been thinking..." They've reached the car, and Damian leans a forearm on the roof. "What if you signed this house over to us?"

Curtis's laugh is incredulous. "How would I do that?"

"I don't know." Damian shrugs. "Talk to a real estate lawyer."

"This is Sydney's house, too. Her name is on the deed. How would I convince her to just *hand over* our dream house to you?"

Curtis is mocking him and his idea, and Damian feels a strong urge to smack the condescending look off his face. But he takes a breath, stays calm. "Tell her you miss New York and want to go back. You can say you sold the house, then lost the money in a bad investment or something."

"That would never work. Sydney's way too smart to fall for a story like that."

"I'm trying to help you out here," Damian snaps, eyes glowering at the other man. "Bianca wants you to fail, you know. She wants an excuse to tell Sydney everything. To share that video with everyone you know."

"But I didn't do anything," Curtis whines, but it's half-hearted. He knows how easily he could be destroyed.

"I want you to get the money so you can live happily ever after with your wife, and I'll do the same. You're going to have to get creative."

"I will. I'll get it. Don't—" He stops talking when they hear the door open. Bianca emerges, her face stormy.

"Beach day, babe. Grab your stuff."

Without a word, Bianca moves back inside. Damian turns to Curtis. "Use your time wisely."

Driving a stick is more challenging than anticipated. Thankfully, Damian doesn't have to worry about burning out Curtis's clutch. As long as he can get them back up the hill, he doesn't care what happens to the car. After a couple of stalls, a few hops, they arrive in Cadaqués and park in the dusty lot.

Bianca had been quiet in the car. Yesterday, they'd celebrated putting their plan in motion. They'd had sex in the van, sunbathed in the nude, drank beer in the sunshine. But now Bianca is sullen. Her encounter with Curtis upset her yesterday, and she'd spent the night in tears. The conversation he needs to have with her is not going to improve her mood.

They lay their towels on the patch of sand in the center of town and run into the surf. There's a raft floating several yards from shore, and Damian suggests they swim out to it. With strong strokes and focused breathing, he churns toward the platform. But when he arrives, Bianca is not in tow. Grabbing the ladder, he pulls himself up to the wooden surface and sits there catching his breath. He looks back to shore, watches Bianca wade out of the water, wringing out her long hair. She's wearing her red bikini, and he notices some older men on a nearby bench watching her with open admiration. His partner is undeniably sexy. So why can't he stop comparing her accessible beauty to Sydney's cool elegance? He pushes away the thought and dives back into the sea.

Bianca lies on her back, face placid, eyes hidden behind dark shades. She doesn't lift her head when Damian settles himself next to her and he wonders if she might be asleep. For a few moments, he's silent, savoring the stillness, the peace of the moment. But he has to broach this subject.

"Curtis is having a hard time getting the money."

"Too bad." Bianca doesn't look at him, doesn't even move. Her indifference is clear.

"He may not be able to get the whole five mill."

"So? Then we'll tell Sydney everything. We'll tell his mom and all his friends back home, just like we planned."

"But what about us?"

She lifts her head then, lowers her sunglasses, and peers over them. "What do you mean?"

"We need a certain amount of money to stay here. I'm not going back to the States, Bianca."

"I know."

"We need to be flexible. If Curtis can't get *all* the money, maybe we settle for three million. Or the house."

"Sydney owns half that house. She'd never give it to us."

She's right. He lies back, imagines living in the Spanish house with Sydney. He can't abandon Bianca, but maybe the three of them...? But that's a teenager's wet dream. He knows Syd would never entertain it. Neither would Bianca.

"We need a good chunk of money to get ourselves set up," he continues, eyes on the cloudless sky. "We need to do some calculations to figure out what we're willing to accept."

Bianca rolls on her side to face him. "I want *all* his money. I want him in debt, and starving, and in the dark. I want his wife to leave him and all his friends to turn against him. That's the only punishment I'll accept for what he did."

She returns to her back, ending the conversation. Damian glances over, sees the grim line of her lips, the tense set of her jaw. But behind her dark glasses, a tear seeps from her eye.

He watches it trickle down her cheek, untouched.

40

When Bianca found her sister crumpled on that filthy sidewalk, she'd picked her up and helped her stumble toward her building. She'd found Lyric's keys in her small purse and let them both into the lobby. With her arm around the girl's waist, she half carried her into the elevator and up to the apartment. It was a cramped one-bedroom littered with clothes, shoes, makeup, and other girlish accoutrements. There was no sign of the roommate who'd hung up on her, but she noted a closed door next to the bathroom. Lyric had another roommate too, but she appeared to be out.

The sisters crawled into Lyric's futon bed, and Bianca held the girl while she slept. Bianca's flight was leaving soon, and she wouldn't be on it. If she didn't call Damian before the plane landed, he would go to the airport, and she wouldn't be there. She needed her phone, but it was in her purse on the floor, and she couldn't let go of her sister's small, limp body. So she lay there, holding her as the hours ticked by.

From behind the thin paper screen, Bianca heard the roommate get up, shower, and leave. Silence followed, and she felt sure they were alone. She didn't know how long they'd been lying there, but her arm had fallen asleep under Lyric's weight. What time was it? Could she still change her flight? She needed her phone. Gingerly, she attempted to extricate herself, but Lyric stirred. She turned over in Bianca's arms, smiled weakly at her.

"You're here."

"I'm here."

Lyric's face crumpled then. "I'm sorry."

Bianca shushed her, stroked her hair. "Tell me what happened..."

Lyric shook her head, still confused and discombobulated. Her eyes filled with tears, and she looked so young, so afraid. She was not hard like her older sister. Bianca had handled their cruel mother with no one in her corner. Lyric had always had Bianca as a buffer, a safety net. That love and support had allowed her to grow up soft. It had made her weak.

Bianca cradled the girl in her arms and made soothing noises until she stopped crying. Delicately, she began to ask questions.

"Why did you quit the restaurant?" There was no judgment, only curiosity.

Lyric's voice was small. "This lady came in for dinner. She was so classy and sophisticated. She invited me to a party."

"You went to a party with a stranger?" Bianca's gentle tone was slipping.

"She was a regular. She seemed super nice."

"Where was this party?"

"The first one was small, more like a get-together. It was in a fancy high-rise apartment. I had fun that time. I drank champagne and met all these cool people. Everyone was rich, and some of them were even famous," Lyric continued. "The lady—her name is Fay—told me everyone liked me a lot. And if I'd come to more parties, they'd pay me."

"Pay you for what?" There was only the slightest tremor in Bianca's voice.

"Fay said I'd be like a hostess. All I had to do was chat to people and make sure they had drinks and stuff. She said I'd work less and make way more than I did at the restaurant. I thought it seemed legit."

Then why did you lie to me about it? But Bianca couldn't scold her, not now.

"So I quit the restaurant. I—I only went to two parties." She was getting emotional again, but Bianca needed her to keep talking.

"What happened at these parties?" she asked softly.

"The next party was much bigger. It was in an office tower, in a big empty space. There was no furniture except some couches and a few bars. I—I must have drunk too much that night. I felt sick and kind of scared. I wanted to leave, but Fay said I had to stay or I wouldn't get paid. The next day, I couldn't remember what happened or how I got home."

Bianca felt her body tense, her skull squeezing her brain, but she forced herself to relax, to listen.

"A few days ago, Fay called and invited me to another party at some big warehouse. I told her I didn't want to go, that I was going to get another job at a restaurant, but... she said I had to." Lyric's voice wavered with shame and regret. "Fay had a video of me doing things that I don't remember. *Sexual* things."

Bianca felt her body quaking with rage toward this horrible Fay woman, but she stilled it, focused on her sister. "It's okay," she said. "It's not your fault."

"I went to the party, and I tried not to drink. I held the same cocktail glass all night. But somehow, something happened to me. I don't remember anything after that, until you found me on the sidewalk."

Bianca held her close, kissed her hair, and rubbed her back. "You're safe now. I'm here." She waited until the sobs subsided before she said, "But you're coming home with me."

"No..." But it was a weak protest, because she knew. Lyric was too young, too naïve, to survive alone in New York City.

When her sister went back to sleep, Bianca called Damian. "I missed my flight. I'll be home tomorrow. I'm bringing Lyric."

"What happened? Is she okay?"

Bianca explained about the man dumping her on the sidewalk like a bag of garbage.

"She must have been drugged," Damian said. "She could have been raped. Take her to a doctor. Call the cops."

"I'm not going to put her through all that," Bianca responded. "The cops won't believe a young, drunk girl over a bunch of powerful assholes. And she doesn't remember anything. That's probably for the best."

"She's *your* sister," Damian muttered, clearly disagreeing with her approach. "I suppose she's going to be living with us?"

"Of course she is," she snapped. "If you don't like it, you're free to leave."

"Calm down, Bianca. I'm fine if she stays for a while."

Damian needn't have worried. Lyric wouldn't live with them for long.

Within the year, she'd be dead.

SYDNEY AND CURTIS

41

Sydney had been attempting to sleep off her hangover when she'd been jarred awake by the sound of music. It was coming from the speakers by the pool, a loud, bassy song permeating her closed window. This wasn't the type of music she and Curtis listened to. They preferred classical or smooth jazz. This was rock 'n' roll with a country twang. It had to be the Australians.

She felt a stab of irritation at their lack of consideration, but then she glanced at the clock. It was almost two in the afternoon, a perfectly reasonable time to play music. Still, her guests knew she was trying to sleep. And why had Curtis let them play this frankly awful song at such a high volume?

Dragging herself out of bed, she moved to the window. Her blinds were closed tightly against the afternoon sun, but she pulled back a corner and peeked out to the pool. At first glance, the area appeared deserted. But over in the corner, not far from her jam jar full of cigarette butts, were two deck chairs. One was empty. On the other, Damian lay out, sunning himself. He was stark naked.

Objectively, she could admire his muscular bare back, his perfectly round ass, but Syd was too annoyed to feel any sort of desire. She'd already asked Bianca to keep her top on, and now Damian was baring it all in the sun. The nudity was overly familiar and downright rude. And after last night's antics, Curtis was sure to feel disrespected. As if on cue, she heard Curtis's car start in the driveway. He was leaving.

Grabbing a pair of shorts and a T-shirt off the floor, Sydney struggled into them as she hurried to the front door. She burst outside half dressed, waving her arm at Curtis, but the Citroën had already backed down the driveway, was turning onto the main road. Curtis put the car into first, his eyes forward, focused on his getaway. The car raced off toward the main highway.

Shit. Sydney went back inside, cursing herself. This was all her fault. This morning, Curtis has been gentle with her, had assured her he wasn't angry, but he had to be hurt. She'd crossed too many boundaries last night, and now her guests were taking advantage of it. Damian flaunting his spectacular nude physique was adding insult to injury, rubbing Curtis's nose in what happened on that dance floor.

Syd found her phone, tried to call her husband, but he didn't answer. He was driving, focused on the road. Or maybe he was upset and screening her. Keeping her voice low, she left him a message:

"Curtis, please come home so we can talk. I think... maybe the Aussies should leave. I know we need help with the building, but I just want it to be you and me again... I love you." She hung up, her throat tight with emotion.

Syd went to the coffee machine and turned it on, waited for it to warm up. Surely Curtis would agree that their guests had worn out their welcome. Syd had been titillated by them at first, distracted from the hard work of making a marriage work, but she didn't want them here anymore. She didn't judge their lifestyle, but last night had cemented her monogamous nature. She wanted her marriage to work. She wanted Curtis to forgive her error in judgment so they could move forward with their healing. Now she knew how easy it was to make a mistake.

Filling her mug with coffee, she turned around and startled. Damian had slipped into the kitchen while her back was turned. He was shirtless but wearing a pair of shorts, thank God. Being alone with him in such close quarters, in such little clothing, might have excited her before, but not today. She felt nothing for him now but mild irritation.

"I need to apologize to you and Bianca," she began curtly. "For my behavior last night."

"You were fine." His smile was cocky. "We were all having a good time."

"I wasn't." It was a lie. She couldn't deny she had enjoyed herself in the moment, but shame warmed her cheeks, made her stomach churn. Regret was a waste of her energy. Her focus was on establishing boundaries, a sense of decorum. "Curtis and I are committed and monogamous," she continued. "It was wrong for me to betray him like that."

Damian cocked an eyebrow, leaned his arms on the countertop. "Bianca said Curtis betrayed *you*."

Thanks, Bianca. Sydney had shared that information with her in confidence. Now she felt defensive of her relationship, compelled to explain the complexities of a committed marriage to this nearly naked Aussie who was bashing the man she loved. "We have history," she said. "And we have a future. And that's worth fighting for."

Damian nodded slowly. "Are you sure you trust him?"

Syd saw the opportunity to get some clarity, and she took it. "Is this about Curtis flirting with Bianca? She told me about that. If you saw something, I'd like to know."

But he didn't answer. Instead, he said, "You need to look out for yourself. Just look out for yourself, Syd. Emotionally and financially."

"*Financially?*" Acid churned in her empty stomach, and she set down her mug. What did this virtual stranger know about their finances? More than she thought.

"Your mom left you money, right? Make sure Curtis can't get to that."

She pressed him, but Damian was cagey, offering platitudes about relationships and trust. He moved to the sink and filled a glass with water. "Bianca's taking a nap in the van," he said. "I should go check on her." And he left.

The conversation had rattled her. She had no reason to mistrust her husband about money. Curtis had been transparent about everything, even his affair. But why would Damian bring up their finances unless Curtis had said something shady? It would be foolish not to at least check.

With her mug of coffee, Syd went into the living room. Her laptop rested on the ottoman next to a novel she hadn't picked up since their guests arrived. Taking the computer to the sofa, she booted it up and accessed their bank accounts. Everything was in order; there were no unusual withdrawals. She logged into her private account. Curtis had suggested, even *insisted*, that she keep her inheritance separate from their household finances. There was no activity, not since they'd had to buy the new fridge and stove.

Why had Damian said something so incendiary? Why did he want to stir up her mistrust? Sydney wondered if the Aussie was trying to damage her marriage, but to what end? Damian had been flirtatious with Sydney, but he wasn't *in love* with her. He and Bianca had been together since they were kids! Destroying Sydney's marriage seemed pointless. And cruel. It was time for their guests to leave.

As she sipped her coffee, her eyes flitted to the desk in the corner. It was piled with papers, most pertaining to their visa applications. Curtis's laptop was there, plugged in, under a stack of invoices from various tradesmen. She had his password. He'd shared it in therapy, a gesture of his commitment to regaining her trust, but she hadn't checked it in months. Snooping through his devices felt like undermining all the work they'd done. And she trusted him now. Didn't she?

On stealthy feet, she hurried to the desk and grabbed her husband's sleek laptop. She brought it back to the couch and turned it on. Her heart fluttered as it booted up, the screen jumping and flickering at first. Then the log-in page loaded, and Sydney typed in Curtis's password. It was the name of his elementary school and the year he was born. The response was instant.

Incorrect password. Try again.

Her stomach dropped, but she told herself she'd been careless, had typed the school name wrong. There was no reason to panic.

"Hair of the dog?" Damian was back, holding up a beer.

"God, no," she snapped. The thought of alcohol turned her stomach; his presence irked her. Damian seemed intent on enticing her to join him out by the pool, but she dismissed him, told him Curtis would soon return to keep him company. Luckily, he got the hint and disappeared.

Carefully, methodically, she retyped the password.

Incorrect password. Try again.

If she entered it wrong one more time, the device would lock up. Curtis would know that she'd tried to access his computer, that she was aware he'd changed his password. He had locked her out of his computer because he was hiding something from her. But what?

And what the hell did Damian know about it?

Sydney Cleary and Curtis Lowe, Couples' Counseling Session
Ellen Dwyer, Psychologist, PsyD
July 22

TRANSCRIPT 5.

Ellen:
Let's talk about your relationship before the affair. Tell me what was good about it.

Sydney:
Curtis always made me feel special. Like I was chosen. And treasured. He seemed so solid and steadfast. I felt like he'd always take care of me.

Curtis:
You *are* special, babe. And I *will* take care of you.

Sydney:
I'm not special. Not if you could sleep with some random client who means nothing to you. Not if you could hurt me like that.

Curtis:
I was drunk. And high. You and I were so far apart. You're the most special person in the world to me.

Ellen:
Curtis, what do you value about Sydney?

Curtis:
Everything. I mean, look at her. She's beautiful. And smart. And successful. And she cares so much about people, and justice, and doing the right thing. Sydney makes me a better person.

Sydney:
I make you a better person? You just did molly and cheated on me. I'm doing a great job.

Ellen:
Sydney, what do you need from Curtis to feel emotionally safe in this relationship again?

Sydney:
I don't know. Curtis works all hours. He gets late-night texts and leaves the house at a moment's notice. How can I ever trust him again?

Curtis:
You can have all my passwords, Syd. You can track me on my phone.

Sydney:
I shouldn't have to snoop on you like you're some naughty teenager.

Ellen:
Maybe it's just a temporary measure. Until Curtis can prove to you that he'll never betray you again.

Sydney:
What if he can't prove it to me? What if I never trust him again?

Curtis:
If you want to read every text or email I send for the rest of my life, you can.

Sydney:
I don't want to. And I shouldn't have to. That's my point.

Ellen:
There are strategies that can help you to rebuild your trust. *If* that's what you both want.

Curtis:
I'll do anything to earn her trust back. Whatever it takes.

Ellen:
Sydney? Is that what you want, too?

Sydney:
I think so.

42

Moments after Bianca spat in his face, Curtis had jumped in his car and taken off. He had no destination in mind, but he couldn't stay at the house and play nice with the two grifters camping in his driveway. When Sydney woke up and found him gone, she would worry and wonder. But after her behavior on the dance floor last night, she'd blame herself. She'd assume Curtis had gone somewhere to lick his wounds. She had no reason to suspect that their guests were scammers who were trying to destroy him.

As he shifted gears at a roundabout, Curtis berated himself for his gullibility. He'd known it was too much of a coincidence that the pair had broken down so close to the house, but the Australian accent had thrown him off. There was no way a couple of Aussie travelers could have any dirt on him. Still, it had felt wrong in his gut. He hadn't wanted to invite them in. He certainly hadn't wanted them to stay. He'd done it for Sydney. And now, thanks to them, he could lose her.

"Fuck!" He smacked the steering wheel with his palm. "Fuck, fuck, fuck!" This move to Spain was supposed to wipe the slate clean. The mess he'd been involved in back in New York was not supposed to follow him here. Emotion was building in his throat, tears threatening his vision, but he'd already spent the morning falling apart. He'd taken the wooded path toward town and sobbed, wailed, and cursed his bad luck. Now it was time for action. He would protect the life he and Sydney had built, at all costs.

The exit to Roses loomed ahead, and he took it, winding down the hill toward the seaside resort community. He hadn't planned to stop here, but it was a good place to blend in, to be another anonymous tourist. Roses was larger than Cadaqués, full of high-rise hotels and lively bars. He'd get a drink to calm his nerves and figure out how to make his problems go away. One way or another.

He parked the car in a lot and bought a ticket, stuck it on his dashboard. He walked with purpose along the main strip, stopping at a small tourist bar, a cluster of empty tables out front. Suddenly, he remembered his sweaty, bedraggled appearance, his eyes bloodshot from crying. But the attractive waitress didn't bat an eye at him when he sat down and ordered a double margarita.

As he waited for his drink, Curtis revisited Damian's blackmail threat. The fake Australian claimed to have in his possession a compromising video of Curtis, but he refused to show it. Curtis knew a video of him existed. The footage had already been used against him once. How the hell did Damian and Bianca get their hands on it? They were likely bluffing. Could he call them on it? Risk them showing it to Sydney or making it public?

The drink arrived, and he took a grateful sip. It was tart and strong, just what he needed. After a couple of gulps, the tequila softened his anxiety, blunted his rage. It allowed him to assess the situation more calmly. Curtis was not a bad man. He'd made some serious mistakes, become entangled with some evil people, but he was not a killer. Damian and Bianca had gotten it all wrong. He needed them to listen and be reasonable, to let him explain. But he could never explain what he'd done to Sydney.

Emotion clogged his throat again, so he took another drink and forced himself to swallow it. An affair Sydney could understand, eventually forgive. But what Curtis had done was much more complex, more nuanced. His wife existed in a world of rights and wrongs, of law and order. She'd defended rapists and murderers and con artists because it was due process, because she believed they deserved to be punished fairly. But punished nonetheless.

The last swallow of tequila washed away the emotions, and he focused on the business at hand. Damian and Bianca needed to go away before they could talk to Sydney. The easiest way to make that happen would be to pay them off. He signaled the waitress for another drink and perused the banking apps on his phone. Calculating in his head, he added up his checking, savings, and a handful of investment accounts. If he was willing to liquidate everything—which he wasn't—he'd still be short. There was no way he could convince Sydney to sell the house. Even if he could, it could take months to sell. Five million was a ridiculous ask, even if he *had* killed someone.

Sydney had some money from her mother, but he couldn't get his hands on it without arousing her suspicion. And it would only be a drop in the bucket. He considered applying for a bank loan, but he had no credit history in Spain and no job. Even if he were approved, no bank would give him a huge lump sum within a week. He knew about *hard money* loans, high-interest loans secured by valuable property. But when Curtis inevitably defaulted on his payments, they'd seize his house and his car. Syd would have questions, obviously.

The second drink arrived, and he drank heartily, licked the salty rim. Curtis had plenty of friends with money back in New York, but he couldn't ask them for help. He'd cut ties so completely after leaving the country. And calling for an urgent loan was desperate and pathetic. It meant admitting that he was a fuck-up, that his life was on a precipice. They'd all talk and speculate, but they'd be judging his failings. Moving to Spain and opening a winery had been met with eye rolls by plenty of them. Begging for money would be admitting he'd been delusional. That he'd failed.

That left Simon, his former partner, his former friend. Simon knew the mess Curtis had left behind in New York. He was angry, he felt betrayed, but they also had a history. Simon had known him since college; he knew Curtis was a decent guy who got caught up in something beyond his control. It was worth a shot.

Curtis finished his drink and signaled for the bill. As he waited, he checked his voicemail. It had to be Sydney, wondering where he'd gone, asking him to pick up milk or painkillers or toilet paper. But he heard her voice, full of emotion.

"I just want it to be you and me again... I love you."

His throat tightened. They were the words he'd been longing to hear from Syd, but were they coming too late? No. Because he was going to fix this.

He strolled along the seaside path again, rehearsing his script. He knew the best way to spin the story, the narrative most likely to elicit the desired outcome. After about ten minutes, he felt ready. It was midmorning in New York. Simon would have been at his desk for hours. He got up at 4:30 each morning to run on the treadmill, then headed to the office by 6:00. (He was one of those guys who did cold plunges and ate one meal a day.) Curtis swallowed deeply and dialed.

His friend answered on the second ring. "What do you want, Curtis?"

"I need some help. I'm sorry to ask, but I have nowhere else to turn."

"Why would I help you after the mess you left me in?" Simon snapped.

"I'm being blackmailed," Curtis explained. "There's a video of me that casts me in a bad light." He cleared his throat, went in for the kill. "It would reflect badly on the business if this footage was made public."

"Are you threatening my business now?" Simon's voice was a growl. "You really are a piece of shit."

"It's not a threat, Simon, it's a fact. My name's still on the masthead."

"It's nothing a good crisis PR team can't handle," Simon retorted, and it was clear he'd thought about this eventuality. "We already put out a press release that you're no longer part of the company."

"You know me, Simon." Curtis's voice hitched. "I made some mistakes, but I'm not a bad guy."

Simon's voice dripped with contempt. "You deserve whatever happens to you, Curtis. You lay down with dogs, you get fleas."

"I did it for the company!" he cried into the phone. "I did it for both of us!"

"Fuck you." And Simon hung up.

Anxiety seeped through the tequila fog, making Curtis's heart race, his vision blur. He stepped off the sidewalk, onto the sandy beach, and stumbled toward the water's edge. He stared out at the sea, the sun glinting off the turquoise water, and felt an overwhelming fatigue. His bone marrow had turned to lead, and he sank to his knees in the damp sand, dropped his head to his chest. For a moment, he considered weeping, but there were toddlers in the water, which meant their parents were nearby.

He stood, collected himself, focused on his final option. There was one more person he could call, a man with a vested interest in helping him make this problem go away. The thought made him feel sick and scared, but it was his only hope. He couldn't call this man after drinking tequila on an empty stomach, though. He needed to be stone-cold sober.

Curtis dragged himself off the beach and went to get a coffee.

43

Sydney was propped up in bed with her laptop when she heard Curtis's car creep down the driveway. Her chest tightened. Her husband could not come in here and discover what she was doing. As she listened to Curtis get out of the Citroën, let himself into the house, she stayed still, silent. After her husband admitted his affair, he'd felt like a stranger. But now it was worse than that. He felt like an enemy. Hopefully, Curtis would think she was napping, doing battle with the hangover from hell. Only when she heard him head to the kitchen did she allow herself to exhale and continue her search.

She may have been depressed, medicated, and hungover, but Sydney wasn't stupid. The fact that Curtis had changed his computer password meant he had something to hide from her. And given Damian's oblique warnings, her guest knew what it was. Syd could only assume this had something to do with Collette. Not long ago, the woman had blocked Syd from her Facebook account. Curtis and Collette must still be in contact.

Syd's mind had gone instantly to the worst-case scenario. Not only was Curtis still in touch with Collette, but he was in love with her. He had told Damian about his feelings, his plans to leave Sydney and build a life with his supposed one-night stand. Curtis was going to clean out their bank accounts and run away with the biotech exec. But then why had he confessed to the affair in the first place? And why had he moved them all the way to Spain? It made no sense for Curtis to invest so much in their future only to end it.

Sydney was an analytical person, a litigator. She knew the dangers of making assumptions, so she calmed herself and continued her research. But the internet provided no new information on Collette Jasper or her company, Anderson Technologies. It was almost as if neither entity existed online. That made no sense in Collette's industry, in today's connected world.

Sydney had heard the term *reverse image search*, but she didn't know how it worked. Thankfully, instructions were readily available online. Setting the laptop aside, Sydney grabbed her phone. She still had Collette's images stored in her photos. As instructed, she opened Google Lens and uploaded one of the pictures she'd screenshotted from Collette's Facebook page. It was the one where Collette held that fruity drink, laughed with the photographer. Almost instantly, Google recognized the photo from Instagram. Sydney clicked on the link, read the caption beneath the cheerful image.

lilabetts Having the best time in Mazatlan with my boo @bradhikes22 #blessed #Mexico #cocktail

Sydney clicked on the profile, saw another image of Collette in the top right corner. But the bio read:

Lila Betterave
Wifey, Dog-mom, Soup-lover
Vancouver, BC

What the hell was going on? Sydney scrolled through the images of Collette/Lila with her fit husband, her midsize rescue dog, her not-so-photogenic bowls of soup. The face that had haunted Sydney's dreams was not Collette Jasper. It belonged to a happily married aspiring online chef in Vancouver. So who the hell was Collette? Did she even exist?

With only the slightest prompting, Curtis had fallen on his sword about the affair, told Sydney he couldn't bear to keep his horrible secret from her. But had he made Collette up? Why would he hurt his wife like that? It was cruel and sadistic. Unless Curtis was covering up something even worse. Had Curtis been sleeping with someone Syd knew? One of her friends, even? Why else would he concoct such an elaborate lie?

"Sydney!" It was Damian bellowing her name from another room.

Tossing her phone aside, she crawled out of bed, moved tentatively down the hall. She found her husband and their guest in the kitchen, the tension between them palpable. But Curtis forced a smile when he saw her. "Damian suggested a frittata for dinner. Does that work for you?"

She took in his forced cheerfulness, the upbeat façade. "Sure. Whatever," she replied. "Call me when it's ready."

Syd had considered opting out of the meal like Bianca, but she hadn't eaten anything all day and realized she was starving. At the table, Damian held court, tried to draw Syd into the conversation, but her mind was stuck on Lila Betterave's Instagram profile, her husband's new password, and all that it implied. She knew Curtis had grown up in a house full of tension and secrets, but he'd assured her he'd done the work to heal from that toxic environment. Had he? Or was he hiding his true self from her, too? As soon as she'd washed her plate, she headed back to the bedroom to continue her research.

Curtis joined her about an hour later, looking pale and fatigued. Keeping secrets was clearly exhausting, but he gave her a wan smile as he sat at the foot of the bed. "Feeling any better?"

She put down her phone. "Yeah. How about you?"

"I'm good." His smile was forced. "I didn't sleep well last night after everything that happened."

Sydney caught the edge in his voice, but she would not be guilted. She'd already apologized for what she'd done at the nightclub. Curtis was the one who'd been lying for months. Digging in the drawer of her bedside table, she extracted a small bottle of pills. "Take one of these," she offered. "You'll feel better after a good night's sleep."

"Nah." Curtis pulled his shirt over his head. "I'll be fine."

"You're overtired," she urged. "That can make it hard to sleep and then you'll feel even worse tomorrow."

It was rare for Curtis to accept pharmaceutical help for any of his maladies, but she saw him waver. Smiling tenderly, she passed him a glass of water, put the pill into his hand. "Take it," she said gently, her eyes radiating care and concern. Curtis smiled weakly, nodded, and swallowed.

Syd waited until her husband was in a drugged sleep to climb gently out of bed. Slipping into her thin silk robe, she moved down the hall and into the kitchen, where she grabbed her pack of cigarettes from a drawer. *May as well kill two birds with one stone.* And if Curtis woke up, caught her outside the house in the night, she'd have an excuse handy.

The air was warm and still, smelled faintly sweet as she crept out to the small brick patio off the living room. She was on the opposite side of the house from the pool, away from their bedroom. She lit her cigarette and inhaled deeply. For a moment, she closed her eyes, let the nicotine do its thing. Then she pulled out her phone and dialed.

It was evening in New York, but she'd still be able to catch Curtis's former assistant, who regularly worked late. Felicia Elliott had been her husband's right hand for at least five years. When Curtis left, Simon kept her on, moved her into a contracts position. Felicia and Sydney had been on friendly terms, joking at the holiday party about their dual roles managing Curtis's life.

"Hi, Sydney! Or should I say *Hola*?"

"How are you, Felicia?"

"Can't complain. How's life in Spain?"

"Good." Syd got to the point. "Could you look up a contract for me? A company called Anderson Technologies. On Franklin Street."

Sydney had an excuse ready (a friend looking into leasing a space Curtis had previously mentioned) but Felicia didn't ask for one. Her fingers tapped on the keyboard. "There's no record of a lease for that company."

"Try the client's name. Collette Jasper."

After a moment, Felicia said, "There's still nothing."

Sydney considered confiding in Curtis's former admin assistant. If Syd's husband had been having an affair, Felicia had been in a good position to know. But the woman had been retained for her loyalty and discretion. She wouldn't betray Curtis, even now. For all Syd knew, Curtis could have been sleeping with Felicia herself.

"That's so strange," Sydney said. "I appreciate you trying."

She slipped the phone back in her pocket, took a deep drag on her cigarette. Suddenly, she sensed a presence behind her. Whirling around, she saw Bianca's still form lurking in the doorway.

"Jesus Christ!" Syd pressed a hand to her hammering heart. "You scared me." Why were the Australians always sneaking up on her? It was unnerving. And creepy.

"Sorry." Bianca smiled. "What are you doing out here?"

None of your business. "Sneaking a cigarette," Sydney fibbed, dropping her butt on the bricks. "Don't tell Curtis."

"Your secret's safe with me." Bianca walked toward her. "I thought I heard you on the phone."

Syd muttered an excuse about work, but Bianca was not deterred. "Who's Collette Jasper?"

She was prying, but Sydney was ready for it.

"No one. An old client of mine."

"Why are you looking for her?" the other woman pressed.

And that was when Sydney noticed it. Or the lack of it. "What happened to your accent, Bianca?"

It was Bianca's turn for excuses. She'd stammered a lame explanation, offered to make Sydney eggs, then backed her way into the house.

"Good night, Syd."

"Night."

Syd wanted another cigarette—she wanted to smoke a whole pack—but she stopped herself. She was overwhelmed, confused, and her mind was racing with suspicious thoughts. Collette Jasper did not exist. The Australians were not who they said they were.

What the fuck was Curtis hiding from her now?

Sydney Cleary and Curtis Lowe, Couples' Counseling Session
Ellen Dwyer, Psychologist, PsyD
July 22

THERAPY PROGRESS NOTES—SESSION 5.

Sydney doubts Curtis's authenticity in trying to regain her trust. She feels that his attempts are too contrived to be true. She fears they could be manipulative and that once she allows herself to trust him, he'll betray her again. She's not ready to risk her emotional safety with him.

Curtis needs to take concrete <u>actions</u> (not just words) to restore his wife's trust. Sharing his passwords was a positive gesture, but he'll need to continue to be transparent or Sydney will retreat into her pain and mistrust.

When asked what he values about Sydney, Curtis said: She makes me a better person. This is a very self-centered response. Are the reasons he's fighting for his marriage coming from a place of love for his partner? Or from his ego?

44

That morning, Curtis stood in the driveway watching Damian and Bianca take off in his Citroën. It was evident by the grinding of gears that Damian didn't really know how to drive a manual transmission. Curtis would likely have to replace his clutch, but it wasn't like he could refuse Damian's request to use the car. And he wanted the visitors gone. Their lingering presence made him tense, angry, and sick to his stomach. Besides that, he had a lot to deal with today.

Curtis had been hiding his burner phone under the driver's seat of his car since they began tearing the shed apart. Luckily, he'd brought it inside with him last night, turned it off, and hid it in the pocket of a winter coat buried in the front closet. Entering the house, he digs into the closet and retrieves the device, hides it deep in the pocket of his shorts. He has an essential call to make, but there can be no record of it on his regular phone. Any connection to this man would be the kiss of death for his marriage, his entire reputation. But first things first...

Sydney is waiting at the table, hands on a mug of coffee, her expression dark. He sits across from her and picks up his cup, takes a sip. The coffee is cold, and the milk has curdled. Or maybe it's just the sour taste in his mouth. He sets down the mug, pushes it away.

"Bianca and Damian need to go," Sydney says. Again. "He's not even able to help around here, so what's the point of having them stay?"

"*You* invited them," he replies, because he can't help himself. He hadn't wanted the travelers to move in in the first place, and now he's forced to fight for them to remain. The cognitive dissonance is exhausting.

"And now I'm going to disinvite them," she retorts. "If you're too afraid to do it."

It's a dig, but he won't rise to it. He must convince Sydney not to ask the fake Aussies to leave. If she does, they'll refuse. Damian might come up with an excuse, but Bianca won't. She'll relish the opportunity to destroy his marriage, to tell Syd about his connection to some dead woman he doesn't even know. And then everything else will come out, and his marriage will fall apart.

He keeps his voice calm. "They've done a lot of free labor around here, and I think kicking them out—and sticking them with a massive towing bill—is a shitty way to repay them."

Sydney appears to take this in, but then her eyes narrow. "Is there anything you want to tell me, Curtis?"

Does his wife know something? Or is she simply suspicious? Curtis can't reveal his secrets now, not when he's so close to making all their problems go away. So he plays dumb.

"Like what?"

"Anything you'd like to tell me about Collette?"

"For God's sake, Syd. I told you everything in therapy."

"Damian's been acting weird. Is something going on with you two?"

"I just watched him make out with my wife at a nightclub," Curtis retorts. "Some tension is to be expected, don't you think?"

Her eyes drift down to the table. "I said I was sorry."

"I know. And I forgive you. But it's going to take some time for me to feel comfortable around Damian and Bianca again."

"Then why don't you want them to leave—*now*—like I do?"

"I *do* want them gone." He reaches for her hand. "I can't wait until it's just the two of us again. But in a few days their van will be fixed. Then they can leave without any bad blood. And without us seeming like a couple of privileged assholes who took advantage of their situation."

"Fine," she sighs. She gets up and takes their cups to the sink. "I'm going to do some sanding in the downstairs bathroom."

"Great. I'll be out in the shed. Holler if you need me."

Curtis walks toward the dilapidated building, but he continues past it, toward the wooded patch at the back of the property. The big oak tree will provide privacy. It had shielded the *mysterious smoker*, who he knows wasn't Collette or Teddy Drew flown in from New York to spy on them. It wasn't a random farmer either. It was Bianca or Damian smoking back there, hiding the machete and gloves to fuel fear and paranoia in their hosts. When he reaches the tree, he stands behind it, surveys the property to ensure he's alone. He can't risk Syd overhearing this conversation.

He pulls out the burner phone and dials. The man he is attempting to contact is nearly impossible to reach, protected by a phalanx of gatekeepers tasked with screening out all but the most vital communications. West Beatty is rich, respected, and high profile in the business and tech communities, but rumors swirl around him. He's adept at ensuring none of them stick, that loose ends are always tied up. Curtis had called his number twice yesterday, had expressed the urgency of the situation. He needs West to answer this time.

Thankfully, a receptionist patches him through to a PA who puts him on hold. His heart thuds in his chest as he waits for West to come to the phone.

"You disappeared on me, Curtis." There's no greeting, just the smooth voice, the subtle, indistinguishable accent of a citizen of the world. "That wasn't very cool."

"I set you up, though," Curtis replies quickly. "Simon will take care of you."

"Let's hope so."

Curtis ignores the subtle threat, forges ahead. "I've run into a problem. And it affects you, too."

"I'll call back." Abruptly, the line goes dead.

Curtis waits, pulse pounding, mouth dry, for the phone to ring. If West has abandoned him, blocked his calls, he's truly fucked. Thankfully, the phone buzzes moments later.

"This is a secure line," West says. "Continue."

The words pour out of Curtis, a stream of desperate verbal vomit. He tells West about the travelers who turned up at his home, how they pretended they were Aussies, how they knew things that had happened back in New York. He explains that a young woman is dead, that he doesn't know how she died but they (mistakenly) think Curtis had something to do with it. He tells West that they're blackmailing him, that they want five million dollars or they'll go public with everything they know.

West asks, "Was my name mentioned?"

For a moment, Curtis ponders the most beneficial response. If he says yes, West will feel more vulnerable, more likely to come to his aid. But he may blame Curtis for leaking his name to the pair, and he can't afford to piss this guy off.

"No."

"Oh, Curtis..." West says his name like he's scolding a puppy that pissed on the carpet. "How did you let this happen?"

"*I* didn't let it happen. They found out through this dead girl."

"I don't know anything about a dead girl."

"Neither do I!" Curtis cries but quickly composes himself. "You know my role in this whole thing was peripheral."

"Was it, though? You were essential to making the whole operation work. And you were well aware what was going on at those events."

"I didn't want to be involved. I had no choice! Why should I have to pay the price alone?"

"Because you're the one who got caught."

Five million bucks is pocket change for this tech bro. He's got money to invest in new technologies, in films, in experimental anti-aging drugs. He owns houses around the world, islands in the middle of nowhere. It would be so painless for him to end Curtis's nightmare.

He chokes on a sob, blurts the words. "It's just five million, West. Why won't you help me?"

"If you pay these two off, do you really think they'll disappear for good?"

The rhetorical delivery slips past Curtis. He's never been blackmailed before, but Damian had sounded sincere. He has plans for his future as a multimillionaire, a life of privilege and hedonism.

"Yeah, I think they will."

"Really?" Curtis hears the clink of ice in West's drink. Curtis doesn't know where in the world the magnate is, but it must be evening there. He's likely sipping an eighty-year-old Scotch. "Someone this couple cared about is dead. A girl. And they blame you. But you think they'll ride off into the sunset with their five mill? Live happily ever after and forget the information that would destroy us both?"

There's no missing the skepticism this time. Curtis's face burns. He's been so naïve, so foolish.

"I learned a long time ago not to fall for grifts," West continues. "Paying this couple off is not the solution. They need to disappear. For good."

"You're right." Curtis's voice trembles. "Can you...help?"

"I could." The ice cubes clink again. "But that could get messy. I couldn't guarantee your safety. Or your wife's."

"So you want *me* to do it?"

"Didn't your mother teach you to clean up after yourself, Curtis?"

"I'm not a killer. I wouldn't know how!"

"You're a smart guy. I think you can figure it out."

"No. I won't do it." He feels perilously close to tears. "I—I can't."

"Fine." He hears the oily smile in West's voice. "At some point in the next twenty-four hours a man is going to show up at your house. He'll have a semiautomatic weapon, and he's going to open fire on this couple. Of course, he may not be able to distinguish you and your wife from these blackmailers. And he won't want to leave any witnesses."

The threat is overt. Terrifying.

"I'll take care of it," Curtis says, voice shaking. "Don't send anyone."

"Let me know when it's done." The ice cubes rattle as West finishes his drink. "It's a great house, Curtis. Love those arched windows."

The compliment is a ruse. West knows the house. He's been keeping tabs on Curtis all along. He could send someone there in a heartbeat.

"It's handled," Curtis croaks. "I promise."

He hangs up.

45

Peeking out the living room window, Sydney watches her husband walk toward the winery shed, then continue toward the back fence line. He glances briefly over his shoulder to see if she's watching, so she ducks her head out of view. Curtis is moving toward the secluded area behind the big oak tree, with its tall grass and thick brush. It's the spot where the farmer had been smoking. *If* it had been a farmer. Sydney doesn't trust Damian's assurances anymore.

Curtis clearly wants privacy. He must be making a phone call. Syd is desperate to know who her husband is calling and what he's saying, but there's no way she can approach him without being noticed. There's nowhere for her to hide and eavesdrop. So she will take advantage of her time alone in the house. She will find out who Bianca and Damian really are.

Despite her solitude, Syd finds herself tiptoeing down the tiled hallway, holding her breath as she opens the door to the guest bedroom. She exhales in a puff of disgust as she takes in the mess. Clothes are tossed carelessly on the floor. The bedside table is littered with bottles of sunscreen, tubes of lip balm, crumb-coated plates, and half-empty water glasses. A cup of coffee perches on the dresser, growing scum on its surface. And there's a discarded beer bottle tossed in a corner, as if their beautiful home is a frat house. Syd feels a surge of anger at the lack of respect, but she channels it into determination. She enters the room, closing the door behind her.

Sydney rifles through the drawers of the nightstand and dresser, but she finds nothing of interest. Dropping to her knees, she digs through the duffel bags on the floor. Damian's contains only clothes—a mix of dirty and clean—that she would rather not touch. She moves on to Bianca's bag, sorting through her bikinis and T-shirts, her tiny shorts and a couple of sundresses. At the bottom of the sack, Syd finds a packet of birth control pills and a small box of tampons. She tips the box upside down, the tampons falling out onto the floor. She hears the clink of metal hitting the tile.

It's a single key on a ring. Picking it up, Syd reads the tag. It's the name of a secondhand car dealership in Barcelona. She's found the key to the van. Inside that vehicle, she will find all of Damian and Bianca's secrets. Syd stuffs the tampons back into the box and shoves it into the duffel bag. Clutching the key in her hand, she hurries outside.

The air is still and quiet as she crunches across the gravel toward the van. Thankfully, there's no sign of her husband or of the guests returning in the Citroën. Sticking the key into the lock of the van's panel door, Syd slides it open and climbs inside. It's oppressively hot in the vehicle, almost airless, but she closes the door behind her. If Damian and Bianca return, she doesn't want to be discovered. And she doesn't want to explain her sleuthing to Curtis either.

In contrast to the guest room, the van is tidy. The couple spends very little time in here, and it's *their* space. They treat it with respect, unlike Sydney's house. She starts by opening the top storage bin and finds it largely empty except for a few camping staples: matches, bug spray, and a small Swiss Army knife. It's not nearly the supply one would expect for a couple who's been living in their van for over a month.

Taking the lid off the next bin, she inhales sharply. Inside is a coil of yellow rope, a roll of electrical tape, and a small hammer. Damian is a builder. Owning these items is far from suspicious. He could have bought them for the winery or another building project. Or he could be planning to beat Curtis to death with the hammer, tie up Sydney with the rope, and tape her mouth shut so she can't scream. Perhaps she's overreacting, but she no longer trusts Damian and his partner. Her head swims, and she feels nauseated in the stifling heat.

The final storage bin contains a pack of cigarettes, a bottle of drugstore perfume, and a pair of leather work gloves. Sydney recognizes the gloves instantly. They were hidden behind the oak tree next to the machete. So it was Damian sneaking cigarettes out there, not some creepy stranger. He must have been hiding his habit from Bianca, because of her asthma. But where is the machete Sydney had found?

Dropping to all fours, Sydney digs under the camping bed. There's nothing there but dust bunnies and sand. She moves to a kneeling position and lifts the mattress, steeling herself to find sex toys or condoms or dirty tissues, but there's nothing there. She's about to lower the mattress when something catches her eye in the far corner.

Passports.

Sydney reaches for the dark blue booklets. A lot of countries issue passports in this color, and Australia could very well be one of them. But before she even looks at the front cover she knows. The words, embossed in gold, validate her suspicions.

Passport
United States of America

Opening the first one, she looks at Damian's photo. His hair is shorter, his expression serious. His full name is Damian Iain Walsh, born in Everett, Washington, in 1997. Bianca Leigh Muller was born in Indiana later that year. The pair has been lying about their provenance. Why?

It could have been a game. Sydney can see the fun in pretending to be someone else, talking with a foreign accent. It's a little immature, but Damian and Bianca are younger. Or does this couple have a reason to hide the fact that they're American? Do they know Curtis and Syd from back home? Damian and Bianca were born in states that Sydney has never even visited, but it doesn't mean they still live there.

They could live in New York. They could have some connection to Curtis and Syd.

In Syd's former career, she'd made plenty of enemies. Normally, she'd assume the couple were here because of her. But Curtis has been acting so strange, keeping secrets, making surreptitious phone calls. She'd given him a chance to come clean this morning and he'd refused it. All his talk in therapy about honesty and transparency had been bullshit. He's hiding something. But what?

She sifts through a few empty cubbyholes before climbing into the van's cab. Opening the glove box, she rifles through the insurance papers, the registration, some napkins from a café. She pulls out a small square device that resembles an electrical plug. At first, she thinks it's an electrical adapter, transforming American voltage to European, but upon further inspection she realizes it's a part for a car. She hurriedly snaps some photos before returning it and slams the glove compartment closed.

Back in the house, she returns the key to the tampon box, then moves into the living room. On the sofa, she uploads the photos to her new favorite tool, Google Lens. The pluglike device she found is a fuel pump relay. When removed, the fuel pump won't work, rendering a vehicle useless. So Bianca and Damian had broken down on purpose. By installing that relay, their van is fully operational. The discovery is not unsurprising. The couple is here for a reason.

Setting her phone aside, Syd feels regret and shame press down on her like a landslide. Her chest is weighted, her breath trapped in shriveled lungs. She'd been so lonely in her pain, so desperate for company, that she'd invited the couple to stay. She'd flirted with them, and kissed them, and now the remembrance turns her stomach. It's more than just "the ick." This pair could be dangerous, and she wants them gone. But now Curtis won't let them leave.

She considers going to her husband, telling him everything she knows. She could demand the truth, insist on the transparency he's always promised her. But she realizes that would be pointless.

Everyone has been lying to her, including Curtis. She can't believe anything he says.

Sydney needs to find out what the hell they're hiding from her before someone gets hurt.

Or worse.

46

Curtis sits on the ground a couple of feet from the puddle of bile he just spewed into the grass. Tears run unchecked down his face, comingling with the snot streaming from his nose. He's having an emotional breakdown. It's pathetic. And disgusting. Damian has continually taunted Curtis for his weakness, his softness, and he's right. Curtis is a coward, far too tender for the task at hand. He wipes a sleeve across his face, but it has little effect. He's a mess. He needs to pull himself together. But he can't, not yet. The ugly truth of his situation twists his insides, rattles his psyche.

He'd been stupid to think he could pay off his blackmailers, that the money would make Bianca and Damian go away for good. But what the hell did he know about extortion? He had been a legitimate businessman until West Beatty entered his orbit last year. Curtis remembers the moment he met him, the excitement, the sense of opportunity. He'd lunged at the chance to be involved with Beatty's empire, ignored the rumors that swirled around the mogul. And now he'll pay the ultimate price...unless he acts.

Curtis has made some enormous mistakes in his life. He's done things that were legally gray, ethically ambiguous, morally repugnant... but he's not a criminal. And he's definitely not a killer. Soon he will be. There's no other choice. If he doesn't take care of Damian and Bianca—and fast—one of West Beatty's hired guns will show up here with a semiautomatic weapon. This man will kill them all, leave no witnesses. Curtis crawls onto his hands and knees and vomits again.

Even as a boy, Curtis was never physical, never strong. He didn't have a sibling to teach him to wrestle and play fight. He's never thrown or felt a punch. The world he inhabited valued intelligence, wit, money, and education. Not brute force, not physical aggression. The sports he played were noncontact, like tennis and golf, sports that relied on skill over power. And now he's being called upon to murder two people. How the hell did he get here?

Wiping his mouth with his sleeve, he finds his footing. It's tempting to crumple again, to curl into a ball and moan and wail about his hopeless situation, but there's no time to waste. Curtis must come up with a plan to exterminate his guests and save his wife. He takes a step on watery legs, and then another, moving away from the house, following the fence line. He can't see Sydney yet. Not until he's concocted a plan that will protect them. But how?

Curtis can almost imagine shooting Damian and Bianca. A gun is the kind of weapon that provides physical and emotional distance. He might even enjoy watching Damian beg for his life before he puts a bullet in his chest. But Curtis knows that guns are hard to get in Spain. He'd investigated acquiring one for protection when they first bought this remote house. He would have had to take lessons and undergo background checks. And Syd was against it, so he'd given up. *Fuck.* It would have made this so much simpler.

Stumbling on the rutted hillside, he slows his gait, focuses his attention on a solution. Could he hire a hit man on the dark web? He knows enough about the shady side of the internet to know he'd need to download a special browser, and then... what? Would he type in "hit man wanted, Cadaqués"? What are the odds that a murderer-for-hire lives in the general area? There are likely hit men in Spain, but could he communicate his needs without the help of Google Translate? (Duolingo hadn't covered employing assassins.) If Curtis managed to find someone, how long would it take him to get here? Could he arrive and kill Bianca and Damian before West Beatty could send a thug here to take care of them all?

He rustles through the tall grass, moving numbly down the incline of the north property line. Brainstorming about gun licenses and hit men is simply procrastination, avoidance. Because Curtis knows he will have to take care of these two himself. And he'll have to do it tonight. But how? Damian is so strong. Curtis will have to get him drunk, maybe crush some of Sydney's sedatives into his drink. If he's drugged, Curtis will be able to strangle him to death or smother him with a pillow. If Bianca wakes up, he could slit her throat with a kitchen knife. These methods sound slow and gory, and his guts churn, but there's nothing left in his stomach to throw up.

Heading east at the bottom of the hill, he slows his gait. He's nearing the house now, coming up toward the pool. But he can't face Sydney until he's calmed himself, until his plan to save their lives is solidified. When he takes a heavy step, the toe of his shoe hits a rotted log, pitches him headfirst into the tall grass. He lands on his right forearm. He'll likely have a deep bruise tomorrow, but he feels no pain now. His nervous system is too overwrought to deal with anything else.

As he attempts to drag himself up, his shin hits something hard. Something metal. He pauses, crouches down on his haunches. His hands sift through the tall stalks and land on an object. It's the machete.

Damian had told Curtis the weapon was locked in the van, but he'd obviously lied. The machete has been hidden here so no one can find it. Damian must be planning to use it. Will he hack Curtis to pieces if he doesn't come up with the money? Or will Damian get the money first and *then* chop him up? What about Sydney? Would Damian attack her, too? Would Curtis be able to protect his wife from a bigger man armed with a blade like this?

Finding the weapon is a sign. It's a gift. Gripping the handle, Curtis feels the power and the potential. He will put the machete in his bedroom closet. When the time is right, he'll strike. Tonight. He refuses to think about the spurting blood, the crunching of bone, the brain matter sprayed on the guest bedroom walls. He blocks out Bianca's screams as Curtis cuts into her partner's carotid artery, Sydney's desperate pleas for him to stop the massacre. He has to kill the other couple. It's the only way to keep his wife safe.

He'll be caught, of course. Curtis will go down for murder, pay the ultimate price. He'll be branded a psychopath, a monster, and will spend his life in jail. Maybe he'll swallow Sydney's personal pharmacy, wash it down with a bottle of booze, and take the easy way out. Because he knows Sydney will call the *policía*, that she'll turn him in. He will beg and plead and try to explain, but she'd never cover this up for him. She's too decent. She's too good. That's why he loves her. It's why he has to save her.

Concealing the machete at his side, he heads back toward the house.

DAMIAN AND BIANCA

47

Damian watches his partner pick at the piece of white fish on her plate, moving it around without taking a bite. She'd complained of being hungry at the beach, but now she's barely eating. She's drinking, though. Bianca is halfway through her second glass of white wine. She brings the glass to her lips, eyes fixed on the stunning view their patio table offers.

"Look at the color of the water," Damian says, keeping the conversation upbeat. "You never see anything like this back home." He forks up some fish from his own plate, stuffs it into his mouth. "And this fish is so fresh. You should eat, babe."

"I had too much pan con tomate," she mumbles, setting down her wineglass. "I'm full."

"Save room for dinner. Curtis will make us anything we want." He's trying to make this fun—they should savor Curtis's servitude—but Bianca doesn't want to play.

"I've lost my appetite." She fixes him with glare. "Since you told me you want to let Curtis off the hook, I feel sick to my stomach."

Damian had expected this. He exhales through his nose, maintains a calm tone. "I'm not *letting him off the hook*. But I'm not going to walk away with nothing either. We have our future to think about."

"My sister doesn't have a future thanks to Curtis Lowe." Bianca picks up her wine and drinks. "That's all I care about."

"That's a foolish attitude."

"Fuck you," she snaps, and he sees a woman at the next table glance over at them.

Damian leans forward, keeps his voice low. "We came here to hurt Curtis, and we will. But we had an agreement. We had a plan."

"You're the one backing out of our plan. You're so worried about Sydney that you're willing to let Curtis skate for what he's done."

"He'll still suffer, Bianca. He'll still lose his wife. And his house." He leans back and takes a sip of his cold Spanish beer. "If we're too rigid, he might break down and tell Sydney everything. We should be ready to accept a couple mill if that's the best he can do."

"I'm not haggling over my sister's life."

Damian's temper swells, and he feels heat flushing his face. "What about *my* life?" he growls. "I've given up so much for you and that fucking kid. It's about time I got what *I* wanted."

For a tense moment, Bianca doesn't speak; she just stares at him with her wild eyes. They're so cold, so dangerous. He expects her to toss her wine in his face or throw the glass. But she scrapes her chair back. "I'll meet you at the car later. I've got some errands to run."

Damian sips his beer, breathes, tries to get his heart rate to return to normal. When their server passes by, he signals for the bill. As he waits, he picks up Bianca's glass and finishes the rest of her wine. He knows his partner will calm down eventually, but he also knows she won't change her mind. She's always been so stubborn, so immovable. To Bianca, five million dollars equals Curtis Lowe's ruination. Anything less means he got away with murder.

Damian pays *la cuenta* when it comes, leaving a decent tip. He's slightly embarrassed by his public fight with Bianca, and besides, soon money will be no object. He nods to the woman at the next table who'd heard his girlfriend curse at him and walks out toward the bay. Bianca needs time to cool off, so he steers clear of the shops and strolls the seaside path toward Portlligat.

For the first time since they met, Damian can envision a life without his childhood sweetheart. He's loved her since they were kids, but he can picture a future on his own now. He can imagine himself happy—happi*er*—without Bianca's dark, wounded presence. If he's forced to choose between his partner and a couple million, he'll take the money. He can't go backward, not now that he's come this far. He'll take whatever Curtis offers, and he'll split. Bianca can stay behind and wreak her havoc.

Damian has never articulated the thought out loud, but he doesn't believe Curtis killed Lyric. Not *technically*, anyway. Is Curtis culpable? Probably. But he's just one of a confluence of factors that contributed to the girl's death. Deep down, Bianca knows it's true, but she's so desperate for someone to blame that she's convinced herself that Curtis is responsible. She believes the only way she can find any peace or healing is by ruining him.

Bianca had been foolish to think that Lyric would recover from her trauma simply by changing her scenery. Moving back to Indiana, moving in with them, was not going to be a cure-all after the abuse she'd suffered. The kid was damaged, she probably needed therapy, but Bianca didn't think that way. And they couldn't afford it. Lyric was still Yvonne's dependent, and the woman couldn't keep a job long enough to get insurance.

Lyric had only been living with them a month or so when the problems started. Bianca had convinced her sister to return to high school, to get her diploma. Or so she'd thought. A call from the school counselor informed her otherwise. The counselor had already called Yvonne but had been met with indifference, so she contacted Bianca.

"Lyric hasn't been coming to class," she said. "She's on academic probation. If she doesn't start turning up, she'll be expelled."

"I'll talk to her," Bianca promised.

"There's something else..." the counselor had said. "I suspect your sister is abusing drugs. I gave your mother the name of a substance abuse counselor, but Lyric hasn't gone to see him. She needs help, Bianca. She can't do this on her own."

"I'll take care of it."

But Bianca couldn't heal a traumatized, drug-addicted child. She was too young and damaged herself. She'd made a valiant effort, though. Bianca read books on teen addiction, watched YouTube videos with drug counselors. At first, she tried patience and understanding with her sister. When that had no effect, she came down hard, setting boundaries and offering ultimatums. But Lyric had always been adept at manipulation and the drugs made her even more wily. She played her mom and her big sister against each other, lied to get what she wanted. Lyric was too far gone. The tragic ending was already written.

Damian has reached the end of the paved path where the road turns inland, gets hot and dusty. He takes off his cap, pushes back his sweaty hair. His mouth is furry from too much beer and not enough water. He turns back toward town and sees the dark clouds gathering in the distance. He's grown accustomed to endless blue skies, but a storm is brewing. Bianca will need more time to cool off, but he's not going to stand out here and get drenched. As he heads to the car, his mind drifts back to Indiana, to that terrible night.

Bianca's phone had rung around 2:00 a.m. Damian had smoked a joint before bed, so he'd been slow to wake up. He was still coming to when Bianca answered and started screaming. He heard her terror, and he heard her rage. It was Yvonne on the phone. Lyric was in the hospital. She'd overdosed.

By the time they arrived, the girl was dead. Well, her brain was dead; her young body was refusing to shut down, clinging to life out of habit, not desire. But there was no hope of recovery. The doctors counseled Yvonne to let her go, but Bianca refused. She held Lyric's limp hand and begged her to come back, as if she could repair the girl's damaged brain through sheer force of will. But of course, she couldn't. The next day, they let her go.

Damian had taken Bianca home, held her in his arms, tried to soothe her with his words.

"You were a good sister. This isn't your fault."

"I know."

"Lyric was an addict. There's no one to blame."

Bianca had turned her dry eyes up to his. "Yes, there is. His name is Curtis Lowe."

48

Bianca wanders through the winding streets of Cadaqués on autopilot, unmoved by the bright sprays of bougainvillea spilling over the quaint passageways, the tourists posing for selfies against the stunning backdrops. She pauses to look at sun hats and sarongs, inspects earrings and bracelets made of shells, stones, and strings. From the outside, she appears to be any other tourist shopping for clothing and mementos. But inside, she's seething.

Damian has betrayed her, lured her here under false pretenses. She knew their objectives were different, but she'd thought they were aligned. Now Damian has revealed that they're not. When had her partner become so self-serving? Is his infatuation with Sydney playing into his selfishness? All he cares about is getting enough money to get out of Indiana, to spend his life posing as a sophisticated expat. He'll accept whatever cash he can get so he can build a new European life. He doesn't care if Curtis Lowe suffers at all.

His indifference isn't entirely surprising. Damian knows what Bianca told him, but he wasn't there. He didn't see Lyric's visceral reaction, didn't see her terror and pain. Bianca was the only eyewitness to the moment when her sister recognized her tormentor. And unlike Damian, that scene is seared in her memory.

On their last day in New York, Bianca had collected the remnants of Lyric's big-city life and shoved them into two backpacks. The roommates were upset to be losing a third of their rent, so Bianca Venmoed them eight hundred bucks and told them to find a replacement for her sister. It wasn't enough, but it was all she could afford. The Chicago roommate looked about to complain but then thought better of it. Bianca knew she could be intimidating.

She put a backpack on her back, balanced the second one on top of her rolling suitcase. Lyric was feeling better, but she still seemed brittle, fragile, and so small. Lyric carried her sister's purse, held on to her arm as they walked through the bustling streets to the subway. They'd take the train uptown to the Port Authority, catch the express bus to the airport. And then they could put this disturbing chapter behind them.

They were about a block from the station when Lyric abruptly stopped walking. Bianca turned, the heavy backpack swaying, making her stagger.

"What?" Bianca asked, but her sister was mute. The girl's face drained of color, became a mask of anguish, even fear. Lyric bent double and vomited on the sidewalk.

"Jesus!" Bianca cried, resting a comforting hand on her sister's back. "What's wrong? Are you still sick?"

Lyric righted herself, her eyes fixed on a building just ahead of them. She pointed with a shaking hand, breathed a single word: "Him."

Bianca followed her sister's gaze to a large sign in the window of a vacant building: FOR LEASE. In the bottom corner was a man's smiling face, technically attractive but too slick, too greasy. Beneath his smarmy face were the words:

Call Curtis Lowe today!

"Who is he?" Bianca demanded.

"He was there," Lyric whispered. "I...I remember his hands on me." She scrunched her face, shook her head against the memory. "His breath."

"We're going home. He can't hurt you anymore."

They continued down the street, but Bianca glanced over her

shoulder at that sign. She took in the face and the name, branded them on her brain. This was the man responsible for her sister's pain. She would never forget him.

The sky is darkening, clouds covering the narrow strip of sky above her. Rain is imminent, so Bianca pops into a shop, buys herself a bracelet. It's a cheap bauble to commemorate her first trip to Spain. Despite the ugliness of her mission, she likes it here: the scenery, the people, the way afternoon naps are a part of their culture. But she'll be gone soon, one way or another.

Outside, fat raindrops have begun to fall, and she hears a crack of thunder. She could head to the car, hope Damian is already there, but she's not ready to go back to the hillside house, to return to playing the sweet, stupid Aussie. Continuing down the sloping passageway, she walks by a small bar. It's just a hole-in-the-wall, dark and dank in contrast to the bright open restaurants. This is a bar for people like her, whose inner turmoil is at odds with the brilliant scenery. It's also shelter from the coming storm. She's already had two glasses of wine; one more and she'll be officially drunk, but still she backtracks and enters.

There are two round tables occupied by older Spanish men drinking vermut, snacking on olives. She sees four empty stools at the bar, so she perches on one. The bartender approaches, a young Spaniard with dark eyes, a slight frame. She orders a glass of white wine in English, and he nods, heads to the fridge. Bianca plays with the bracelet on her wrist as she waits, listens to the Spanish music playing, the men behind her bickering and laughing. She likes it in here. It feels good. She might stay all day, let Damian go back without her.

The bartender returns, balancing a glass almost full to the rim. She laughs, makes a comment on the heavy pour.

"You look like you need it," he says in heavily accented English.

"Do I?" She's flirting. It comes so naturally. This young man is into her; it's obvious in his gaze, his body language, not to mention the enormous drink he's offering her.

She already knows what comes next. It's probably ill-advised, but she will do it. Because sex with this random bartender will allow her to stop feeling. For those eight to twelve minutes, it will make the pain and rage go away, expunge her disappointment and disillusionment.

The bartender leans on the bar, his face close to hers. His eyes are deep and sexy, and Bianca focuses on them, choosing to ignore his rather tiny hands and how he needs to trim his nails.

"Where are you from?" he asks.

"Canada."

"My name is Carlos."

"Melissa," she lies. Because Melissa the Canadian doesn't have a dead sister. And she didn't come to Spain to seek revenge for her murder. Melissa is just a girl on vacation, day-drinking in a dingy bar, about to have fast, rough sex in a bathroom or a storage closet. Melissa doesn't have to feel bad about what she's about to do.

She doesn't have to feel anything at all.

49

Damian sits in Curtis's car, listens to the rain pummeling the metal roof. Bianca is still wandering the streets, getting drenched, so focused on her rage and hate that she's impervious to the weather. He's texted her a bunch of times, tried to call, but her phone is off or set to Do Not Disturb. That means she's still not ready to play nice. But how long is he supposed to sit here and wait for her to calm down? As long as it takes. He has no choice.

He can't leave Bianca in town in the middle of a rainstorm. The steep trail that leads back to the house would be treacherous in this weather, and Spain's tragic history with floods runs through his memory. Besides, returning without his girlfriend would elicit too many questions. Sydney would be concerned, of course, would insist on searching for Bianca. If she found her, who knows what Bianca would say to Syd one-on-one. If Bianca chose to reveal all of Curtis's dirty secrets, their mark would have no reason to pay them the money. Damian can't let that happen.

In the distance he can just make out a couple headed his way. The man holds a canvas jacket over their heads, providing a little shelter from the deluge. The woman is laughing, clutching his arm. She's wearing shorts and a T-shirt, and she's a little unsteady on her feet. Tipsy, probably. The couple has come from a boozy lunch or an afternoon at a bar.

As they move closer, he realizes the woman is Bianca. The couple's heads are obscured by the jacket, but he doesn't need to see her face to know it's her. He recognizes her walk, her body, her clothes. And the way she holds on to this man like she gives a shit about him when she really doesn't.

The pair stop several yards from the car, and Bianca puts her lips close to the man's ear. The guy (Christ, how old is he? He looks fifteen.) peers over at Damian, waiting in the car like a cuckold. The man's surprise and confusion are visible even from here. Bianca kisses his cheek and runs through the rain to the Citroën.

"Who was that?" Damian asks as she climbs into the passenger seat.

"I made a new friend. His name's Carlos."

"Cool," he grumbles.

Damian starts the car and blasts air on the windshield to combat the condensation obscuring his vision. Backing out of the parking lot, he grinds it into first gear and pulls back onto the main road. Bianca sits next to him, lips curled into a placid smile. There's something smug in her expression, like hooking up with Carlos was a big *fuck you* to Damian. They've never been monogamous, have worked to separate the physical from the emotional, but he can't help but think she did this to punish him. For having feelings for Sydney. For looking out for himself.

They climb the hill in tense silence, the wipers slapping rhythmically at the torrential rain. Damian keeps his eyes on the road, focuses on gearing down to grip the steep incline, but his mind is trapped on their predicament. Bianca will not budge from their initial demand of five million dollars. If Curtis can't come up with it, she'll wreak havoc. And then what? They'll go home to their shitty little town, to their shitty little jobs, content that they've avenged Lyric's death. No way. He's never going back. He'll do what it takes to ensure his future.

Reaching the turnoff to the house, Damian slows the car, stalling it briefly. But he starts it up again, lurches forward into the driveway. As they creep down the gravel path, Bianca seems to shed the afterglow of her fling. She sits forward in her seat, suddenly tense and on edge.

Like him, she must be wondering what the next few days will bring. How this is all going to play out.

Before Damian has even turned off the ignition, Curtis appears on the doorstep, holding two black umbrellas. He pops one open and approaches the driver's side. As Damian climbs out, Curtis hands him the second umbrella and says, "We need to talk." He hurries around to the passenger door and holds the umbrella over Bianca as she emerges. The three of them huddle together for a moment.

"I've found someone who can float me the full five million," Curtis says, fiddling with the umbrella in case Sydney is observing them. "I should have it by end-of-day tomorrow."

Relief surges through Damian's veins like an infusion. "Great."

"Wiring that much money to your bank will raise red flags," Curtis continues. "Bitcoin is best."

"Yeah, I know," Damian snaps. He'd already asked for the money in crypto. Curtis is such a condescending douche bag. "I'll send you my wallet details."

"I'll send mine, too," Bianca pipes in. "Half the money to me, half to Damian."

He looks at his partner in surprise. Since when does she not trust him to share the money with her? This was never discussed. It's an unnecessary added complication. But Curtis shrugs it off.

"No problem." He glances toward the house. "We'd better get inside before Sydney wonders why we're standing out here in the rain."

The men take a step, but Bianca doesn't budge. They turn back to face her. Her eyes are locked on Curtis.

"Does this mean you accept responsibility for what you did to Lyric?"

Damian watches Curtis's face, the flicker of recognition, the struggle to remember. Then he says, "*Lyric*. The young woman from the party."

"She wasn't a *young woman*," Bianca spits. "She was a child. And she was my sister."

Curtis flushes, his voice wobbly as he speaks. "I'm sorry that she got wrapped up in that whole scene. And I apologize for my role in it."

"For what you *did* to her," Bianca growls. "Say it."

"I—I'm sorry for what I did to her."

But he's not. He just wants to make them go away. For some reason, Bianca seems to accept his lame apology. She nods briefly. "Okay."

They hurry through the rain toward the house.

Damian and Bianca head to their room to dry off and change. He strips off his damp T-shirt, grabbing a dry button-down. "Crisis averted," he whispers, but he can't keep the jubilation out of his voice. They no longer need to worry about negotiations with Curtis, about their conflicting goals.

His partner doesn't speak as she peels off her soaked top. He hands her a towel, watches as she dries off her wet skin. Her expression is dark and troubled despite the good news.

"So someone's going to lend Curtis five million dollars, with no questions asked," she states, dropping her wet shorts to the floor, stepping out of them.

Damian buttons his shirt. "These rich assholes have piles of money lying around. It's not a lot to them."

"But how will Curtis pay it back?" She pulls a sweatshirt over her head. "He has no income. He can't build his winery without startup money."

"That's his problem."

Bianca tosses the damp towel on a pile of clothes, steps into a pair of cozy sweatpants. "If Curtis used the house as collateral, they could seize it. And Sydney would find out everything."

Damian keeps his voice calm, but it's tinged with irritation. "We asked him to get the money, and he did. Why do you care how he pays it back?"

She looks at him with those cold, hard eyes. "I don't."

He may as well ask. "When did you set up your own crypto wallet?"

"Back home," she says, grabbing her phone. "Did you think I wouldn't look out for myself, Damian? That I wouldn't make sure I got my share of the money?"

"No, but I thought we..."

But she's already moving toward the door. Without another word, she leaves the room.

50

The aroma of fried onions, of meat and seasonings, wafts through the air as Bianca walks toward the kitchen. Curtis stands by the stove, wearing an apron and stirring a large pot. He's surrounded by dirty pans, chopped herbs, an open bottle of white wine. He must have been cooking for hours, preparing their final meal.

Damian is on her heels. "Smells great," he says, Aussie accent in place though there's no sign of Sydney.

"Hope you like beef stroganoff." Curtis seasons the massive pot. "You had the car, so I had to make do with what I had in the fridge and freezer."

"Love it," Damian replies, and Bianca mumbles her agreement.

Sydney emerges from the basement stairwell and joins them in the kitchen. Her hair and clothes are dusty. She's clearly been working downstairs while the rest of them took the day off. She smiles at Bianca. "Did you get caught in the rain?"

"Yeah," Bianca says. "But we'd already had lunch and a swim, so it was okay."

Syd turns to Damian. "Were you able to swim with your sore shoulder?" Her delivery is benign, but Bianca sees the sharp glint in Sydney's eye. Does she think Damian faked his injury to get out of working on their winery? Is she resentful that they enjoyed themselves while she sanded the basement walls? *Fuck her.* Bianca and Damian don't owe her any more unpaid labor.

But Damian's reply is chipper. "I just paddled around a bit. It was fine." Either he has missed the edge to Syd's remark or Bianca has imagined it. She's not sure which.

Sydney moves toward her husband at the stove. "What's for dinner?"

"Beef stroganoff." He gives her a wink. "Don't worry, I made a separate batch with no mushrooms for you."

Syd kisses his cheek in thanks. "I'm going to have a quick shower before dinner."

Curtis says, "We can eat in an hour. I'll make negronis."

Bianca and Damian lean against the counter and watch as Curtis mixes the cocktails. He pours the three liquors into cut-glass tumblers, slices the fresh oranges, their citrus scent permeating the strong cooking smells. Bianca's never had a negroni; she's not sure she'll like it, but she stays mute, not wanting to dampen the celebratory mood. She's never seen Curtis so upbeat, almost manic in his happiness. And Damian is cheerful for obvious reasons. Bianca should be, too. Soon, she'll have everything she wanted: millions of dollars and Curtis Lowe's decimation. But for some reason she can't get there.

Something feels off about Curtis's obvious jubilance. Of course, he's happy that they're leaving. He wants them gone so they can't fuck with him anymore, can't tell his wife that he's a monster. But how can he be so happy about being five million dollars in debt with no obvious means of paying it back? And why is he so sure he can trust them not to talk to Syd once they've received their cryptocurrency?

Curtis hands her a drink, and she takes a small sip. It's cloyingly sweet and bitter at the same time, but she nods and smiles her thanks. Bianca doesn't plan to drink it. She's already had too much wine today, and she feels the need to keep her head on straight. She needs to be ready for any and all eventualities.

Glass in hand, she leaves the men chatting about Formula 1 racing like old friends and heads toward the French doors. She stares out at the pool, the underwater lights illuminating the raindrops pummeling the surface. The trees are blowing in the distance, and the moon casts an eerie glow from behind the cloud cover. The whole scene feels creepy, even ominous. But maybe it's all in her head. And then Bianca sees a tiny red dot glowing in the darkness. Sydney is huddled under the overhang of the house, smoking a cigarette.

Bianca wants to stay inside, warm and dry, but she's uncomfortable around Curtis and Damian. Their sudden camaraderie feels like a betrayal. Now that Curtis has found the money, Damian seems to have forgotten that he's an abusive predator. That what he did to Lyric was so disgusting, so heinous, that she descended into addiction and lost her life. Setting her drink on an end table, Bianca opens the door and creeps outside.

The roof offers about a foot of overhang. Bianca slinks down the side of the house to join Sydney and stay out of the rain. "Can I bum one?"

Syd's hair is wet from the shower, combed back from her face. She holds out the pack to Bianca. "I thought you had asthma?"

"I don't." Bianca takes one, lights it with Syd's lighter. "I just said that so you didn't smoke around me. I'm trying to quit."

"I've been trying to quit, too," Syd says, staring out at the rain. "It's going really well."

Bianca chuckles, takes a drag. They smoke in silence for a few moments, and it's surprisingly comfortable. But Bianca can feel the malaise emanating off her host, the aura of discontent.

"Sounds like we'll have our fuel pump soon," she says to lighten the mood. "Maybe even tomorrow."

"That's good news." Sydney blows smoke into the darkness. "Are you excited to continue your adventures?"

"Yeah. It'll be good."

Syd's gaze is intense. "I feel like I never really got to know you, and now you're leaving."

Bianca arches an eyebrow. "We made out."

Syd laughs, rolls her eyes. "There's still a lot I don't know about you." She takes a drag on her cigarette, speaks on the exhale. "Tell me about your sister."

Bianca's flinch is imperceptible... at least she hopes it is. How the hell does Sydney know about Lyric? "I don't have a sister."

Syd cocks her head. "Damian said you did."

Drawing smoke deep into her lungs, Bianca composes herself. Damian must have slipped up, mentioned Lyric in an offhand comment. He wouldn't have told Sydney anything that would impact their plan. "I have a half sister," she covers. "We're not really in touch."

"Where does she live?"

"Back in Freo. Last I heard."

"Why aren't you close?"

Bianca shrugs a shoulder. "Different dads. Big age difference."

"How old is she?"

"She's just a kid." A kid who would never get older. She tosses her half-smoked cigarette onto the wet bricks. "Why are you so interested?"

"I always wanted a sister," Syd says. "Someone who'd look up to me. Someone I could take care of."

Bianca's throat tightens and tears prick at her eyes, but she shuts down the emotions. Once the money hits their accounts, she will tell Sydney all about Lyric, every vile, disgusting thing that Curtis did to her. Then she can cry and scream and fall apart, if she needs to. But not now. Not yet.

"We were close when she was young, but she grew up. And it got complicated."

"What happened?"

She's prying. She's onto them. Bianca needs to shut this conversation down now. "I don't want to talk about it. It's painful."

"Sorry."

"Curtis made negronis," she says, forcing a cheerful tone. "Let's go in."

Pressing themselves against the house, the women scurry to the French doors.

51

When Bianca and Sydney enter the kitchen, Damian can tell they've been smoking. The scent of cigarettes emanates from their hair and their clothes, causing him a knee-jerk stab of irritation. But as he takes the last sip of his negroni, he lets his annoyance go. There's really no need for Bianca to hide her smoking habit anymore. The lies, the secrets, and this fucked-up game are almost over.

"Sit," Curtis says, ushering the women toward the table. "Damian, can you open a bottle of red?"

"Sure." Damian moves to the wine rack and pretends he has a clue which wine to select. He grabs one, brings it to Curtis at the stove. "Is this okay?"

Curtis drops egg noodles into a pasta bowl, tops them with a scoop of aromatic stroganoff. He glances at the label on the bottle. "Excellent choice," he says, taking the bowl to the table and setting it in front of Bianca.

Damian twists out the cork and fills four glasses. As he carries them to the dining room, he takes in the scene. There are candles on the table, their flames flickering as Curtis places bowls of food on the place mats. Syd takes her seat at the end nearest the kitchen. With her hair wet and no makeup, she looks sexy, but wholesome and ethereal. Bianca is seated beside her, looking drawn but placid. On the surface, this appears to be a rustic but upscale dinner party, four friends enjoying comfort food on a stormy night. Underneath, there is so much more at play.

Handing each diner a wineglass, Damian sits next to Bianca. Curtis has served him a heaping bowl of food, and he realizes he's starving. He scoops up a forkful, stuffs it into his mouth, and chews.

"Mmm," he mumbles appreciatively, glancing around at his companions. He knows this is all fake, that the collegial atmosphere is forced for Sydney's benefit, but that doesn't mean he can't enjoy it. The plan he concocted back in Indiana has come to fruition. Curtis has promised to deliver on their demands. They can stop punishing him for one night before he's left in ruins.

"This is delicious," Sydney says, taking a delicate bite.

"Thanks," Curtis responds. "It was my grandmother's specialty."

She glances at her husband. "I thought your grandmother was British?"

"On my mom's side. But my grandma on my dad's side was half Hungarian."

"How did I not know that?" Syd's question is light, rhetorical. But her husband's ancestry is just one of his many secrets.

As they eat, they discuss the weather, the fear of flooding and mudslides. Curtis and Sydney fortified the hillside above their property with sandbags as soon as they moved in, and they're hopeful they'll hold. The trauma of Spain's deadly floods lingers.

Syd eats her special serving sans mushrooms and changes the subject. "Bianca says your fuel pump should be in tomorrow."

"If all goes well, we'll be out of your hair by tomorrow night." Damian glances at his partner, who gives him a wan smile. She's picking at her food like she did at lunch. Unlike Damian, Bianca is unable to compartmentalize her hatred, to put it away and enjoy herself for a few hours.

"Hopefully the roads won't be affected by this rain," Syd says.

"They should be fine," Curtis responds quickly. He smiles at Damian and Bianca in turn. "We're grateful for all your help. You've done so much around here."

"We are," Syd agrees, clearly missing the subtle barb in her husband's compliment.

"A toast." Curtis holds up his wineglass. "Though our paths will diverge tomorrow, may all four of us have bright and happy futures."

They all clink and drink. Then Bianca sets her napkin on the table. "If we're leaving tomorrow, I need to get packing."

"You've barely touched your food." Curtis sounds concerned.

"I think I'm coming down with a summer cold," Bianca says, standing. "It was really good, though."

Curtis jumps up, too. "I'll save it for you. You might be hungry later." He hustles into the kitchen with Bianca's plate, leaving Sydney and Damian alone at the table.

"Is she feeling okay?" Syd asks him.

"She had some drinks at lunch and didn't eat much then either. She's probably just tired."

"She could be dehydrated."

"I'll check on her." But he doesn't move. He's too content here in the low light, with this tasty meal, the quality wine. And Sydney.

Syd leans back in her chair. "Is everything okay between you two?"

"Why do you ask?" He refills her wineglass, tops up his. "Did Bianca say something?"

"No. Just a vibe I picked up from her."

"What kind of *vibe*?"

But Curtis returns then, digging into the food on his abandoned plate.

"Does Bianca seem okay to you?" Syd asks him.

"I think she's just a little stressed." He turns to Damian as he chews. "You two have made yourselves at home here. Now you've got to pack up your entire lives and move on."

"We travel light," Damian counters. "I can throw everything I own into one backpack. B. doesn't have much more."

"I guess she likes to be prepared." Sydney smiles, and they finish their meals.

Even though he cooked, Curtis insists on cleaning the kitchen. Damian and Sydney take the bottle of wine and their glasses to the living room, sink into opposite ends of the sofa.

Syd tops up her glass with barely more than a tablespoon. "Where are you and Bianca off to next?"

"Greece, I think. I've heard Milos is beautiful. And fairly cheap."

"I've heard it's got amazing geography." Syd takes a sip, stares at him over the rim. Her gaze feels intense, magnetic. Are they having a moment? He's had several drinks, and his infatuation with Sydney may be skewing his judgment. Damian doesn't know what's real between them or if he can trust his own judgment. He just knows the clock is ticking. He needs to try.

"I might stick around Spain a little longer." His words are loaded with subtext. "I seem to have grown attached."

"Oh yeah?" Syd swirls her wine gently. She seems receptive, but it could be wishful thinking. "And how does Bianca feel about that?"

"Bianca and I are going our separate ways." The words have been uttered before he can think them through. "We're not angry or fighting. We just want different things out of life. Our futures will be better if we spend them apart."

"That's a big decision."

"It's the right one." And it feels true. Two and a half million is enough for both Damian and Bianca to move forward, to be happy, separately. And as his eyes connect with Sydney's, a confidence fills him. A sense of knowing. He's creating the life he's always wanted.

Curtis enters, wiping his hands on a dish towel. His timing is impeccable. "How are your drinks?" he asks brightly. "Shall I open another bottle?"

"Why not?" Damian tears his gaze from Syd's, smiles up at her husband. "It's our last night, after all."

52

Bianca stands outside in the rain, watching Damian and Sydney through the arched windows. They're having a cozy chat in the living room while Curtis does the dishes. They look good together, like a real couple. Sydney is so cool and elegant while Damian is strong and masculine. Their body language belies their attraction: legs crossed toward each other, torsos tilted inward. Damian is watching her like she's an angel, a beautiful apparition that could vanish at any moment. Bianca's heart feels tight in her chest, as if it's being crushed by her rib cage. She's not jealous, though Damian's infatuation is obvious even from here. She's disillusioned and disappointed. But mostly, she's scared.

When Sydney asked about Lyric, Bianca knew they were screwed. The other woman was onto them. Syd used to be a lawyer, adept at solving puzzles and building cases. Bianca had smoked her cigarette, tried to throw Syd off the scent, but she'd been caught off-guard. Her stammered denials and excuses were not convincing. And Sydney is far too intelligent to have been fooled.

Later, as Bianca picked at her meal, questions had run rampant in her mind. She and Damian had planned and rehearsed their Australian personas for months before they arrived in Spain. Damian wouldn't have *casually* mentioned that Bianca had a little sister, not when Lyric was the reason they were here. Damian's feelings for Sydney are evident, but he's too greedy, too focused on the five million, to jeopardize their plan. If he told Sydney what Curtis had done to Lyric now, the payoff would never happen.

Curtis would never have mentioned the girl to his wife. Lyric is his darkest, ugliest secret. Or is she? Bianca wonders if Curtis could spin the story of what he did to Lyric in a way that would convince his wife to forgive him. It's not impossible. She knows women sometimes stay with—even fall in love with—brutal murderers. There are mothers who look the other way when their children are abused by the men they adore. Sydney already knows she's married to a liar and a cheat. Is she so desperate, damaged, and lacking in morals that she'd absolve Curtis of his heinous crime?

It was Curtis's cheerful toast to the future that triggered Bianca the most. If he's feeling optimistic, they've done something very wrong. Curtis should be stressed and worried, wondering how on earth he's going to pay back five million dollars with no job, no business, while keeping it a secret from Sydney. He shouldn't be cooking his grandma's favorite meal and making upbeat statements about happy days to come. Bianca knows something is off. Unfortunately, Damian is too excited, too drunk, too enamored with Sydney, to see it.

Turning away from the windows, Bianca creeps past the pool and away from the house. As she moves farther into the darkness, she stumbles on the uneven ground. But she can't use her flashlight and risk drawing attention to herself. How would she explain her presence out in this field, under the driving rain? No one can know what she's doing out here. And what she's planning.

Gingerly, she picks her way through the tall grass, moving down the hillside behind the pool. She slips on the slick ground, going down hard on her knees, but she gets back up and presses forward. Soon, she reaches the barbed wire fence that lines the bottom of the property. Sticking close to it, Bianca moves toward the rotted log, the hiding place for the machete.

She can't be sure what Curtis has planned for them, but she'll be ready. If he double-crosses them, if Sydney has known everything all along, if the couple plans to eliminate their guests, Bianca will attack. She's not going to accept defeat like a defenseless lamb. Or allow herself to be manipulated like her gullible, lovestruck boyfriend. Bianca will wreak what havoc she can. For Lyric.

When she reaches the rotted log, she drops to her knees. The soft ground squelches under her weight, water soaking through her sweatpants, but she ignores the unpleasant sensation. She feels around the crumbling wood, sifts through the tall grass. She knows the machete was here, pressed against this fallen log.

And now it's gone.

Terror grips her, usurping all rational thought. Her intuition has been screaming at her that something isn't right, that she could be in danger, and now it's confirmed. Curtis found the machete. Or Sydney did. Maybe even Damian discovered it. It doesn't matter who has possession now. Bianca trusts no one. And she knows what she must do.

Dragging herself out of the grass, Bianca retraces her path back toward the house, edging around the pool to the front door. Breathing on her hands, she rubs them vigorously together, tries to make them functional again, but they're so cold, so stiff. When some sensation has returned to her fingers, she gently, soundlessly opens the door.

Cheerful conversation drifts toward her from the living room, Damian's jovial fake-Australian voice reaching her ears as she tiptoes down the hall. He sounds so happy, so in his element. At the door to their bedroom, she pauses, a hand on the wood surface. If she summoned Damian, told him they weren't safe, would he listen? Or would he grill her on why she'd removed the machete from the van and hidden it from him? Knowing her lover's machismo, he'd insist that he could handle Curtis and his weapon, that the threat was too minor to jeopardize their plan. But her every instinct is telling her to run. She presses the bedroom door open and slips inside.

With her cold and filthy hands, she shoves her clothes into the duffel bag. Everything will be wrinkled, covered in dirt, but she doesn't care. Zipping the bag closed, she finds the box of tampons. She tips it upside down, dropping the contents onto the floor. The key to the van clinks gently on the tiles, but it sounds like a thunderclap to Bianca.

She freezes, listens. But Damian's upbeat diatribe drones on. She shoves the key into the pocket of her soaked pants, hoists her bag, and slips out of the house.

Rain pelts her as she scurries toward the van, lugging her belongings. Her hands are trembling with cold and fear as she fumbles the key into the lock. It takes a couple of tries, but she manages to unlock the panel door and slide it open. Gratefully, she climbs inside and closes it gently behind her. For a moment, she sits on the floor of the van, allowing her heart rate to return to normal.

The rain on the metal roof is rhythmic and soothing, and her pulse begins to slow. After so much time with Damian, Curtis, and Sydney, the solitude is a relief. There have been moments she's enjoyed, instances that almost felt like friendship, but they weren't real. Bianca feels supremely alone in the world, but it's natural and familiar. She's only ever been able to rely on herself.

She finds an old T-shirt tossed carelessly aside and dries her face, pats at her neck. She's soaked through, covered in mud, but there's no time to change. Someone inside that house has the machete, and they'll be willing to use it. A crime so messy and bloody seems incongruous with the sophisticated pair, but who knows to what lengths they would go to protect their money? And their secrets. Bianca needs to get the hell out of here. Then she'll regroup, find another way to exact revenge on Curtis Lowe. But she needs to stay alive to do it.

Climbing into the cab, she opens the glove box. The fuel pump relay is there. The day Damian removed it feels like months ago and yesterday at the same time. Her hands tremble as she picks it up, slides it into her pocket. She reaches over to the driver's side and pops the trunk.

The rain pummels her as she heads to the back of the vehicle and unlatches the cover. She's grateful the van's engine is in the rear, so she can use her phone flashlight undetected. Peering into the engine bay, she finds the black plastic box that houses the various relays and fuses. Thank God she'd paid attention when Damian removed the relay. Even then, when she thought her relationship was solid, she must have known she might need to look out for herself.

Despite the trembling of her hand, the pluglike gadget slides neatly into its spot. If she's done this right, the van should be fully operational. She can back down this driveway and disappear, save herself. For a moment, a wave of guilt gives her pause. Can she abandon Damian after all they've been through together? She has loved him for so long, but she's always been emotionally prepared for the end. Her father's abandonment and the sudden death of Lyric's dad have wired her brain to be prepared for the worst. Bianca knows good things don't last. She slams the cover closed and takes a step toward the driver's-side door.

And then, a pain so intense it's almost blinding doubles her over. Bianca crumples to her knees on the wet gravel, impervious to the rocks cutting into her skin. Something is wrong, but her brain can't compute. She's exhausted, she hasn't been eating, and the acuity of the ache usurps all rational thought. She vomits onto the wet ground, clutches fruitlessly at her abdomen. What the hell is wrong with her? Bianca needs to get away from here, but she's losing consciousness. And she's paralyzed. She's blacking out.

She lies unmoving, a wounded dog in the rain.

53

Damian is feeling warm, content, and a little buzzed after a delicious meal and several glasses of red wine. But it's been the one-on-one time with Sydney that produced this unfamiliar lightness in his chest, this effervescing sensation in his brain. He's finally articulated his desire to stay in Spain, alluded to his hope of a future with Syd. She'd seemed receptive—cautiously so. But once she learns the truth about her husband, she'll need him.

"Top up?" Curtis holds the bottle of wine out to his guest. He'd joined them after cleaning the kitchen, his presence like a parent chaperone at the prom.

"Sure." Damian holds out his glass, and Curtis pours a few ounces of the bloodred liquid into it.

Curtis turns to his wife. "Last splash, Syd?" But she shakes her head, holds a hand over her glass. It's still half full.

"Come on," Damian cajoles her, his eyes dancing with flirtatious energy. "It's our last night together."

"I'm good." Syd smiles. "Besides, someone has to drive you to Girona to get your fuel pump tomorrow."

Right. The supposed fuel pump has finally come in. "Good point."

"I'll drive you," Curtis offers, dumping the remains of the wine into his glass. "As long as you didn't burn out my clutch today."

"Nah," Damian says, sipping his wine. "I got the hang of it pretty quick."

Curtis cocks an eyebrow. "That's not how it looked when you came lurching into the driveway."

It's an attack on Damian's masculinity, and he feels the urge to shut the prick down with a well-placed barb. But he restrains himself. The evening has been so pleasant. Sydney has been so warm and open to him. He doesn't want to ruin it by getting into a pissing match with Curtis. Soon, he'll have two and a half million reasons not to give a shit what that asshole says.

"When we pick up the fuel pump, you can get your clutch replaced," he jokes, and he's rewarded when Sydney laughs.

They finish their wine and call it a night. It's late now, and tomorrow is a big day. It will be the culmination of Damian's master plan and the beginning of an exciting new chapter. He must be well-rested, remain vigilant for tricks or double crosses. He'd let his guard down tonight and enjoyed himself, but he'll be on high alert tomorrow. He's so close to the life he's always wanted he can taste it.

He enters the guest room and finds it empty. He'd expected to see his girlfriend curled up in bed, exhausted from a day in the elements. But Bianca must be in the van. He looks out the window through the wall of rain and finds the vehicle dark and quiet. She must have decided to sleep out there. Bianca will still be pissy about their fight at lunch. Could she have heard him flirting with Sydney? Telling her that he and Bianca have decided to part ways? Bianca has never cared what Damian did with other women, but this is different. Sydney is so mature, so wise, so accomplished. His feelings for her are so valid. They're so *adult*.

Shaking off his concerns, he grabs his phone and flops on the bed. He must ensure the money transfers seamlessly into his crypto wallet. He opens his Bitcoin app, copies the chain of letters and numbers from his wallet, and texts them to Curtis. He's likely sending the info to Curtis's burner phone, the one he keeps hidden from his wife. Obviously, Syd can't know that her husband is about to transfer a huge amount of money to their houseguests in a desperate attempt to save his marriage.

A futile attempt.

Setting his phone on the nightstand, Damian slides between the sheets. As he settles into bed, he wonders if Bianca has sent her wallet details to Curtis. Probably. Despite her denials, Bianca wants the money as much as he does. They'd developed their blackmail plan together, come up with a figure, decided that cryptocurrency was the simplest and safest method of payment. Damian had offered to set up a wallet to collect the Bitcoin. One account was the most streamlined. But at some stage, Bianca had stopped trusting him. When?

He lies on his back with his arms behind his head. He's exhausted, a little drunk, but he can't sleep. His eyes are wide-open, and his heartbeat is erratic. It's the red wine. Or it's the anticipation and anxiety. Tomorrow, once the money is received, Bianca will tell Syd that she's married to a killer, that her husband is part of something debauched and insidious. And then Bianca will vanish. But Damian will hang around to pick up the pieces of Sydney's broken life.

Of course, Syd might reject Damian's offers of comfort and support. She'll likely be disgusted that Bianca and Damian profited off her husband's vile behavior. But Damian plans to put it all on Bianca. Monetary compensation was the only way she could move forward after her sister's death. Poor guileless Damian had no choice but to support her. Sydney is all alone in Spain. He'll be the only one she can turn to.

His eyes are finally getting heavy, and he rolls onto his side. Soon he drifts off, finds himself in a troubling dream. Something—or someone—is after him. Damian is running from sharp claws, or maybe a dagger, but he's weak, his legs barely functional. Suddenly a thud jolts him awake. It's the sound of an object hitting the tiled floor. It could be nothing—a dropped book or a phone—but he bolts upright, listens.

Is there someone in the hall? He tries to quiet his own breath and heartbeat and listen. There's nothing but silence now. No voices. No footsteps. The house is quiet, and he assumes his hosts have gone to bed. He lies back down, but his nervous system won't settle. Is he wound up from the ugly dream? Or is his intuition warning him of danger?

He's tried to ignore his doubts and fears, but they bubble to the surface now. Does Curtis Lowe really trust his guests to get their money and ride off into the sunset? To accept five million bucks as compensation for the death of a beloved sister? Curtis was a savvy businessman in the cutthroat world of New York real estate. Are they to believe he's suddenly become so gullible?

If Damian was being blackmailed, he knows what he'd do. He'd erase the problem. He'd play along, make like he was going to pay the money, and then, when the extortionists dropped their guard, he'd strike. But Curtis Lowe is a pussy, a coward, a creep who preys on little girls. He could never summon the courage to take on Damian, even though Curtis's marriage, reputation, and everything he cares about are on the line. Could he?

No. There's no way the smaller man would try to physically attack him. It would be a death sentence. Damian is stronger, faster, and tougher in every way. Only a gun would tip the balance of power in Curtis's favor, but he'd assured Damian that he didn't have one. In fact, he'd been highly offended when Damian had suggested he might own one that night at dinner. And this is Europe, where it's famously difficult to obtain a firearm. Reassured, he drifts away into sleep.

The room is dark, silent but for the rain pattering on the roof, when the pain shocks him awake. It's a ripping, tearing sensation in his lower intestines, a powerful wave of nausea. Damian rolls over and vomits on the floor, a cascade of red wine splashing the tiles. Jesus. He didn't think he was *that* drunk. In fact, he knows he wasn't. Another surge of intense cramping curls him into the fetal position, and he grits his teeth against the anguish.

It's food poisoning. And it's bad. Damian tries to remember what he'd eaten that day, but the searing pain is too distracting. His viscera are being torn apart, and he groans audibly. He needs to get to the toilet, though the thought of standing upright makes him whimper. But he's not going to shit the bed, not in Sydney's house. Doubled over in pain, he staggers across the hall to the bathroom, slams the door behind him.

Immediately, he collapses onto the cold tiles, hands reaching for the cool porcelain of the commode. A cold sweat prickles his skin, and his entire insides feel liquefied. He's sick. Really sick. He needs Curtis to drive him to the ER, but he can't leave the bathroom. Not yet. In the distance, he hears a braying, wounded animal. It must be a wild boar, shot by a hunter with a gun or a crossbow. The creature is dying slowly and painfully, its anguish echoing through the quiet hillside.

Just before he loses consciousness, Damian realizes the sound is coming from him.

CURTIS AND SYDNEY

54

Curtis vividly remembers the first time they saw the Spanish house. The Realtor, José Sainz, had picked them up from the small apartment they'd rented in Girona, had driven them toward the sea. Curtis had sat in the cramped back seat, allowing Sydney to sit up front and take in the views. José had regaled them with tales of the area, its medieval history, its culture of passion and bravery. It was imperative that his wife fall in love with Cap de Creus. This was where they'd rebuild their life together.

The villa that would become their home had been vacant for several months. José apologized for the state of disrepair as they meandered down the hillside toward it, but his words barely registered. The view had them mesmerized, glimpses of the whitewashed town and the sparkling Mediterranean seducing their attention. Eventually, José turned into the gravel drive, and they jostled toward the house.

José's business motto was clearly underpromise and overdeliver. While there were repairs to be made, upgrades desperately needed, the bones of the house were good. And the magnificent windows! The sweeping views! The charming beamed ceilings! Curtis had never felt a visceral longing to live somewhere before, but he felt it now. Sydney felt it, too. They'd fallen instantly in love with the place.

They hadn't even tried to play coy with the salesman; they couldn't. Wandering through the rooms, they'd estimated the work required, tallied up the costs on a notes app. It was significant, but

Curtis and Syd were up for the challenge. They needed a project that would bring them together, a shared goal. That was why they'd moved here.

When they'd surveyed every inch of the house, José took them outside, walked them around the fence line. "It's one of the larger plots on this hillside," the Realtor told them. "With full sun most of the year at the west fence line. You could grow vegetables or fruit."

"Grapes?" Curtis queried, and caught Sydney's eye. Her smile was small but optimistic, and she'd never looked more beautiful to him.

"Of course," José insisted, moving toward the massive oak near the back fence. "This hillside would be perfect for Airén grapes. You could make a beautiful small winery here."

Curtis could envision it. An aspirational new business. He and Sydney working side by side to create their own wine. It would be hard work, long hours, and it was unlikely to be financially rewarding. But it would be theirs.

José had reached the tree now and rested a hand on the trunk. "This beautiful Holm oak tree is hundreds of years old," he said. "It will give you shade for picnics. And it will be perfect for your future children to climb on."

It was a patriarchal assumption, and Curtis's eyes had darted to Sydney's. But she seemed unfazed, comfortable with the decision they'd made together to remain a family of two. She kept her gaze on the massive tree. "It's beautiful," she responded.

José squatted next to the base of the thick trunk and plucked a small mushroom from a cluster growing there. "These mushrooms are very poisonous. Extremely dangerous."

Curtis bent over to look at the offending fungi. "They look a bit like straw mushrooms."

"That is the problem," the real estate agent said, righting himself. "Many people make that mistake and pick them. They taste quite good, apparently. But even cooked, they can kill you."

"Thanks for the warning, but I'm allergic to mushrooms," Syd said, even though she wasn't. She wandered up the hill to take in more of the view.

"We'll steer clear," Curtis assured their guide, but José wasn't finished.

"People get very sick, and then, a few hours later, they feel better. They think it was simple food poisoning, so they don't go to the doctor. But the poison is still inside them, destroying their organs. And then, they die."

"Brutal."

"You call these death caps in English," José stated.

"I think we have those back home," Curtis said, but it wasn't like he'd been foraging for food in the sidewalk cracks of Manhattan.

"Curtis!" Sydney called from the upper fence line. "Look at the view from up here!"

He'd hurried to join her, the death caps forgotten.

Until today.

The memory had revisited him shortly after he'd discovered the machete, wrapped it in an old sweater, and hidden it at the back of the shelf in their bedroom closet. He'd known he'd never be able to use it. As desperate as he was, he couldn't hack Damian and Bianca to death. It was so gory, so bloody. And Damian was much bigger and stronger. He'd wrestle the weapon away from Curtis and likely cleave him in half.

But poison was relatively clean, hands-off, and should be effective. Traditionally, it's been considered a woman's method of murder. Damian would have had a field day with that one... except he wouldn't because he'd be dead. And unlike a bloody machete attack, this would look like an accident. Bianca and Damian had gone out for lunch, had accidentally ingested the mushrooms. Curtis would dispose of his tormentors and get away scot-free. The plan was perfect. He felt elated, practically high.

While Sydney was sanding the basement bathroom and Bianca and

Damian were at the beach, Curtis had crept out to the big oak. Dropping to his knees at its roots, he'd plucked several of the innocuous-looking fungi. José had informed him that they were safe to handle with his bare hands, that their power wouldn't be diminished by cooking, that ingesting even a few would be fatal without medical intervention. Storm clouds were gathering by then, foreshadowing a heavy rain that would send their guests scurrying back home. He had no time to waste.

In the kitchen, he prepared the death caps carefully, treating them with a deserved reverence. He washed them, sliced them uniformly, and then sautéed them with butter and sprigs of fresh thyme. Sydney didn't eat mushrooms, so she was in no danger. But Damian and Bianca would be suspicious if Curtis didn't partake. He found a few conventional mushrooms in the fridge, slightly withered with age. He sliced them to match the death caps, sauteed them in a different pan, and hid them in the stove. While his guests were at the beach, he prepared the stroganoff, adding all the ingredients except the death caps. He set two servings aside: one without mushrooms for Sydney, one with the regular mushrooms for himself. It was simple enough to dish up their meals and serve himself last.

And now, lying next to his wife in bed, he stares sightlessly at his book, and waits. It will take a few hours for the amatoxins to take effect, to begin attacking the blackmailers' gastrointestinal systems. José had been so detailed that Curtis hadn't even needed to research the effects. If the police check his devices, they'll find no searches for poisonous mushrooms, nothing suspicious. It's a foolproof plan, and he bites on a smile.

Sydney drops her hardcover on the floor with a loud thump. Curtis flinches. He's tightly wound, on edge. "Sorry," she says, reaching over to turn off her lamp. "I hope I didn't wake the guests."

"Damian had a lot of wine," Curtis says. "And the rain on the roof is pretty loud."

"Good night." It's slightly cool but not unusually so. And there's no kiss, which has become the norm since his "affair." The tender voicemail she'd left him earlier seems to have been forgotten. Syd snuggles down under the covers, presents her back to him. Curtis flicks off his lamp and curls around her. He feels her stiffen slightly, but soon she relaxes into him.

"I'm glad they're finally leaving," he whispers, his mouth close to her ear. "I just want it to be us again."

At first, his wife doesn't answer. She's so still, so quiet, that he wonders if she's already asleep. Eventually, she mumbles something that sounds vaguely affirmative. It sounds like she's agreeing with him, like she's eager for their guests to go, too. Syd's been hard to read lately, has seemed trapped in her own head. But once Bianca and Damian are gone, they can work on restoring their closeness.

And that will be very soon.

Sydney Cleary and Curtis Lowe, Couples' Counseling Session
Ellen Dwyer, Psychologist, PsyD
July 29

TRANSCRIPT 6.

Ellen:
How are you both doing?

Curtis:
I feel like Syd's shut down. Like our relationship is regressing.

Ellen:
Healing from an affair is really hard. Sydney, why don't you share what's been going on with you so we can sort this out?

Sydney:
Curtis came home late the other night. I started to worry.

Curtis:
I had a client dinner that ran late. I'm co-owner of the company. These things aren't optional.

Sydney:
I know that. But when you stay out late, I can't stop worrying that you're with Collette. Or with someone else.

Curtis:
I don't know what else to do. I came clean, Syd. I told you everything. I've given you access to my phone and my computer. Do you want me to quit my job? Because I will.

Sydney:
You built that company. I'd never ask you to abandon it. I know you need to go out and network and schmooze. I know that dinners and drinks are part of your job. But... I'm just not sure I can stay married to you.

Curtis:

You're more important to me than the company. Far more important. I'll sell my shares. I can do something different. Or we could move. Start over.

Sydney:

Are you serious?

Curtis:

Deadly serious.

Ellen:

That sounds like a pretty drastic measure to rebuild trust. Can we focus on some other possibilities?

Curtis:

Thanks, Ellen. But I think we're done here.

55

Sydney is lying awake in the dark, her mind racing as it tries to slot all the pieces into place. Her body is tense, a block of stone against her husband's touch. And then she hears it: the distant cry of a tortured beast. The sound rolls over her like a wave, a cold chill pricking her skin. It's a moan of anguish like she's never heard, the guttural cry of an injured animal. Or it's Damian, dying on the bathroom floor.

"Curtis," she says, shaking him awake. "What's wrong with him?"

Her husband sounds fully alert when he answers. "I have no idea."

"I'll go check on him." Syd twists her legs out of bed, but Curtis stops her with a hand on her shoulder.

"I'll go." He climbs out the other side in his boxers and T-shirt. "This could be messy."

Sydney waits, her pulse skittering, her mind running over the possibilities for spontaneous and excruciating pain. It could be a twisted bowel or a kidney stone. Damian could have had a preexisting condition that's just flaring up now. His moans continue, and she grabs her phone, considers calling 112 for an ambulance, but she waits for Curtis to return.

"Seems like a case of food poisoning," her husband says, climbing back into bed. "He'll be fine in a few hours."

"What did he eat?"

"I don't know. They probably had something spoiled at lunch today."

"Is Bianca okay?"

"She's not there." He fluffs his pillow, sounds remarkably unconcerned. "She must have slept in the van."

"We should check on her." Syd moves to get up. "She might be sick, too."

"Give her some privacy. If she's puking and shitting herself, she may not want witnesses."

Sydney pauses. He has a point.

"Besides," Curtis continues, "she's not as dramatic as her boyfriend." Damian's moan, quieter but no less agonized, punctuates the sentence, and Curtis snorts. "He acts like such a tough guy, but a few bad mussels and he wails like a baby."

Disdain drips from her husband's words. He's more than indifferent to their guest's suffering; he's enjoying it. The picture begins to form, a puzzle she's been trying to solve all evening.

"Did you do something to them?"

"What?" Curtis sounds incredulous, offended. "Like what?"

"I don't know... Did you feed them something that was off? Or spoiled?"

"Are you serious?" He sits up. "Why would I want them to be sick in my house? That makes no sense."

Syd's confidence wobbles in the face of his outrage. But she won't be manipulated, not anymore.

"Don't lie to me, Curtis."

"I'm not lying." He reaches out, touches her hair. "I've always been honest with you, babe. Even about the affair."

"But you didn't have an affair, did you?"

His hand falls from her hair, and his eyes turn wary. "How much did you have to drink tonight?"

He's trying to gaslight her now. But she knows more than her husband realizes, the information festering inside her. It's time to let it out.

"Collette Jasper doesn't exist. You made her up."

"You saw her Facebook page, Sydney."

"You created that Facebook page using someone else's photos. You knew I'd be curious and try to search for Collette online." She watches his expression for traces of guilt, but Curtis's face is closed, a mask. "I wondered why the page disappeared, but Meta must have taken it down because it was fake."

He shakes his head, like he's shocked and confused. But it's a ploy. "I don't get it, babe. Why would I admit to an affair I didn't have?"

"Because you were covering up for something else. Something worse."

He reaches for her again, his eyes pleading. "What could be worse than cheating on the woman I love? You know how much I adore you."

Her stomach churns at his words, and she recoils from his touch. Because there are worse things. Far worse things. "Come with me," she commands, sliding out of bed.

"Where are we going?" he grumbles, but he trails her through the house, Damian's agonized groans growing fainter as they move toward the stairs. They descend silently to the basement. Syd had spent much of the day down there under the auspices of painting prep, but she'd been otherwise engaged.

The antiquated security system had been ignored since they moved in, its wires tangled, the console covered in dust. At first, video surveillance of their private oasis had seemed unnecessary. Sydney and Curtis had felt so safe and comfortable in their idyllic hideaway. After they discovered the machete, the video cameras had felt insufficient to protect them from a lurking psychopath. So the system had remained untouched, inoperable. But it had been included in the real estate listing as an asset. If it couldn't be made functional, why would José have mentioned it?

Sydney had approached the system with patience, determination, and a pair of pliers. She'd painstakingly untangled the cords, snipped the wires that needed repair, and carefully reconnected them. Her first attempt had been unsuccessful, and she'd felt a swell of panic, of desperation. She knew her husband and her houseguests were hiding things from her, keeping dark secrets. The surveillance cameras felt like her only hope to learn what the hell was going on in her own home.

In the distance, she heard a car chugging up the steep hillside. Could it be Damian and Bianca returning from their rained-out beach day? Her heart pattered in her chest, and her fingers slipped on the wires as she heard the Citroën lurching up the driveway. Above her, the front door opened and closed. Curtis was going to meet the guests outside, away from Sydney's prying eyes. She had mere moments to make these cameras operational, to capture their exchange.

The small screen flickered to life just as the car's engine turned off. The image was nearly obfuscated by dust, but she rubbed it clean with the side of her fist. For a moment, she worried that the cameras outside would light up, would catch their attention, but luckily, the rain obscured them. And as Bianca and Damian huddled with Curtis, umbrellas sheltering them from the deluge, they were far too intent on their conversation to be distracted. Sydney turned up the volume, strained to listen over the driving rain. And what she heard made her cold. And ill. And desperate for answers.

Now, she presses rewind and plays the scene for her husband. His face has gone pale, a sickish hue of gray as he watches himself on-screen with Damian and Bianca. In the tiny room, his voice rings out loud and clear as he offers them five million dollars to make them go away. And as he accepts responsibility for what he did to Lyric. A child. Bianca's sister.

Curtis turns to face his wife, and she sees the defeat in his eyes. The game, his narrative, is over. It's time for him to tell the truth. Sydney will not accept anything less.

"What the fuck did you do to that girl, Curtis?"

56

Curtis is not the villain in this story. He was just a pawn, a man trapped, used, and manipulated. What he did wasn't *that* bad. Not compared to the acts he witnessed, the vile things he saw others do. He felt sick about those for weeks, even months. Because he is decent and good, deserving of an amazing woman like Sydney. It is time now to be honest. To come clean. To make Syd understand that he never hurt Bianca's sister.

He leads Sydney upstairs and pours her a bourbon. She sits on the sofa holding the glass, but she doesn't drink. She looks pale, and ill, and furious. He knows her mind is going to dark and disturbing places, but he can explain everything. It will all be okay once she hears him out. Thankfully, Damian's soundtrack of moans has ceased. He's likely passed out, overcome with pain and dehydration. Curtis and Sydney are alone. And so, he begins...

It all started with a call from West Beatty's head of property, a man named Michael Lucan. Curtis had been excited to hear from him. Beatty was one of the biggest players on the East Coast, well known for having a conglomerate of diverse businesses. Bringing him on board as a client would be a coup for Waters and Lowe. For Curtis himself.

"We're looking for space for our expanding ventures," Lucan told him over the phone. "West has heard good things about your firm."

"I'll handle your needs personally," Curtis offered, though he rarely saw clients anymore. But this was an enormous opportunity, too big to be handled by an underling.

He'd toured Michael Lucan around for weeks, visiting properties across the boroughs. Lucan was a taciturn Brit, elegant in his bespoke suits and French cuffs. He wasn't an easy man to be trapped in a car with for hours on end, but Curtis was a salesman. He knew how to charm even the most difficult clients. He knew when to fill the silences and when to let them be. Eventually, they found a new office tower in Long Island City ideal for Beatty's biotech company. The significant commission was well worth Curtis's time investment. And he knew he'd delivered. There should be more opportunities to come.

Curtis took the lease to Lucan's FiDi office for signing. "We're having a little kick-off party in the new space," Lucan told him. "West would like you to come."

Of course Curtis would attend. It was good for the relationship, a great networking opportunity. "Should I bring my wife?"

Lucan's eye had twitched slightly. He was too sophisticated to wink. "You'll probably have more fun on your own."

So Curtis had gone alone, expecting something naughty like strippers or topless waitresses, but the party was sophisticated. It was held on the top floor of the tower, in an empty space with sweeping views of the New York City skyline. The suite had been furnished with white leather sectional sofas, white acrylic bars, and an elevated DJ booth. The music was loud and bassy, the lighting low and strategic. Curtis got a martini and wandered through the crowd, awed by the high-profile attendees: athletes, rock stars, politicians. He'd heard West Beatty threw elite parties, but this was next level.

Soon, Michael Lucan found him. "West would like to meet you."

Curtis was led to a secluded sofa where West was engaged in an intimate conversation with an A-list actor. Curtis couldn't help but feel intimidated, but West stood and shook his hand. He was shorter than Curtis, with a soft physique and pasty complexion, but he had a regal air about him. He was a unicorn, and he knew it.

"Lucan has told me good things about you," West said in his unique accent.

"I'm glad I could find you this space."

"It's perfect. And we'll be needing more properties going forward."

"I'm your guy."

West introduced Curtis to the actor (as if an introduction was necessary) and invited him to join them. The A-lister was considering opening a restaurant, and Curtis blabbered on about a few of his listings. He tried to be professional and knowledgeable, but he was starstruck, out of his element. Until West pulled a small gold box from his pocket and flipped open the enamel lid. He dropped a tiny pill into Curtis's palm.

At first, Curtis just stared at it. He didn't do recreational drugs. Even in college, he'd steered clear of chemicals. But he watched West swallow the pill, and the movie star took one, too. It would have been rude not to join in. Highly uncool. So he placed it on his tongue with practiced nonchalance and washed it down with gin.

They talked for a while, and when the drugs kicked in, it made him comfortable and confident. It didn't matter that West was a billionaire, that the movie star was a household name. Curtis felt on their level, deserving of their attention. He, too, was successful, exceptional, and interesting. He was also extremely thirsty.

Curtis excused himself and headed for the nearest bar. He got a glass bottle of water, drank heartily, bathing his parched throat. With the bottle in hand, he wandered through the crowd. It was late now, and the space had filled up. Everyone there was so attractive they were practically luminous. He'd never felt so warmly toward complete strangers. In retrospect, he knew it was the serotonin flooding his brain from the pill West had provided. But in the moment, it all felt magical. Curtis perched on another white sofa, drank his water, and savored the ambience.

At some point, several young women emerged from the elevator, strolling past him in slinky dresses, short skirts, and heavy makeup.

He watched them wobbling on their heels, whispering and giggling to each other. They ordered drinks, were rewarded with pink concoctions that seemed to thrill them. They stayed as a gaggle, a tight little clutch of bare skin, long hair, snatches of fabric.

A burly man in a suit approached them, said a few words, and they dispersed. As one of the women tottered past him, Curtis realized she wasn't a woman at all. She was a girl, barely old enough to drive. He watched as the teen stumbled, spilled her drink on the shiny floor, but kept moving forward obediently. There was something trancelike in her propulsion. He watched her with detached concern until she disappeared, enveloped into a group of men in their fifties.

A frisson of wrong ran through him, despite his altered state. He swiveled in his seat to view the other partygoers, but no one else seemed disturbed by the presence of these children. In fact, the girls were mingling with the adults like it was completely natural. Normal. Not sick. Not criminal or even immoral. Curtis watched a reality star give one of the kids a line of powder. A female singer was kissing a girl while a couple of tech bros watched. All around him, these teenagers were being touched and fondled and fed alcohol and drugs. And no one blinked an eye.

One of the girls sat down next to him. She was fucked-up, her eyes glassy and unfocused. "Hi," she said in a small voice, intentionally subservient. "I'm Lyric."

He hadn't remembered the name until Bianca said it. He'd assumed it was fake. *Lyric*. But he remembered the girl. Her long hair, her thin frame, her gentle eyes. "I'm Todd," he said.

"Do you mind if I sit here, Todd?" The flirtatious tone was forced, almost comical. She'd probably never had a boyfriend, and now she was meant to come on to men three times her age. His instinct was to tell her no, to send her away, but he knew what would happen to her if he did. He felt protective of her.

He kept that girl beside him for the rest of the night so that no one would hurt her. Around him, things were happening to the other young women, things that weren't right. He wasn't going to take advantage of a child who was clearly drunk and high. He wasn't going to do anything she didn't want. He had wrapped an arm around her, sheltered her, and kept her safe. The girl opened up to him, told him her hopes and dreams. She was sweet, funny, and vulnerable. Eventually, a woman in her mid-forties collected Lyric, shepherded her away. The party was over. He felt like he'd done his job.

About a week later, Michael Lucan scheduled a meeting. They met at an expensive French restaurant, sat at a secluded table near the kitchen. Curtis was upbeat, hopeful for another big contract. But Lucan had something else in mind.

"Did you enjoy yourself the other night?"

"Sure," Curtis replied, eyes on his steak frites. His skin felt hot and prickly. He wanted to forget the party, forget what he'd seen there.

"These events need to be kept secret. For obvious reasons."

"Of course. I won't say anything."

Lucan smiled, revealing his small uniform teeth. "We like to change venues regularly. A moving target is harder to hit."

Something was coming. Curtis could sense it. But what?

"You've got so many listings. Office buildings and warehouses that are sitting empty. We'd like to hold our parties there."

Curtis audibly swallowed a chunk of steak. "My clients would never stand for it. Not to mention my business partner."

Lucan's smile was cool, unreadable. "They'd never have to know. We're very discreet."

"I'd like to help you out, I really would, but there are huge liability issues." Curtis set his fork on his plate with a soft clink. "I can't have my company involved in something like this."

"But you're already involved, Curtis." Lucan reached inside his suit jacket and pulled out his phone. He tapped at it for a moment, and then he passed it across the table.

The video that played out on-screen starred Curtis Lowe and the girl who'd told him her name was Lyric. He watched himself sitting next to her on the white sofa. Even in such a tiny image, she was so clearly a child. Why was he sitting so close to her? The kid was practically on his lap. He'd wrapped his arm around her for protection, but on film it looked lascivious, disgusting. How had his hand gotten on her knee? He watched himself lean in, whisper in her ear, his lips brushing her neck, her mouth. Soon, he was kissing her, and it turned his stomach; he feared he might vomit at the table. He watched as he took the girl's hand and led her out of frame.

"I—I never..." But the words stuck in his dry throat. He reached for his wine and drank, coughing and sputtering.

"You did," Lucan said. "Would you like to see the next video of you two together?"

"No!" Curtis barked, because he couldn't stomach it. He'd pushed the memory so far down, buried it under a barrage of denials and excuses. He'd created a narrative that he was a good guy, a savior even, and he'd locked it in as fact. But the truth of what he'd done, who he was, snaked its way into his psyche now. It was too much to bear.

His voice was an outraged whisper. "You set me up. You drugged me, and you filmed me without my consent."

"You willingly took a recreational drug you were offered." Lucan tucked the phone back in his jacket pocket. "And we have security cameras for the safety of our attendees." His face contorted in feigned sympathy. "You slept with a child, Curtis. I can see how this would be hard for your wife to forgive. And your friends. And your colleagues..."

Curtis had no choice but to play ball. He arranged for West Beatty to use vacant spaces, provided him keys or access cards. But Curtis never attended another party. Not because he wasn't welcome or because he didn't trust himself. But because he knew what was happening there was illegal and wrong. Curtis was a decent guy who made one mistake, an error that got him wrapped up in something debauched and disgusting. He'd had no power to stop it. But it ate him up inside. He couldn't sleep. He lost weight. And when Sydney finally confronted him, asked him what was going on, he made up the affair.

It had killed him to hurt her that way, but Sydney was too smart, she knew him so well. If he didn't admit to something huge, life-altering, she'd know he was lying. So he'd concocted the fling with the fictional Collette Jasper. It was bad, but it was forgivable...he hoped. He'd agreed to go to counseling, but the sessions were torturous. The therapist's questions were so probing, he felt like she could see right through him. He was suffocating under the weight of his lies. And then, he found a way out.

Their new life in Spain was the reprieve he'd been longing for. Sydney still had to heal from the pain he'd caused her, but Curtis felt lighter, happier, than he had in years. He had a few loose ends to tie up back in New York—notably Simon. But his friend would provide the party spaces; he'd honor the agreement. Curtis had passed on an invitation that Simon had been all too happy to accept.

Curtis had no idea that the girl he'd met at the party, the one he'd tried to protect, had died. He still didn't know how—he assumed suicide, maybe a drug overdose. But he knew Bianca and Damian had gotten it all wrong. Her death was not his fault. What happened between them was undeniably wrong, but it hadn't been violent or ugly. It had been gentle, tender even. She hadn't cried or complained; she'd never asked him to stop. When Curtis apologized to Bianca for what he'd done to Lyric, it wasn't an admission of guilt. It was just a way to make them go away. Surely, Sydney could see that.

She had to.

Sydney Cleary and Curtis Lowe, Couples' Counseling Session
Ellen Dwyer, Psychologist, PsyD
July 29

THERAPY PROGRESS NOTES—SESSION 6.

Counseling terminated via email from Curtis Lowe. He advised that the couple is moving to Spain for a fresh start. I suggested they continue therapy via telehealth or find an English-speaking couples' therapist near their new residence. There has been no response.

Account paid in full.

57

The glass in Sydney's hand is empty now, but she has no memory of drinking the hard liquor. She can feel it burning in her chest, though, warming her belly. The alcohol seeps through her nervous system, tries to numb her to the horror and disgust she's feeling. But it's no match for the vile tale she's just heard. She sets the tumbler on the coffee table. Only then does she meet her husband's eyes, shining with desperation, a glimmer of something more positive... It's hope.

When Sydney speaks, she sounds like the attorney that she is. But she barely recognizes the faraway, professional voice coming out of her. "You're a child rapist."

"It wasn't like that, Syd. I never hurt her. I—I was gentle."

Her stomach churns, but she maintains her cool. "You were involved in human trafficking. And child abuse. And sexual slavery."

"I wasn't *involved*. I was forced to provide the venues. That's all."

"That's being involved. That's being an accessory."

"The things I saw, Syd." His voice trembles. "The things they were doing to those girls. What I did was nothing by comparison."

"Stop minimizing what you did!" Her throat is filled with acid. "You had sex with a drugged teenager! You're disgusting!"

She gets up, moves away from him. The fact that she had ever loved him, that she had ever let him touch her, that she had moved across the fucking ocean with him, makes her want to puke. What happened to the man she'd married? The guy who'd made her coffee and ensured she ate properly? Who'd made her feel safe and cared for and chosen? When had he been replaced by this sick bastard making excuses for his role in a sex-trafficking ring?

"I—I'm not the villain here, Sydney. I protected Bianca's sister. I took care of her."

"But the video of you *protecting her* was used to blackmail you," she spits. "You had sex with her. She was a *child!*"

He clutches at his head like her words cause him pain. "They gave me a pill. I was so fucked-up. I—I wasn't myself. But Lyric felt safe with me. I didn't do anything she wasn't okay with."

"She was an abused and exploited girl! She couldn't give her consent!"

"There were famous people at that party. Movie stars and athletes and business moguls. Everyone was doing it! Far worse things than I did!"

"Stop!" Sydney feels a nearly overwhelming urge to violence. She's never struck another person in her life, but now she wants to attack. She wants to hit and punch and claw this man. This *stranger*. Because this is not her husband. There's a monster trapped inside his familiar form, a demon. She's never felt such overwhelming hatred.

She rushes out of the room to the kitchen, desperate for distance from Curtis. She knows he'll follow her, that he's not done begging for absolution, but she needs space. Collapsing her arms onto the counter, she presses her forehead to the cool surface. Tears pour untouched down her face, and her body shakes with sobs. She can sense her husband's presence in the room like a toxic gas, but she takes her time, lets out the pain. Eventually, her sobs subside, and she wipes her face with a tea towel. She feels calm now. Focused on what she needs to do.

"I'm going to call Brian Hale. He'll put me in touch with the DA in New York."

"You can't." Curtis's voice is adamant. "I won't allow it."

"You can't stop me," she snaps. She takes a few steps toward the bedroom to get her phone, but Curtis grabs her arm, yanks her back. He holds her roughly, his voice a growl.

"There are huge, influential names involved in this, Sydney. They'll do what needs to be done to protect themselves. West Beatty is fucking ruthless. That's why I had to get rid of Bianca and Damian."

"You poisoned them." After what she's heard today, nothing can surprise her anymore.

"I had to." He loosens his grip slightly, allows her to extricate herself. "West would have sent a hired killer here to take care of them. It wasn't safe for you."

Syd crosses the kitchen, turns back to face him. "What did you give them?"

"Remember the death cap mushrooms the Realtor warned us about?"

"Of course. But you ate mushrooms, too."

"I had some regular mushrooms in the fridge. I added those to my plate."

"Jesus." The lengths he's gone to to protect himself are astounding.

"Once Bianca and Damian are dead, no one can implicate me anymore. Simon is providing the venues now. I sent him to a party, and he got himself wrapped up in it." He takes a tentative step toward her. "We can still have an amazing life here. We can still build the future we've always wanted."

She looks at her husband, his expression so desperate, so pleading. He's been lying and manipulating for so long. He must be exhausted. And he's tied up all the loose ends, except for one. Her. Because Curtis and Sydney could have an incredible future in their beautiful Spanish villa. If not for the simple fact that Sydney has a conscience. And her husband knows it.

Wordlessly, she moves to the fridge and pulls open the door. Inside, she finds Bianca's leftover meal covered in plastic. She removes the plate of poisoned food and sets it on the counter. It's cold and congealed, looks unappetizing but completely benign.

"What are you doing with that?" Curtis asks, but she ignores his question.

"You know I can't let this go. I couldn't live with myself if I didn't try to stop it."

"You can't stop it, Sydney. You'll be erased."

"The feds could build a RICO case," she continues, as if he hadn't spoken. "You'll likely be charged as a co-conspirator. You'd go to jail as a pedophile. And a sex trafficker."

"And you know what would happen to me there!" he cries. "But I'd never make it to jail. Ratting on Beatty is a death sentence. For both of us."

For a breath, Sydney wonders if she should be afraid of her husband. She's the only thing standing between Curtis and a blissful life in Spain. But everything he's done—the move, the lies, the poisoning—has been for her. He is a corrupt, weak, and selfish man, but he loves her.

"I'm offering you a way out," she says, pushing the plate of food toward him.

"You want me to kill myself? Are you serious?"

"I'll make an anonymous call to the DA and leave both our names out of it." She moves to the kitchen drawer and pulls out a fork. "If you die of an accidental poisoning, I can go on with my life without the shadow of what you did. It's the only way that I won't be painted with your disgusting brush."

"After all our years together, you want me to die a slow, agonizing death? To suffer like Damian is?"

"But Damian's weak, remember?" She sets the fork on the counter. "Surely you'll handle it better."

Curtis stares at the plate of poisoned food, his expression a blend of shock, disbelief, and grief, almost like he can't believe involving himself in a pedophile ring has had such a dire outcome. He looks up at his wife.

"If I eat this, you have to promise me you'll call the DA from a burner phone. And you won't tell them your name."

"I promise."

"I—I love you so much," Curtis blubbers, letting the tears pour from his eyes. "You mean everything to me."

Sympathy grips her heart, but just for a breath. It's undeserved, and she pushes it aside. "Then you'll eat. Or the world will know you're a pedophile. And we'll both suffer the consequences of that."

A sob bursts out of him as he picks up the fork.

Sydney turns and walks out of the room.

BIANCA AND DAMIAN

58

At some point in the night, Bianca managed to drag herself out of the rain and into the van. Now, she wakes on the linoleum floor, shivering in her damp, dirty clothing. She feels weak and nauseated, but the sharp pains in her stomach are gone. Her bones ache from sleeping on such a hard surface, and there's a pounding in her skull. But she has recovered. She's survived.

Hauling herself upright, she realizes the thudding sound is not just in her head. Someone is knocking on the panel door. Last night, she'd been afraid for her life, desperate to flee. But today, she feels resigned, too exhausted to care if Curtis Lowe is standing outside with a machete. Bianca fumbles with the handle, but she's so frail, her grasp too weak. "Come in," she croaks through her damaged throat.

The door slides open to reveal Sydney standing in the predawn light. The sun is rising behind her, its gentle rays highlighting her ghostly pallor, the lines around her eyes and mouth. Sydney looks to have aged ten years overnight. Was she sick, too? Before Bianca can ask, Syd speaks.

"I just found out what Curtis did to your sister," she says. "I'm disgusted. And I'm sorry."

If she's come to Bianca for absolution, she's deluded. "Do you expect me to believe that you had no idea your husband was a sexual predator?"

"I was naïve and stupid to believe his lies. I know that now. But I loved him."

"You were beyond stupid," Bianca snarls. "You were a fucking idiot."

"I don't care what you think of me, Bianca." Sydney's expression is stony. "You used your sister's death to make five million dollars."

"I never cared about the money," Bianca blurts. "That was all Damian's idea. He said it was the best way to hurt Curtis. The only way that wouldn't send me to jail for murdering him."

"Well, he's not going to pay you," Sydney continues, unfazed. "He fed you poisonous death cap mushrooms last night. You need to get to a hospital."

That devious piece of shit. Damian had convinced her Curtis could be trusted, but Bianca should have known he'd never pay for what he did.

"Joke's on Curtis," Bianca says, struggling out of the van. "I survived. I feel better now."

"The poison is still in you, attacking your organs. Go to a hospital. You didn't eat that much. You might still be okay." Sydney turns and walks toward the Citroën.

Bianca is weak, dehydrated, and the tsunami of information in her delicate state has made her woozy. She takes a few steps to follow Sydney, but she stumbles on the gravel, drops down on a knee.

"Wait!" Bianca drags herself back to her feet, moves gingerly forward. "Where are you going?"

"I'm not sure," Syd says, eyes on the sun rising above the sea. But she's lying. She doesn't want Bianca to be able to find her. Fair enough. Sydney turns her gaze back to Bianca. "I'm going to call the DA in New York. And an investigative journalist I know. I'll do everything I can to stop the sex-trafficking ring." Her face softens, and her eyes are damp. "I know it's too late for Lyric, but maybe some other girls can be saved."

There are things Bianca needs to say, but her throat is tight with emotion, still raw from her violent illness. She struggles to push the words past the blockage, to maintain her composure, but she won't be able to speak without crying. And Bianca doesn't do that. She's too hard, too strong. But Sydney is opening the car door; she's about to leave. It's now or never. Bianca reaches out, clutches Syd's arm. "I have more information."

With tears spilling from her eyes, Bianca tells Sydney about the restaurant where Lyric worked, a high-end establishment that hired a pretty teenager with no education and no experience. She tells her about the woman who called herself Fay, who preyed on the young girls who worked there. Bianca mentions Lyric's roommates, who may have information about these parties, and Sydney types the address into her phone.

Bianca has one last question. "Where is Curtis now?"

"He ate the rest of your poisoned meal." Sydney puts on her sunglasses. "It's what he deserves."

Bianca nearly chokes on a sob. Of relief. Of gratitude. "Thank you."

"Save yourself," Sydney says. "Save Damian if you want. I don't care." Then she gets in the car and backs down the driveway.

Bianca knows she should get in the van, drive to the nearest hospital. She's been poisoned, and time is of the essence. But something draws her toward the house—curiosity, maybe? She needs to know that Curtis really ate that meal, that he's truly suffering. Or, despite all they've been through, is it concern for Damian?

The house is eerily silent as she slips inside, wanders through the vacant rooms. The bathroom door is closed, locked. Someone is in there, but they're quiet. She knocks tentatively.

"Damian?"

His response is a groan, followed by, "Fuuuuuuck."

He's alive. For now, at least. But where is Curtis?

Bianca walks into the kitchen, rifles through the drawers for a knife. In her weakened state, she's unlikely to be able to defend herself, but she can't approach Curtis without protection. He tried to kill her, even if it was in the most cowardly way possible. And he could still have the machete on his person. She selects a steak knife, sharp but light enough for her to grip. As she turns toward the stairs, she notices the empty plate on the counter, the discarded plastic wrap next to it. It appears Curtis has poisoned himself. Would he really end his life in such a torturous way? She needs to be sure.

She grips the banister as she descends to the basement, the knife pressed against her thigh. The chill and the damp have made her tremble, but now anxiety takes over. Curtis ate the meal last night. He may be feeling fine by now. He could be lying in wait for her, ready to finish her off. She clutches the knife in her tremulous hand. But as her feet land on the concrete floor, she hears an unmistakable sound.

Sobbing.

Bianca hesitates, listening to the outpouring of self-pity. It's Curtis—there's no mistaking it—weeping for all he's lost. He's wailing about the end of his marriage, crying over the imminent and highly unpleasant end to his life. And maybe he feels some regret for what he did to Lyric, to all the girls who were used and exploited and discarded. Soon, the poison will torture him to death. As if she's willed it, he gasps and groans. The process is underway. She can leave now.

59

Damian stumbles into the kitchen and fills a glass with water. It hurts to swallow, but he forces the liquid down. He's dehydrated and woozy from last night's gastro attack. What the hell caused such horrible symptoms? Was it food poisoning? Some strange Spanish virus? It doesn't matter now. He's survived the worst of it, and he'll be feeling a hundred percent soon. He has to be strong and ready. Tonight, the money will arrive, and Damian will begin his new life.

A presence behind him makes him jump, but it's just Bianca lurking in the entryway. God, she looks like shit. It's clear she suffered the same illness he did, but she endured it out in the rain. In addition to her ghostly pallor, her clothes are damp and dirty, her hair matted and tangled. And then he notices the small steak knife clutched in her hand.

"What are you doing with that?"

"I went to check on Curtis," she says, setting the knife on the counter. "He's sick, too."

"And Sydney?" He feels a sharp jab of concern. She's so fragile, so delicate. A bad case of food poisoning would take its toll on her.

"She left," Bianca says.

"Where did she go?"

Bianca shrugs. "Maybe to get some Pepto-Bismol?"

She's making light of their shared sickness, and he allows a small chuckle. But there's nothing funny about what he just endured. Last night, he'd been sure he was going to die. As he lay on that cold tiled floor, his life had run through his mind like a film. It was so small, so pedestrian. And that was all Bianca's fault. If not for her, he'd have left their small hometown, made his way in the world. He'd have been looking back on a life full of travel, adventure, and experiences. But Damian's been given a second chance, and he's not going to squander it.

"I won't be going to Greece with you," he says.

Her reaction is mild: a slight narrowing of the eyes, a subtle nod. She's been expecting this. She moves past him to the sink and fills a glass from the tap. He watches her drink, rivulets of water running down her cheeks. She sets the glass on the counter and looks at him. He continues.

"You can take the van. Go wherever you want." His tone is magnanimous. "Once the money comes in, I'll tell Sydney what Curtis did to Lyric. She's going to be upset. I want to stick around and make sure she's okay."

"That's nice of you."

Is she referencing him giving her the van or supporting Sydney? Either way, the compliment sounds disingenuous, even sarcastic. He's been diplomatic for so long, but he lets himself lash out.

"It's time I put myself first, Bianca. I sacrificed my dreams and my future for you. I stayed in Indiana so you could support your little sister and you failed. Lyric ended up a prostitute and a drug addict. And now she's dead."

The words are harsh, even cruel, but his partner has always been adept at shutting down her emotions, presenting a cold, unreadable facade. She does it now, meeting his eyes with her icy blank stare. Then she steps up to him and presses her lips to his cheek. They're dry, lifeless, but she holds them there for several seconds, the connection between them strong and constant.

"Good luck with your future, Damian."

She turns and walks out of the room.

* * *

He takes a long, hot shower, scrubbing away the remnants of his illness and his past life. He's fresh, clean, and ready for the next phase of this plan as he heads out to the pool. The sun will nourish him, help him regain his strength. And he needs to get away from Curtis's tortured moans rising from the basement. His host is in the throes of the illness now, his insides twisting and tearing. Curtis is smaller and weaker, the bacteria hit him harder. Damian got over it so much quicker. In fact, he feels almost normal now.

Last night's raindrops cling to the grass, the trees, and the deck chairs. The morning sun hits them, makes them sparkle like diamonds. The whole scene is surreal and magical, like an omen of good things to come. Damian feels an awesome sense of possibility. He can imagine that this house, this land, these glittering views are all his. When Sydney learns the truth about her husband, when she turns to him for comfort, his dream could become a reality.

Wiping the surface of a deck chair with his sleeve, he lays himself down on it. The morning rays warm his skin through to his bones, restoring his energy and vitality. An unfamiliar feeling settles on him, and he sits with it, ponders it. It's true contentment. No, it's more than that. It's a sense of achievement. Because he *made* this happen. He'd been stuck for years, and he got himself unstuck. He's built the perfect fucking future.

Something dark and unusual catches his eye in the pool. He leans forward, but he can't quite see the objects on the pool floor. Struggling to his feet, he moves to the edge, peers through the water. Nestled at the bottom are three phones. He recognizes his own, Curtis's, and the other is a cheap burner phone, likely the one Curtis had been using to call his shady friends. Who threw the phones into the pool? And why?

It had to be Bianca. She was angry with him, for obvious reasons. Still, tossing the devices into the pool seems childish. Petty. And why would she destroy Curtis's phones, too? Her behavior solidifies his decision to end things, validates his feelings for Sydney, who is more mature, more grounded. Syd would never do something so vindictive.

It's likely too late to save the phones, but he wades into the water to retrieve them anyway. He sets them on the pool deck, attempts to turn them on, but they're dead. What's the hack for a wet phone? Salt or rice? He can't remember. Apparently, his brain is still a little fuzzy, and he wobbles as he climbs out of the pool. He's dehydrated and exhausted. He needs to rest. And he's not concerned about his old, dated device. In a few hours he'll be rich. He can buy a new phone.

He returns to the deck chair, lets the sun dry him off. As pleasant thoughts filter through the brain fog, he slips into a state of lethargic contentment. Soon the money will come in. Sydney will return. And Damian will finally get everything he deserves.

He clings to that beautiful promise as he slides into a delirious sleep.

CATALAN NEWS

CADAQUÉS
English Language

Expat Dies after Eating Poisonous Mushrooms

An American citizen living in the Costa Brava has died after accidentally ingesting poisonous mushrooms. Another man remains in hospital in Girona in critical condition. The coroner is waiting for toxicology reports, but death cap mushrooms were found growing on the property where the poisoned men were discovered. A police spokesman says it appears the men picked, cooked, and consumed the mushrooms at the home about six kilometres from Cadaqués.

Mushroom poisonings are more common in Europe than in North America, which may explain the men's mistake. Death caps bear a striking resemblance to straw mushrooms, used regularly in Asian cooking.

The identity of the men is being withheld until next of kin can be notified.

SYDNEY

60

Sydney sits in a sidewalk café, a glass of white wine in one hand, a cigarette in the other. She smokes when and as much as she likes of late. One day she'll quit, but not now, not while she's still recovering from all that's happened. And not while she's living in France. Her habit helps her blend in with the Europeans, keeps her inobtrusive. One day, when it's safe, she'll return to America and get healthy. For now, she'll let herself lean on this crutch.

It's autumn, a bite in the air, but the sun filters through pale clouds and the café is equipped with tall heat lamps. Syd huddles into her thick sweater, takes a last drag on her cigarette, and butts it out in the ashtray. Her phone rests on the collaged tabletop, and she picks it up, types in the first of her usual search items. Dread tightens her chest, makes her breath shallow as the results load, but it's subtler than it once was. It's manageable.

She only checks for news on the fatal mushroom poisoning near Cadaqués about once a day now. It's been nearly six months since she'd called the police from her Madrid hotel, asked them to do a welfare check on her husband. She hadn't heard from him for several days, she told them, and he wasn't answering her calls. It would take her roughly eight hours to drive home. Could an officer make sure Curtis and his friend were okay?

They weren't, of course, and Sydney knew it. She'd sent the professionals because she'd been too afraid to return and find them dead, their bodies bloated by kidney failure, yellowed by liver damage.

She hadn't wanted to deal with the vomit, shit, blood, and whatever other bodily fluids would have seeped from their beings. The police had found the two men, one of them still miraculously clinging to life, the other deceased. An ambulance was summoned. And the coroner.

The *juez de instrucción*, a woman in her fifties with jet-black hair and a no-nonsense air, had concluded that the death was a tragic accident. A simple mistake. There was no evidence to suggest anything nefarious. No money had ever changed hands between the two victims. And the truth was too complex, too bizarre, to be pieced together by even the most brilliant investigative mind. Before Sydney had fled, she'd had the wherewithal to erase the video footage and disconnect the surveillance cameras. She'd thrown some clothes into a small suitcase, grabbed a few toiletries and some cash. Had she left behind any loose ends? Her head had been a muddle of emotions: Disgust. Hatred. Loss. Sorrow.

But to the police and the coroner, Sydney's absence was completely ordinary. She'd gone for a week of shopping and sightseeing in Madrid while her husband caught up with his *mate* Damian. When the men had fallen ill, they'd logically assumed they had mild food poisoning or a common virus. They were *men* after all. And neither of them was a physician or healthcare professional. When things turned dire, they hadn't been able to call for help because their phones were damaged. They were found on the pool deck, destroyed by water. Clearly, they had been forgotten outside in the sudden rainstorm.

But Sydney knew otherwise. She knew Curtis had his phone beside the bed on the last night of his life. Bianca must have tossed the devices in the pool before she left, ensuring there was no way Curtis could save himself. One of them, likely Damian, had fished the phones out of the water, but it was too late. They were destroyed. Useless.

Sydney assumed Bianca had taken her advice, gone straight to the hospital. But which one had she visited? Surely another death cap poisoning would have raised suspicion with the medical staff. Perhaps

Bianca had driven to a different hospital than the one that processed the poisoned men. With appropriate and timely medical care, she could make a full physical recovery. Had she made it in time?

The authorities hadn't mentioned Bianca's presence in the house. There were no feminine accoutrements that couldn't be attributed to Sydney. The other woman has vanished without a trace, like she was a sylph, a spirit sent to reveal Curtis's horrible secrets. Her presence had lifted the veil on Sydney's marriage, showed her the toxic truth of the man she had forgiven. Bianca visits Sydney's mind regularly. She wonders where Bianca is, if she feels her sister's death has been avenged. Is she able to move forward now that Curtis is dead? Or is she still hell-bent on retribution, moving up the ladder from Curtis to the next rung?

Sydney takes a mouthful of wine, tries to wash away the dark and ugly feelings that have surfaced. But it will take more than an afternoon glass of Sancerre to erase the disturbing memories. She may not have discovered her husband's body, but the detective had described the scene in remarkable English. And remarkable detail.

They had discovered Curtis, dead, in their marital bed, clutching a framed photo of their wedding. The *policía* had assumed he'd grabbed it off the nightstand in his final moments, grasping for comfort as he slipped away. But that photo had never been displayed in their new home. At some point in Curtis's slow, agonizing death, he'd found the picture in a storage box. He'd taken it to the bedroom, and despite everything, he'd died with Sydney in his arms.

Somehow, Damian had survived the poisoning. He was much bigger and stronger than Curtis (a fact he never let her husband forget), and his size had saved his life. He was found collapsed in the front hallway, going for help, trying to be the hero. Sydney doesn't know if he'll ever recover. Damian has likely suffered permanent organ damage. He may need a transplant to survive. His mother had flown over from the States, had been at his bedside. Sydney doesn't know where Damian is now, and she doesn't care. The Spanish police may have questioned him, but Curtis cooked that meal without Syd's knowledge. Bianca threw the phones in the pool. Syd is not culpable.

Sydney had to call Curtis's mother too, a few hours after she'd identified the bloated, jaundiced carcass that was once her husband. Curtis had never fostered a relationship between the two women in his life. He'd painted his mother as stern, cold, and emotionally stunted. But Curtis was adept at lying. And yet the stoicism, almost indifference, with which the older woman accepted the news of her son's tragic and untimely death told Syd her partner had been honest about that, at least. Curtis's mother didn't request her son's body be brought home, didn't mention a funeral or service. So, Sydney donated his remains to science.

She takes the last sip of her wine and sets down the empty glass. A silver-haired waiter, distinguished in his white shirt and bow tie, approaches. *"Une autre, madame?"*

"Pourquoi pas?"

Why not? Sydney's evening stretches long and lonely in front of her. She loves this charming little village outside of Toulouse, and her French is passable. But she keeps to herself for obvious reasons. She's not officially *on the run*. She may not even be in danger, but she is cautious. She sold her husband's car and bought a nondescript secondhand Fiat in her own name. She uses cash often. She smiles and nods but doesn't engage in conversations.

Sydney had kept her promise to Curtis to report the pedophile ring anonymously. Not because she owed him anything but because she knew West Beatty and his cohorts would be ruthless. They wouldn't hesitate to eliminate her to save themselves. And so, she'd used a computer in the business center of a Spanish hotel. She'd created an alias email address and sent all the details she knew to a New York journalist and the state attorney. And now, she waits. And she watches.

So far, there have been no charges and no arrests. But Syd's a lawyer; she knows it takes time to build a case. And she knows West

Beatty has the resources to cover his tracks, that he can hire the sharpest attorneys to help him wriggle out of accusations. But she hasn't given up hope that all these predators will be brought to justice.

Tapping on her phone, she peruses several American news sites, entering relevant search terms:

West Beatty
New York Sex trafficking
New York Pedophile Ring
Curtis Lowe
Waters and Lowe Property Management

A headline appears that sticks her inhale in her throat. A tight fist of anxiety presses hard on her sternum as she looks at the familiar face beaming in the photograph. He's on a beach somewhere, tanned and handsome. She taps on the article, hunches over her phone and reads.

Simon Waters, owner of Waters and Lowe Property Management, dead at 46

A successful Manhattan businessman has been found deceased in his Midtown office. Simon Waters owned one of the city's largest and most successful property management firms. Waters died of an apparent suicide.

Waters formed the property management business with his college friend Curtis Lowe, who left the partnership last year. Lowe died earlier this year in an accidental poisoning at his house in Spain.

Simon Waters had been divorced for several years from former model Nicole Kwan. The couple had two sons together and remained close. In a statement, Kwan said her ex had been stressed lately and struggling with drugs and alcohol. He was 46.

Three possibilities run through Sydney's mind.

1. Simon killed himself out of guilt for his forced role in the pedophile ring. He was a father; he must have hated himself for facilitating something so exploitive and disgusting. And he would have been terrified of being found out: by his colleagues, his ex-wife, his two boys... He would have been even more terrified of West Beatty.
2. Simon had tried to back out of the role Curtis had foisted upon him, refused to provide venues for the debaucherous events. Maybe he'd even threatened to expose the illegal activities. Simon had become a liability. So, West Beatty had sent one of his henchmen to kill him and made it look like a suicide.
3. Somehow, Bianca got to him.

Whatever happens, Simon's death means the wheels are in motion. The rats are scurrying, hiding, and trying to protect themselves. Syd will need to be extra vigilant now. She glances around, but she's surrounded by locals sipping rosé and beer, engaged in their rapid French conversations. She breathes through her diaphragm, assures herself that she's safe. Curtis's death was ruled an accident. The monsters have no reason to suspect that the grieving widow knew her dead husband was involved in a pedophile ring. But she'd left a reputation as a smart, savvy attorney in her wake. She can't be too careful.

She'd sold the Spanish house shortly after the "tragedy." José Sainz had assured her that her husband's accidental death would not need to be disclosed, that the *mishap* wouldn't affect the value. And he'd been right. Once the mess had been cleaned up, the property had sold quickly and slightly over asking. The money is enough to finance her nomadic lifestyle for years if she wants that.

Her brother, Reid, knows she's traveling, healing, dealing with her grief. He'd been so angry with Curtis when he'd admitted his affair, but Reid was shaken by the news of his brother-in-law's sudden passing. He'd offered to come to Europe, to bring Sydney home, to provide comfort and support. Her brother is all she has left now. But Sydney had explained that she needed solitude to process all that had happened. One day, she'll go back, but she's not ready yet.

Her glass of wine arrives, and she smiles at the waiter, takes a sip. For now, she will stay in Europe, enjoy the culture, the wine, and a cigarette every now and then.

And she'll watch from afar as justice is finally served.

ACKNOWLEDGMENTS

While visiting the Costa Brava, I met a couple of expats living in a beautiful home in the Spanish hills. Thank you, Nicola and Andrew. Your idyllic life inspired me to create this toxic story of secrets, lies, and murder in a stunning foreign setting.

I'm very grateful to my amazing team at Grand Central who works diligently behind the scenes to bring books to readers.

EDITORIAL: Karen Kosztolnyik

EDITORIAL ASSISTANT: Danielle Thomas

DESIGN: Albert Tang

PRODUCTION: Eric Arroyo, Carolyn Kurek

U.S. SALES: Lauren Monaco

CANADIAN SALES: Sara High

PUBLICITY: Staci Burt, Alli Rosenthal, Donna Nopper

MARKETING: Allison Schuster

As always, thank you to my brilliant agent, Joe Veltre, and the enthusiastic gem, Hayley Nusbaum. Your passion for this concept and your support and guidance in developing the idea were invaluable. Also my gratitude to the ever-helpful Joslyn Jenkins.

A huge thank-you to my friend Marilyn Kwong. Her insights as a psychologist helped me navigate the relationships between this cast of messy and dysfunctional characters. I couldn't have done it without her.

Thank you to my go-to early readers for their support, friendship, and insights: Eileen Cook, Daniel Kalla, and Roz Nay. You're the best.

I'm grateful for all my friends in the thriller writing community.

Despite putting murder and mayhem on the page, these writers are warm, supportive, and inspiring.

Thank you to all the librarians and booksellers who bring books and readers together, and all the Bookstagrammers, bloggers, BookTokers, and Facebook groups who spread the word about the books they read. And to the massive Psychological Thriller Readers Facebook group: Thank you for connecting me with so many avid thriller readers, and for getting me invited on the Imagine Greece Readers Retreat with my brilliant author pal Liz Nugent. What a treat!

Thank you to my family and friends for their ongoing support and enthusiasm. And as always, a special thanks to my husband, John... My brainstorming partner, first reader, and biggest cheerleader.

ABOUT THE AUTHOR

Robyn Harding is the bestselling author of *The Haters*, *The Drowning Woman*, *The Perfect Family*, *The Swap*, *The Arrangement*, *Her Pretty Face*, and *The Party*. She has also written and executive produced an independent film. She lives in Vancouver, British Columbia, with her husband and two cute but deadly rescue Chihuahuas.

RAISING READERS
Books Build Bright Futures

Thank you for reading this book and for being a reader of books in general. We are so grateful to share being part of a community of readers with you, and we hope you will join us in passing our love of books on to the next generation of readers.

Did you know that reading for enjoyment is the single biggest predictor of a child's future happiness and success?

More than family circumstances, parents' educational background, or income, reading impacts a child's future academic performance, emotional well-being, communication skills, economic security, ambition, and happiness.

Studies show that kids reading for enjoyment in the US is in rapid decline:

- In 2012, 53% of 9-year-olds read almost every day. Just 10 years later, in 2022, the number had fallen to 39%.
- In 2012, 27% of 13-year-olds read for fun daily. By 2023, that number was just 14%.

Together, we can commit to **Raising Readers** and change this trend. How?

- Read to children in your life daily.
- Model reading as a fun activity.
- Reduce screen time.
- Start a family, school, or community book club.
- Visit bookstores and libraries regularly.
- Listen to audiobooks.
- Read the book before you see the movie.
- Encourage your child to read aloud to a pet or stuffed animal.
- Give books as gifts.
- Donate books to families and communities in need.

Books build bright futures, and **Raising Readers** is our shared responsibility.

For more information, visit **JoinRaisingReaders.com**

Sources: National Endowment for the Arts, National Assessment of Educational Progress, WorldBookDay.com, Nielsen BookData's 2023 "Understanding the Children's Book Consumer"